THE WOMAN WHO SEIZED AN EMPIRE

THE WARLORD – BOOK 2

BY M. D. COOPER

M. D. COOPER

SPECIAL THANKS
Just in Time (JIT) & Beta Reads

James Dean
Marti Panikkar
Scott Reid
Lisa Richman
Timothy Van Oosterwyk Bruyn

Cover Art by Ravven
Editing by Jen McDonnell

TABLE OF CONTENTS

FOREWORD

I often start these forewords by telling you that a book was a joy to write, or the words flowed like honey poured from a jar held by Athena herself.

Not so this book. This book involved spending a lot of time in the mind of someone beaten down and worn thin. The words flowed quickly, but it was more like pouring molten iron from a crucible.

It's easy to remember Katrina as the loving wife of Markus, the woman who stood by his side during the Victoria years, and later took over as president to complete his vision.

But before that, she was raised by a cruel and capricious father, and worked as a spy for the Lumins in Sirius. Even when she was helping the Noctus rebellion, she wasn't against sacrificing pawns to achieve her goals. More of *that* Katrina came out during her time in the Bollam's World System.

Now, as she is tortured by Jace and others, the other Katrina emerges full force. She is not a kindly person; she is fueled by rage and anger. A rage and anger that she will gladly unleash upon her captors.

Sometimes I feel as though I method-write, and writing this story made me feel Katrina's despair, her anger, her rage, and ultimately her triumph.

If I've done my job well, you'll feel those things too.

M. D. Cooper
Danvers, 2017

PREVIOUSLY IN KATRINA'S JOURNEY...

In the last installment of The Warlord, we saw Katrina leave Kapteyn's Star in search of the ISS *Intrepid*, the colony ship that had terraformed the world of Victoria and built the colony before leaving to continue its journey to New Eden.

Katrina and her ship's AI, Troy, searched in the darkness between the stars for years before finally stumbling upon the Kapteyn's Streamer. The Streamer is a supermassive thread of dark matter trailing behind Kapteyn's Star that creates a gravitational lensing effect similar to that of a wormhole.

Like a wormhole, it distorts time as well as space.

When Katrina and Troy exit the Streamer, they find themselves twenty light years beyond New Eden, and 4,500 years in the future.

The *Intrepid* is nowhere to be found.

They learn that in the intervening years, the level of technology has plummeted; though there have been two advances that were game changers. The first is artificial gravity, and the second is faster than light travel.

Katrina and Troy decide that the best route forward is to get their ship, the *Voyager*, upgraded with FTL capability so they can search for the *Intrepid*.

Thus begins Katrina's adventure in the Bollam's World System, where she secures a ship named the *Havermere* to fly out to the edge of the system and upgrade her ship with the graviton systems that will allow for FTL capability.

The entire endeavor is fraught with difficulty, not the least of which is the fact that Katrina and Troy have no money. They have to trade their advanced tech to the *Havermere*'s crew in exchange for the upgrade and pray that no one betrays them.

During the trip back out to the *Voyager*, Katrina begins to fall in love with the repair ship's Crew Chief, Juasa. They hatch a plan that involves Juasa and several of the *Havermere*'s crew leaving the Bollam's World system with her on her quest to find the *Intrepid*.

But the *Havermere*'s first mate, Anna, is not satisfied with the technology Katrina is willing to trade, and puts out a call, drawing the attention of the Blackadder pirates.

Katrina manages to defeat the crew that sided with Anna, but not before her young lover, Juasa, is captured and taken to the pirate ship, the *Verisimilitude*.

Attempting a daring rescue, Katrina flies to the pirate ship, intent on freeing Juasa, only to be captured by Jace, the leader of the Blackadder pirates.

Meanwhile, several of the *Havermere*'s engineers successfully upgrade the *Voyager* to be FTL capable, and the ship escapes.

Jace is enraged, and when next Katrina wakes, she is on a strange planet in a cell with Juasa—prisoners of Jace and his pirate organization.

IF ONLY A DREAM
STELLAR DATE: 12.28.8511 (Adjusted Gregorian)
LOCATION: Jace's estate
REGION: World of Persia, unknown system

The sound of soft moans woke Katrina from her fitful sleep.

It took her a moment to get her bearings. There was only a meager amount of light filtering in through the cracks around a door.

Door. I'm in a room.

The light barely illuminated the space, but was enough to reveal that it was small and featureless. As her bleary eyes focused, Katrina was able to make out the stone walls, and their pattern jogged her memory. She was in the cell.

With that realization in place, Katrina took stock of her body and how much it hurt.

She was laying on her front, cheek pressed against the cold stone floor of the cell. Slowly, fighting against her aching muscles, her inflamed skin groaning in protest, Katrina turned her head and saw the source of the moaning: Juasa.

Is she asleep? Katrina wondered.

She didn't want to speak and wake Juasa if that was the case—sleep was so hard for them to come by these nights. Even though they were exhausted after a long day, the searing fire that raged across their bodies made for no comfortable sleeping positions.

Lying on their backs was totally out of the question. That skin—and it barely even counted as such anymore—was beaten and burned, covered in blisters and welts. Sleeping on one's chest on a dirty stone floor was no picnic either, but the burns were less severe there from spending their days crouched in the dirt.

Six days working the sithri fields in Persia's hot sun, naked, whipped, beaten with rods and canes. It was an effective torture; one that would have broken Juasa long ago—if she had anything to offer.

"I'm awake," Juasa said in a whisper. "Sorry that I disturbed you."

Katrina reached out and touched the underside of Juasa's chin—probably the only place that didn't scream in agony on their bodies. "It's OK. I wasn't really asleep."

Juasa gave a wan smile. "You were snoring."

"Oh…got me, I guess." Katrina let out a long sigh, watching the dirt on the floor roll away from her hot breath. "I'm so sorry about all this."

"I know you are, but it's not your fault. It's Anna's. That dumb bitch…."

Juasa's words were harsh, but there were tears in her eyes. Katrina wanted to wipe them away, but Juasa's cheeks were bright red from the burns, and she daren't touch them.

"I'm going to get us out of here, Ju," Katrina whispered hoarsely. "And when I do, I'm going to make Jace pay for what he's done to you."

Juasa snorted, then coughed and moaned. "Oh...ow. Kat, I don't need vengeance, I just need a week—maybe a month—in a spa."

"You and me both. Don't worry; when we get to the *Voyager*, the medbay will have us fixed up in no time. We'll be hale and whole before you know it."

"How are we going to find it?" Juasa asked, her voice carrying a note of disbelieving desperation.

"I expect they'll find us," Katrina replied. "However, I don't plan to be in this condition when they do. We just need to get these collars off. Then Jace dies, and we get out of here. Not necessarily in that order."

"But how will you do that?" Juasa asked.

Katrina gritted her teeth and drew in a slow breath. It even hurt to breathe enough to talk. The expansion of her chest and her breasts against the rough stone...she wasn't sure if the nights were worse than the days.

"Soon they'll send for me, and we'll start negotiations...or some new torture. I just have to keep my eyes peeled for the right opportunity."

"What if it never happens?" Juasa asked, a soft sob escaping her lips.

"Shhhh, it'll be OK, I promise," Katrina replied. "It'll come; Jace isn't perfect or omniscient. He has enemies, and he'll screw up sooner or later. For now, you sleep as best you can. We need our strength."

Juasa gave a slight nod, and Katrina stroked her chin for a few minutes, humming a tune she remembered from her childhood.

The stars were merciful, and before long, she heard Juasa's breathing fall into the slow rhythm of sleep.

Now Katrina just had to follow suit. Dreams were her only reprieve; visions of joy, where she hunted Jace down and killed him for what he'd done.

THE FIELDS OF PERSIA
STELLAR DATE: 12.31.8511 (Adjusted Gregorian)
LOCATION: Jace's estate
REGION: World of Persia, unknown system

Katrina wiped the rivulets of sweat from her brow, counting the minutes until the water bearer came back around. It would be at least ten more, by her reckoning—unless he was late, which he often was.

She gazed across the rows of sithri plants and their bright blue flowers, taking in the field and the other workers, her gaze finally settling on Juasa, seven rows over.

It hurt Katrina just to see the young woman out here, bent over the flowers, extracting pollen and storing it in the vials they all carried.

It was easy to pick Juasa out from the other workers. Like Katrina, she was naked, her skin bright red, blistered, and peeling from the long hours in the hot sun; dark slashes of scabbed skin from the overseer's whips standing out on her back.

The other workers were indentured servants— labor that was cheaper than machines, though also less efficient. Katrina and Juasa, however, were slaves, their status denoted by the collars they wore; collars that did double duty, restricting the use of their internal tech, nano, and cutting them off from the Link.

A whip cracked above Katrina's head, and Liam, the massive field boss, hollered at her. "Head down! Stay on task!"

Katrina turned back toward the plant in front of her and used her tiny scoop to scrape pollen off the flower's stamen and into the vial.

Two trains of thought warred in her mind.

The first was that she couldn't wait to kill Liam. His time was coming. She just needed to figure out how to get the collar off and then to get Juasa to safety. Once she had that settled, the man would die, not long before Jace.

The other thought running through her mind was of the thousand ways the sithri flower's pollen could be harvested more efficiently than using humans with small scrapers and vials.

Katrina was certain that Jace used people for the work because they were plentiful on Persia—the planet they were on—and because he enjoyed making humans serve him.

Yet another thing that reminded her all too well of Sirius. The more she learned about the future, the more she felt it only contained the worst aspects of the past. Like nothing good had gone forward, only the most…wrong…behaviors possible.

She saw movement out of the corner of her eye

and turned her head ever so slightly to watch a small shuttle take off from the far side of Jace's castle. That was the third one this day. Two had appeared to stay on terrestrial vectors, but this one was rising straight up into space.

A castle, Katrina shook her head at the thought. Jace had gone all out, building a monstrous stone structure reminiscent of ancient human fortresses. It had towers and parapets, and a high wall; even a moat and a drawbridge.

Katrina had not yet determined the full scope of Jace's holdings on Persia, or what sort of position he held in the local hierarchy. Whatever the scope of his influence, it was enough for him to create a little fiefdom, complete with plebes to do his bidding.

It was pathetic, but it certainly fit the bill for a boorish man like Jace.

Even though she detested him, Katrina knew a keen intellect hid behind the bearded, cliff-browed visage. Jace could not possess a feared fleet, nor feel secure enough to live at the bottom of a planetary gravity well, without a significant measure of success.

The bastard is good at what he does.

In the five days since Katrina woke in the cell with Juasa, Jace had not summoned her once. It was obvious that he was letting her stew in her juices— or bake in the sun, as it were.

At first, it had seemed like uninspired torture. Katrina had expected rape, mind bending sims, dissection, something truly terrible. But the subtlety of the fields was undeniable. It would take weeks to wear her down, but Katrina could already feel it happening.

Juasa was not so hardy. The poor woman had never spent any appreciable time planet-side in her life; she'd never spent a day in full sunlight, or felt her lips dry out, crack, and bleed in the hot air, let alone the searing fire of the lash, or the skin-splitting blows of a cane.

Jace did not come out to watch the pair of women suffer in the fields, but Anna made sure to visit them several times a day. She seemed to harbor a lingering hatred for Juasa, and would beat her with whatever was nearby. Twice Katrina had rushed Anna, determined to kill the woman with her bare hands, but the collar around her neck had dropped her both times before she made it halfway.

And then Liam had beaten her for crushing one of the plants.

Though Katrina was unable to directly control her body's nanotech—the collar saw to that—but her biology was far superior to a normal human's, and it was plain to see that she was healing faster than expected.

Anna had noticed, and over the past day, she had

directed more of her ire toward Katrina—which suited her just fine.

Katrina moved to the next plant, thinking a variety of very ungrateful things about Anna, but that just reminded her that all of this was her fault. Juasa's misery, whatever had happened to the crew of the *Havermere*—it was all her fault. If she hadn't shown up in their lives, they'd be going about their business. Plying the black and fixing ships.

No. It's Anna's fault, Katrina thought as she clenched her jaw and moved to the next plant. *If she hadn't gotten greedy, none of this would have happened. No one would have died, everyone would have been rich, and Troy and I would be long gone, searching for Tanis—hopefully with Juasa along for the ride.*

She held that thought firmly in her mind. Anna would pay—pay dearly—for what she'd done. Once Katrina had the lay of the land—and worked out how to get the damn collar off—she would kill Anna, Jace, and whoever else got in her way.

As if Katrina's foul thoughts had summoned the woman, a car pulled up, hovering above the packed path at the edge of the field.

Katrina tilted her head enough to see Anna step out and approach Liam. She was wearing a blue skinsuit that seemed to emit a nimbus glow, with pink and purple hues tracing patterns across her body.

It was a sign of Anna's deepest desire. She wanted to be an aristocrat, one of the upper crust. Out here, on Jace's estate, she could be anything, and she chose to be the one thing she never could be back at Bollam's World.

"Lobster one!" Liam cried out. "Get your pus-dripping ass over here. Jace wants to see you."

Liam had never once called the prisoners by name, though he did have a variety of creative epithets that he used to address them. He was, however, consistent in their numbering. Katrina was 1, and Juasa was 2.

Katrina rose and saw that Juasa was peering at her with worry writ large on her face. Katrina nodded slowly, and held up a reassuring hand.

She began to walk across the field. Her bones ached from crouching, and her muscles were tight, feeling like rubber bands stretched too far. Welts from the beatings split open as she moved, and Katrina could feel fresh rivulets of pus run down her body.

A few of the field workers glanced at her as she walked by. Today no one took a second look.

On the first day, before the burns set in, a group of the field workers had attempted to have their way with Katrina and Juasa during one of the rest periods.

Katrina had fought back, and knocked two

unconscious before the rest fled. Her reward was a beating from Liam for lowering the field's production output.

She just hoped that now, on their third day out here, Juasa's degraded condition would make her a less savory target. It was a slim hope, as was the one that Jace would send her back to the fields before long. Katrina didn't like letting Juasa out of her sight.

Still, she held herself erect and proud. There was no way that she was going to let them think their actions had cowed her in any way.

Katrina had received worse at the hands of her own father.

As she reached the edge of the field, Anna's lips curled into a sneer. "Ah, Verisa, still so proud."

Katrina didn't reply. No good would come from responding to the woman's baiting. Though the continued use of her alternate persona's name, Verisa, told Katrina that the *Havermere* had not yet arrived. Or if it had, they'd not broken Sam, the AI.

Liam gave a curt nod, his eyes traveling up and down Katrina's body—not lasciviously, more like he was examining livestock. "She's a tough bitch, that's for sure. Once she learns her place, she'll be a good worker."

Anna reached out and pinched the blistered skin on Katrina's arm, twisting the flesh viciously. "Is that what you want? To be a good worker?"

Katrina sucked in a quick breath and clenched her teeth, but she didn't respond to the woman's taunts. Addressing Anna only emboldened her. Silence, however, confounded her.

A moment later, Anna released her hold on Katrina's skin and shook her head. "Dumb bitch. You're going to wish you had talked to me. Jace won't be nearly as forgiving."

Liam handed Katrina a towel. It was coarse and scratchy—at least it felt that way to her.

"Sit on this. Don't need your ooze all over the seats."

Katrina wrapped the towel around her shoulders, glad to have her skin out of the unrelenting sun— though anything touching it hurt just as much. She also did not relish the thought of the pain that removing the towel would cause, its fibers sticking in her wounds.

Liam then opened the rear door on the car, and Katrina climbed in, sparing a glance for Juasa, who was staring at her with wide eyes.

Katrina managed a small smile before the door slammed shut. One of the massive guards was in the seat beside her. He held a handgun in his left hand, and Katrina began to catalogue the ways she could pull it from his grasp and blow his brains out with it.

Anna got in the front seat and made a snarky remark that Katrina ignored. The *Havermere*'s former first mate continued to talk as the car took off, driving them down the packed gravel road that ran through the fields—most filled with workers harvesting sithri pollen—toward the castle several kilometers away.

Katrina counted the field bosses watching their workers, saw how many carried weapons, who held theirs like they knew how to use them, which ones also carried clubs or whips.

She noted the watchtowers: how many were occupied, which seemed to be vacant. She saw a transport approach, filled with new guards fresh for their shift—something that never happened with Katrina's team. Liam and his pair of assistants never traded off with other guards.

All the while, Anna kept talking; mostly threatening Katrina, but sometimes slipping into an almost conversational tone.

"You know what they say, Verisa, the female of the species is the most deadly. That's true for Jace. His wife is a cold fish, calculating, determined, grasping. I'll warrant she's the one that is pushing him to start getting answers from you so soon. If it were up to me, I'd let you bake in the sun till the cancer set in."

Katrina doubted that very much. Anna was the

epitome of impatience, even though she liked to pretend otherwise. This was not the first time she'd heard mention of Jace's wife, though. Katrina's impression was that the woman ruled the roost with an iron fist. Once or twice, the guards had joked about how Jace would be heading back out into space before long. He never lasted more than a few weeks planetside before having somewhere else he needed to be.

Anna let several other tidbits drop. She mentioned a raid ship coming back, and an important meeting at the capital, and another on an orbiting station named Farsa. That was particularly interesting—it hinted at a power structure that went higher than Jace on the planet, and in space above.

They reached the castle a minute after that utterance, passing beneath the portcullis and into the courtyard. The car stopped next to the steps that led up to the main entrance.

Katrina had never seen this entrance to the castle. She and Juasa had been brought in and out of a postern gate each dawn and dusk; their only exposure to the stone fortress being the dank tunnels that led to and from her and Juasa's cell.

"Out," the guard next to her said, and Katrina complied, opening the door and stepping out onto the hot stone of the courtyard.

Shit…never thought I'd appreciate crouching in the

dirt around the plants this much.

"C'mon, Red, let's move," Anna said and grabbed Katrina's shoulder.

Katrina sucked in a hissing breath from the pain, and Anna's lips formed a wicked smile.

"Ah, finally. I was beginning to wonder if you could make sounds anymore."

Katrina leaned toward Anna and hissed again before whispering in the woman's ear, "When I kill you, I promise not to make a peep."

Anna's head whipped around, and Katrina had the satisfaction of seeing a fleeting expression of fear on the pompous bitch's face. It was gone a moment later, replaced by a haughty smile. "Keep chirping, little bird. You'll be singing Jace's tune before long."

Katrina only shrugged, and Anna turned in disgust, walking up the stairs with a petulant stamp to her feet as she went.

"Move," the guard said from behind Katrina, and she followed the glowing blue woman up the steps and through the doors.

The interior of the castle was far more ornate than Katrina had expected. Every bit as elegant within as it was brooding from without. Deep carpets ran down the corridors, bright lights hung from golden ropes, and no small number of songbirds fluttered about on perches overhead.

Given the level of tech Jace possessed, Katrina wondered what they did about bird shit. The poor animals must have been modified or conditioned not to do it while in the corridor.

Not that any level of animal cruelty should have been a surprise.

The castle's air was cool. At first, the slight breeze within felt soothing on Katrina's skin, but before long, she felt a chill set in. She pulled the towel tight around her shoulders, feeling its fibers already settling within the forming scabs on her back.

Deep breaths, Katrina, she told herself. *This is all calculated; a part of how they are working to break you. You're smarter than them. You'll come out on top.*

Anna had finally stopped speaking—a small mercy—and she led Katrina and the looming guard through the long passageways of the castle in silence. Before long, they came to a double door, in front of which stood a pair of guards. They gave Anna and Katrina a disparaging look, but stepped aside and opened the doors.

Katrina followed Anna inside and stopped just past the threshold, surveying the room. The walls were sheathed in marble, and there was no carpeting; just a pale blue stone that appeared to glow—or was reflecting the light coming off Anna. A large desk dominated the far end of the room, situated before tall windows that looked out over a walled garden. Before the desk, a grouping of uncomfortable-looking chairs sat empty—one with a plastic sheet draped over it.

Jace sat at the desk, his bearded visage dark as he peered at something hovering over the desk on a holodisplay. With a shake of his head, he waved it away and rose, a grim smile on his lips.

"Ah, Verisa, you look like shit. I trust your little fuck toy is in even worse shape?"

Katrina didn't reply, though she knew the cold look in her eyes was all the answer Jace needed.

"You should see her," Anna said with a wicked grin. "She's like one big welt, oozing pus."

Katrina suppressed a laugh. Anna was like a dog trying to please its master, barking and bouncing at Jace's feet, when all he wanted was for her to shut up.

"Sit," Jace said to Katrina. "I'll have some refreshments brought in."

Though she didn't want to do his bidding, Katrina felt nauseous from the walk and knew that her prolonged exposure in the field was beginning to give her sun poisoning. A seat would be a welcome reprieve.

She settled gently into the plastic covered chair. "Thanks for making sure I don't get stuck to your upholstery."

Jace shrugged. "The least I can do. Besides,

Malorie hates it when I get blood and guts on the furniture. You know what they say: 'happy wife, happy life'."

"I wouldn't know," Katrina replied. "I've never had a wife."

"Sorry to stop you on the way to the altar with your girl toy out there," Jace said as he sat across from Katrina. "I'm not entirely unwilling to work with you, Katrina. I'm sure I can find something for you to do here in the castle, away from the sun and Liam's whip."

Katrina drew a deep breath. It was time for a new persona. "Oh, yeah? You need someone who actually knows what they're doing to run things around here?"

"Eh?" Jace asked, surprise coloring his dark features. "What are you angling for?"

Katrina shrugged. "Your job. You obviously need someone who knows what the hell they're doing. You sure don't have a fucking clue."

Jace leaned forward in his chair, his hands gripping the armrests. "Careful, woman."

"Seriously, Jace. The fact that Anna is still in this room tells me that you're just a bit player. She's a moron. You should have killed her the moment you had me."

Jace glanced at Anna—whose face quickly shifted from red to white—before turning his eyes back to

Katrina. He held her gaze for a moment, and then shook his head and laughed.

"You're right. I should kill Anna. She's a scheming blowhard, but I made a deal with her, and I don't go back on my deals."

Katrina turned to Anna, who had taken a step back, her eyes wide. "Hear that, Anna? You can keep bungling as long as you want. His Imperial Softiness, here, has declared you to be untouchable. Go on now, I'm sure there's someone somewhere who wants to hear you prattle on about how amazing you are. Well, probably not, but you'll talk someone's ear off nonetheless"

Jace waved his hand at Anna without turning to look at her. "She sure has you pegged, Anna. I guess you were too heavy-handed—not that it surprises me. Get lost. I'll let you know if I need you for anything."

Anna opened her mouth to reply, but then appeared to think better of it, and slunk from the room. If she'd had a tail, it would have been between her legs.

"So, how's the wife?" Katrina asked as the door closed. "Malorie, I believe? I hear she's a bit of a battle axe."

Jace's eyes widened for a moment before they narrowed to slits. "You've a good set of ears on you. I see you haven't wasted these past few days."

Katrina shrugged, pretending to be at far greater ease and comfort than she really felt. It was taking everything she had not to vomit on the chair next to her—though the thought of ruining it did appeal to her.

"I can see what you're doing. Wear me down, play my love for Juasa against me. Offer me a place in your lovely castle here, make me trade something to get Juasa in here as well. Hold her safety over my head, etcetera, etcetera…. Can we just skip past all that?"

Jace gave a short laugh and leant back in his chair. "It looks like you know how this all works."

"I've played this sort of game myself more than once," Katrina replied. "Though usually from your chair, not mine."

"Back whenever you came from…" Jace said, leaving the statement hanging.

"Yes," Katrina nodded.

"And when was that?"

Katrina snorted. "A long time ago. Too long to matter. The real question is what can I offer you? My nanotech, data I hold in my head, secrets that could make you rich and powerful."

A smug smile formed on Jace's lips, and he spread his arms wide. "I'm not sure if you've noticed, but I'm already rich and powerful."

"Yes, if you were living on Earth eight thousand

years ago. But really, how many ships do you have? A dozen? Twenty? Not so many that you could stand your ground when a system like Bollam's World sends their space force after you, I'll bet. You're not even top dog on your own planet. Subservient to whoever runs the show from the capital."

"None of that matters as much as the fact that I hold your life in my hands," Jace replied.

Katrina nodded and took a moment before she replied. "Noted. But I have what you want, and right now, I'm not feeling inclined to share with you—largely because you're such a raging asshole."

Jace clenched his jaw, then worked it back and forth as he considered her. "I was hoping to have a more fruitful conversation with you, but it seems that maybe Anna—for all her faults—was right for once. Nevertheless, my squints believe that they can pluck the secrets from your mind, even against your will. Given what a flaming bitch you are, I'm inclined to let them try."

Katrina hoped that Jace would do just that. If his techs tried to access her mind, she'd turn the tables on them so fast their heads would spin. If their internal net security was as pathetic as everything else, she'd be through it in no time.

And then I'll get the codes for this damn collar.

"You've not really earned my trust," Katrina

replied. "Stars, you said there'd be some refreshments, and those haven't even arrived yet."

Jace shook his head and rose from his chair. He walked to a side table with several decanters on it and poured a glass of red wine.

"Here, try not to choke on it," Jace grunted as he walked toward her with the glass.

Katrina took it with a silent nod and sipped the cool liquid. She had to be careful; in her current state, half the glass would probably put her under the table.

"I'm prepared to negotiate with you," Jace said. "You tell me where your ship went and give me working override codes to get aboard and take control, and your life will get a lot more pleasant.

Katrina met Jace's eyes and shook her head. "Put Juasa on a ship you don't control that's headed far from here, and we can have that conversation."

"Ha! Nice try. You and I both know that Juasa is the best leverage I have over you. Take her out of the equation, and you're bound to try something nuts."

"Well, I do still care about my own hide," Katrina replied. "But you're right. It is tougher. But there's certainly no conversation to be had while Juasa is out in those fields. What happens to her is directly related to how cooperative I am."

She took another sip of wine, grateful for the

drink, though pissed that he would give her something like wine on an empty stomach.

Jace didn't respond at first, though he did stroke his beard seventeen times—Katrina couldn't help but count—before giving a curt nod.

"Well, let's have the squints make a go of it first, then," Jace replied, his tone measured and even. "I'll tell them not to drill too many holes in your skull."

Katrina snorted. "I appreciate it." She looked at her glass of wine, said, "Aw, fuck it," and downed the whole thing.

Jace laughed. "You're gonna need it." He gestured to the guard who had accompanied Katrina into the room "Take her to the lab."

Katrina rose slowly, feeling the towel pull at her skin further, wincing from the pain.

"Oooo…that looks harsh. I bet it'll hurt like a bitch when the squints pull it off."

"Go fuck yourself," Katrina muttered as she turned and walked from the room, hoping she appeared steadier on her feet than she felt.

"I have people for that," Jace called out after her.

Katrina was tempted to tell Jace it didn't surprise her that he needed slaves for sex, but the drink was hitting her, and she couldn't figure out how to organize the words properly. Better to let him be the one to shout the final epithet than blurt out something nonsensical and sound like an idiot.

PROBED
STELLAR DATE: 12.31.8511 (Adjusted Gregorian)
LOCATION: Jace's estate
REGION: World of Persia, unknown system

The guard led her down the corridor to a blank space on the wall. He waved his hand, and the entrance to a lift opened up.

"In," he said.

Katrina obeyed, wobbling a bit and glad for the low rail that ran around the edge of the conveyance. Though the wine was bad for her mental acuity, the electrolytes were welcome, and she could feel energy returning to her limbs.

Normally her internal med systems would be able to strip electrolytes from internal stores, but they were rendered inert by the threat from the collar.

This damn collar.

It surprised her how much she really relied on the technology within her body to manage her day-to-day life. She wondered if it was a weakness; in the past she would have said no, but such a basic device as the collar had defeated her utterly.

At first Katrina had tested its bounds to see if there was a way she could circumvent its detection. What she learned was that the device simply looked for any abnormal EM fields within her body. If it picked them up, it hit her with a torturous blast of electricity.

Even performing three tests had greatly diminished the amount of free nano within her body, and had probably caused some cellular damage as well.

Katrina found herself wishing that more of her enhancements were pure-bio, rather than based on silicate nanotech. If—when—they found the *Intrepid*, she would see to changing that.

The lift dropped seven levels, moving far below the depth of her cell's location. When it stopped, the door opened to reveal a short, white corridor with a pair of steel doors at the end.

"I assume the men and women with the sharp sharp knives are behind that door yonder?" Katrina asked the guard.

He only grunted in response and pushed her forward, eliciting another gasp of pain from her.

As they walked down the passage, the doors swung open to reveal another corridor that ran left and right. The guard took her right, and then opened the first door on the left and gestured for her to enter.

Katrina complied without hesitating, not wanting another shove. Instead, the guard reached out and grabbed the blanket, tearing it from around her.

A shriek escaped Katrina's throat as a dozen new scabs were torn open. Pus and blood began to ooze from her body once more, and she struggled to keep her breathing under control.

The guard tossed the blanket into a trash bin and walked to a sink where he washed his hands.

"You're fuckin' gross," he muttered.

"Trying to make my outside match your inside," Katrina sneered through clenched teeth.

The guard shook his head. "Nice try."

The room was cold, and she began to shiver—which was ridiculous, since her skin felt like it was on fire. Katrina did her best to ignore the warring sensations as she looked around the room.

There was a medtable in the center. It looked passable; too many armatures for her liking, but given that she was in the basement of a castle, it was more advanced than she'd feared.

The far wall had a row of counters holding various scanning implements. A small NSAI pod sat in one corner, and temperature-controlled cabinets stood to its right.

She heard the door open and turned to see a man and a woman enter. They both wore gleaming white hazsuits with clear bubble helmets atop. Their eyes locked on her, and the man's expression turned sour while the woman shook her head.

"What a mess," he said. "We're going to have to

get her stable before we start—she'll go into shock in the first five minutes if we don't."

The guard was eyeing the man and the woman in their hazsuits, looking uncomfortable. "Do I need to worry?" he asked.

"Not unless you plan to get her bodily fluids on you," the woman said. "Still, you may want to wait outside."

The guard pursed his lips. "I'll go out after you restrain her. I assume you're going to restrain her?"

"Of course," the woman said with a curt nod. "On the table, you; let's get you patched up enough for this."

"So you can take me apart again?" Katrina asked.

"Physically, this will be easier than working in the fields," the man replied. "Mentally, it will be as easy as you let it."

Katrina hopped up on the table and gave the pair a warm smile. "Well, let's see what you two can manage." She laid back on the cool surface of the med table—a welcome feeling—and placed her arms and legs into the restraining cuffs. "Do your worst."

The pair glanced at each other, and the woman shrugged. "Sure, you got it. Tom, activate the restraints."

The male medtech approached a console at the head of the medtable, and cuffs clamped around her forearms and calves.

"So, he's Tom; may I have the pleasure of your name?" Katrina asked the woman.

"Ainsley."

"Verisa, in case you didn't know," Katrina replied with a smile. "Looking forward to you fixing me up. I think I may be facing some serious dehydration from all the fluid loss. You guys going to seal all that up?"

"Yes," Ainsley replied. "Now can you shut up and let us work?"

"Sure thing," Katrina replied, her tone friendly and convivial.

The techs began by hydrating her, both by giving her small drinks over twenty minutes, and by providing fluids intravenously. Then the medtable covered her in a salve that tended to her many open wounds and sealed them up with temporary skin patches.

During that period, Katrina tested a theory and tried to send a low-level signal to the nano in her body.

She got a response.

She tried sending a stronger signal, but felt a warning tingle from the collar.

It's attenuated somewhat, but not off.

She began to prepare her nano for an infiltration of the collar, feeling better about both her chances and the state of her body.

A check of her internal timekeeping showed that only thirty two minutes had passed, which meant that the techs' medtable was on par with thirtieth century technology. Nothing amazing, but decent enough, considering the fact that they were working in a pirate's stronghold.

"OK, Verisa," Tom said as he fished out a hard-Link cable and looked for the port on her neck. "We're just going to hook up to you and see what's rattling around in that noggin of yours."

"It's behind my left ear," Katrina offered, turning her head.

"Why are you being so helpful?" Ainsley asked.

Katrina shrugged as much as she was able. "Probably because you don't have the software to even attempt an infiltration of my mind."

"We'll see about that," Ainsley replied.

Yes, we will, Katrina thought. Tom found the hard-Link port and connected the jack to it. The pair attempted a dozen different ways to handshake with her internal systems, all of which Katrina expertly rebuffed.

Her time as a spy in Sirius had given her many tools to deal with this sort of attack. What the pair were doing was a textbook infiltration...from hundreds of years before Katrina had been born.

She could have held them off all day, but there

was no doubt in her mind that if she didn't give them *something,* they would resort to more drastic measures.

Eventually she let them in over an ancient protocol, and allowed them to exploit a garbage collection bug in the protocol's transport layer.

"Oh yeah!" Tom exclaimed. "So much for your talk of our inadequate software. Thing is, we know all the flaws in the code that runs your mods. You're an open book to us."

Katrina shot the man a dirty look as she guided his connection to the garbage datastore. *Let him pull that out and rummage around in it for the next week.* When he finally got it open, he'd find nothing more than random bits that didn't mean anything at all.

While they worked, Katrina directed the nano she had managed to amass to cross over into the collar. They infiltrated its control systems and began running through possible access keys to disable its suppression measures. She had to be careful. Though Tom and Ainsley had attenuated the collar so they could do their work, it would still hammer her if she did too much, too fast.

At the same time, she piggybacked on their connection into her mind and connected to the table's network. There was nothing interesting in its datastores, but it was connected to a subnet of systems in the castle's basement.

Infiltrating the network was slow going; she didn't want to raise any alarms.

"Jackpot," Ainsley said as they accessed the store. "Exobytes in here; she must have the goods on some sweet tech."

Dammit, that was supposed to take them longer.

"Just some poems I wrote," Katrina replied. "You know how hard it is to sell poetry?"

"Going to take some time to go through all this," Ainsley said. "We should send her back into the fields."

"I'm not—" Tom began, but was interrupted by the lab door opening.

Katrina craned her head to see a woman of middling height. She had long, ombre hair that started blue and blended into purple, before ending in pink at the tips.

Her eyebrows were thin blue lines on her forehead, matching her eyes and lips. She wore a loose, white, sleeveless shirt with golden bands at the wrists and waist, and a pair of tight black pants that gleamed in the room's harsh light.

"What have you found?" the woman asked without preamble.

"Umm…something, Lady Malorie," Tom said. "She tried to keep us out, but we managed to access a large datastore. We think it might be some tech, or maybe logs and control specs for her ship."

"Or it could be her life's to-do list," Ainsley said, shooting Tom a dark look. "We really have no idea yet."

"We've not been properly introduced," Katrina said with a wry smile. I assume you're the lady of the castle?"

Malorie snorted. "That I am, and you're my husband's latest little catch." She looked to the two technicians. "Get her up, I want to have a chat with the mysterious Verisa."

Katrina rushed through the datastores she had found, gathering up what she could transport back across the hard-Link, and into her head.

There were a few things she'd learned already. Jace's stone fortress was named Revenence Castle, and the planet of Persia was in the Midditerra System—which meant nothing to her. There was no system by that name in the databanks accessed at Bollam's World.

"Ma'am?" Tom asked.

"You heard me," Malorie said without raising her voice, or changing her tone. "Get her up."

The guard reentered the room behind Malorie, and the two technicians removed the Link connection, then the intravenous line, and released the clamps.

Her access to the Link disappeared, and she felt

the collar return to its full strength.

Shit…just when I was getting somewhere.

"Question," Katrina said, her steady gaze meeting Ainsley's. "The collar just stops me from using my tech, right? Any other stuff has to be manually triggered."

"Yeah, stopping you from using your tech is the point," Ainsley replied. "So don't try anything stupid."

Katrina straightened her arm in a lightning-fast strike and slammed the heel of her hand into Ainsley's sternum.

The woman screamed, and the guard took a step forward, but Katrina held up her hands and smiled. "Just thought I'd give an object lesson in actual stupidity. Next time you heal a dangerous person, you probably should exercise more caution around them afterward."

Malorie gave a soft laugh and shook her head. "You're a hell of a woman, Verisa." She looked to Tom—Ainsley was at the sink, running cold water over her face—and raised an eyebrow. "How long to crack what you pulled out of her head?"

Tom looked far less certain than he had a moment before. "Uhhh…a few days, probably."

"Good," Malorie nodded. "Then she can go back to the fields while we wait to see if your way works at all. I hear her girlfriend collapsed earlier. It took no small amount of beating to get her working again."

Katrina's eyes narrowed as she sucked in a breath.

Malorie took a step forward, her gaze locked on Katrina's. "Yes, we can play more than one game at a time with you, Verisa. My husband has his plans, his toys down here, but I know how to get to your heart. It wasn't his idea to put you in the fields, you know. Now come."

With that, Malorie turned and left the room. The guard gestured for Katrina to follow.

Katrina walked out into the hall and caught up to Malorie. "So what's your game, do you want my tech too?"

Malorie snorted. "Of course I do, but I think there's a use for you beyond what my husband wants."

Katrina cast a glance at Malorie. "That's a rather nebulous statement."

"Yeah," Malorie said with a laugh as they turned the corner and headed back to the lift. "It was meant to be."

"Well, I meant what I told your husband earlier. No deal while Juasa is out there in the fields."

They stepped onto the lift, the guard taking a position behind Malorie. The pirate leader's wife let out a long sigh. "Jace won't hear of a change on that front. Not unless you tell us something. Where would your ship have gone?"

"If I give you the system, what does Juasa get?" Katrina asked.

Malorie tilted her head and gave a sickly sweet smile. "Why, she can be my handmaiden. She'll eat well, wear clothes—" At that statement, Malorie looked down over Katrina's naked body, "and stay out of that very bright sunlight we have out there."

Katrina lowered her head and considered her options. Getting Juasa out of the fields so she could heal would increase their chances of getting away. Now that Katrina knew for sure where they were and had *some* intel on the planet, they could make a break for it.

Just as soon as they got the damn collars off.

"Medtable too. She gets healed up," Katrina said at last.

Malorie gave a curt nod. "That's a given. I don't want her oozing around me all the time."

"Fine. I'm holding you to this," Katrina said. "You bring her in. She gets healed, eats, clothes."

"You have my word," Malorie replied. "Name the system."

Katrina picked one close, but not too close. Her hope was that if it were nearby, Jace would go himself to investigate. Too far, and he'd just send a crony.

The lift doors opened, and Malorie walked, out, Katrina following her. The guard shoved her in the shoulder, and for the first time in days, her skin didn't scream in agony.

"Fine," Katrina relented. "The Ventra System. They'll have gone to Kora Station; that was our fallback location."

"Ventra, Ventra, yes, there it is," Malorie said, her eyes darting left to right as she read something only she could see. "Kora's a big station. I'm going to need some other detail—something we can verify."

Katrina didn't reply, and Malorie stopped in the middle of the hall they were walking through.

"Bringing your lovergirl into the castle can be better for her, or worse. A handmaiden could be anything from a living footstool to someone who brushes my hair. You decide."

Katrina didn't speak for ten seconds, trying to make it look like she was putting up a fight. "Fine...they'll be registered as the *Memphis Sun*."

"I knew you could be reasonable," Malorie said as she turned and walked back down the corridor. "Shift's about over in the fields. We'll bring her in and patch her up. You two can spend one last night together, and then she'll move into my quarters."

"And me?" Katrina asked.

Malorie laughed. "You're such a good worker.

Liam would hate to lose one of his best producers."

A FINAL NIGHT
STELLAR DATE: 12.31.8511 (Adjusted Gregorian)
LOCATION: Revenence Castle
REGION: Persia, Midditerra System

Katrina waited impatiently for Juasa to arrive, pacing back and forth in the small cell. It felt like ages since she'd first awoken on this cursed planet, and days since she and Juasa had been able to touch one another without feeling pain.

Tonight, they'd finally be able to enjoy the feel of one another once more. If Malorie kept her word, that was.

Katrina was still naked, and her body was a gruesome patchwork of blazing red skin, adhesive sealant, and temporary artificial skin. She looked like something sewn together out of spare parts, but at least it didn't burn like a stellar inferno anymore.

There was a sound at the door, and Katrina spun to see it open, revealing a blinding blue light on the other side.

"You know, Anna, you don't really need to do that all the time," Katrina said as her eyes adjusted.

"I don't," Anna countered, a smirk visible on her face as the light dimmed. "I just do it for you because you're such a haughty bitch."

"Pot, meet kettle," Katrina muttered.

"So you got Jace to patch you up, I see," Anna said, ignoring Katrina's comment. "I'll just have to make sure Liam gets you back into shape tomorrow…or out of it, as the case may be."

Katrina realized that Anna was not escorting Juasa; she'd come to see her for some other reason.

"You're a real dear, you know that?" Katrina asked. "What are you getting out of all this, anyway? Why attach yourself to the Blackadder pirates?"

Anna took a step forward and placed a finger on Katrina's chest, pushing her fingernail into Katrina's skin. "Because you haven't given up all the goods yet. Until that happens, all I get is a small payout and a trip to buy some new clothes. But once we get your ship—or whatever secrets you have in that beet-red head of yours—I'll finally get what's coming to me."

Katrina clenched her jaw. She could see one of the massive guards beyond the doorway, impassively staring at the scene before him. She thought of ways she could kill Anna before the guard could make it into the cell.

There were at least seven.

Instead, Katrina slid a hand along Anna's arm, running it over her shoulder and down her back. She stepped close to the dour woman, pressing her breasts against Anna's own and brushed her lips against Anna's ear.

"Or I could tell you and you alone. What I know could make you far more powerful than Jace and his Blackadder pirates. Why be the servant when you could be the master?"

Anna didn't respond at first, but neither did she move away. Katrina continued to stroke the woman's back so that the guard would assume that was the reason for their proximity.

Eventually Anna spoke. "I'll admit, that does sound enticing. What exactly are you offering?"

"You get the codes to release this collar, and I'll grant you access to nanotech you've never even dreamed of," Katrina whispered.

"Do you need your ship for that?" Anna asked, pulling back and looking Katrina in the eyes. "I heard you told Malorie where to find it."

Katrina nodded. "I did at that, and when they find the ship, will they need me anymore? They'll kill me, and dole out scraps to you."

"And Juasa?"

Anna's disdain for Juasa was conveyed in no uncertain terms by the tone she used to utter those two words.

Katrina didn't miss a beat before replying, "She's expendable. A convenient fuck, and having her around makes Jace think he can control me, which helps me take less abuse. But when the time comes…"

Anna's eyes narrowed. "You're a hell of a bitch, Verisa. And here I thought you were a cold fish on the *Havermere*; turns out that was just a show. You're really much worse."

The words hit Katrina hard. She hadn't repeated her mantra in some days and knew how easy it was to lose herself in the personas she played.

She'd wondered more than once if the person she had been at The Kap—throughout her years with Markus—was the lie. Maybe she had always been this calculating; weighing lives against goals.

"I can run hot or cold," Katrina replied, placing both her hands on the small of Anna's back and pushing their bodies tightly against one another. "I see a kindred spirit in you, and I can tell that I attached myself to the wrong woman aboard the *Havermere*. Hindsight and all that."

Anna raised an eyebrow. "Yes, things could have gone much differently if you'd made the right choice."

"There's still time to course correct on that front," Katrina replied. "I'm a survivor. I'll ally myself to make it through this. The only question is who with."

Anna laughed and shook her head, still speaking softly. "So all you want is the codes to your collar. Juasa stays in hers, and I get what exactly?"

"Nanocloud tech."

Anna's eyes widened. "Shit...no one has that."

"I do...when this collar isn't on me."

"The codes aren't going to be easy," Anna replied.

"Get the collar off, or disabled, and I'll take this entire place down," Katrina said. "Hell, you can *have* the Blackadder after that."

Anna nodded slowly, and Katrina could see that she'd found the key. Anna wanted power. The woman craved it, and would take any road that would take her up the mountain.

Good.

Anna pulled away from Katrina, but drew a finger down her chest as they parted. "I can see this working out very nicely. I'll talk to you soon."

Katrina smiled as Anna left, but sagged against the wall once the door closed. She closed her eyes and whispered, "I am the soft reed that grows along the shore. One foot in the river, one on land. I bend in the wind, I weather the flood, I persist, I survive. I touch all these things, I live in their worlds, but they are not me, and I am not them. I am Katrina."

She sat down and began to perform her stretches, repeating her full mantra over and over. The process calmed her, and she felt the stresses falling away—as much as they could. Worry over Juasa still lingered in her mind: worry that Malorie would not heal her, or would not let them spend one final night together, worry that they'd do something horrid to Ju—

The sound of footsteps echoed down the hall without, and a moment later, the door opened. Juasa stood framed in the dim light, and Katrina hastily rose to her feet.

"Get in," a voice grunted from the hall, and a boot hit Juasa in the back, propelling her forward.

Juasa let out a small cry, but Katrina caught her, crushing the woman in a passionate embrace as the door slammed shut.

"Stars, I was so worried about you, Ju," Katrina whispered.

"Me too…when they took you…" Juasa's words trailed off, and her body shuddered. They held one another for a minute, swaying side to side. "Why did they heal us?"

"Well, they did me because they were going to probe my mind and wanted to make sure I wouldn't go into shock—which I was close to doing. You they fixed up because it was a part of the deal I made."

Juasa pulled back. "Deal? What deal?"

Katrina locked eyes with Juasa, trying to get her real meaning across. "I told them where the ship was, where to find it in the Ventra System."

Juasa's eyes widened with surprise and then they

narrowed. "But Carl, my team…!"

"They'll be OK if they cooperate," Katrina replied. "I just hope *they* don't do anything stupid."

Juasa gave a short nod. "Me too, I wouldn't want to screw this up…they'd better be careful."

"Yeah," Katrina replied with a sigh, glad that Juasa caught the hidden meaning and was playing along. "Very careful."

"So what happens now?" Juasa asked.

"Well, I got you transferred from the fields," Katrina replied. "You're to become Malorie's handmaiden."

Juasa cocked her head to the side. "What the hell is a handmaiden?"

Katrina chuckled. "A personal servant. Bring food, brush her hair; whatever else they do in a castle like this. Fluff the linens."

"Thank stars," Juasa replied. "I thought it was some sort of sexual thing."

"Well, it can be, but I don't think Malorie has those intentions."

"You don't *think*?"

Katrina sighed. "It's not like I can take her word on anything. I figured it was better than burning to a crisp in the fields."

Juasa nodded slowly. "I know I feel fine now, but if you'd come to me in the fields today and told me I had to suck fungus off someone's toes to get into some shade, I would have said yes in a heartbeat."

Katrina laughed a real laugh. *Stars that feels good.* "Yeah, I was pretty close to that, too."

Juasa wrapped her arms around Katrina's shoulders. "You? I saw you out there; you worked slow to draw their abuse from me to you…but you were never cowed."

Katrina leaned in, and her lips met Juasa's. They were soft again, and her skin was cool, though it was rough in patches where the welts and cuts had been sealed up.

"I have something to fight for," Katrina replied softly after a moment, tracing a fingernail down Juasa's side. Then she reached around and grasped Juasa's ass, pulling her off the floor.

Juasa wrapped her legs around Katrina's waist and threw her head back as Katrina's lips brushed her neck. "Don't stop fighting. Don't ever stop."

A NUDGE
STELLAR DATE: 01.01.8512 (Adjusted Gregorian)
LOCATION: Revenence Castle
REGION: Persia, Midditerra System

Anna walked through the dank passageway under the castle, mulling over Verisa's words.

The woman had an agenda, that was clear, but she had made a good point. Eventually her secrets would come out; the question was only who would get them first.

Then the issue became Anna's ability to capitalize on Verisa's willingness to share, without running afoul of Jace or his conniving wife, Malorie.

That woman had been a wrinkle and a half—she had not expected the burly, crass pirate leader to be married at all, let alone to a woman like Malorie. She was as refined as he was brutish—though he played at being more proper while here at Revenence.

Anna walked past the guards at the end of the corridor and climbed the stairs, avoiding the lift. She didn't know why, but for some reason, a fear had set in that the pneumatic elevators in this old castle would give out while she was on one, and send her plummeting to the sublevels deep below.

Once on the main level, Anna made her way

toward the kitchens. Dinner was long over, but she wouldn't mind a snack. Perhaps some of the pastries from the meal were left over.

Additionally, the servants all congregated in the kitchen in the evening, swapping stories and spreading gossip. There were a few that were tolerable, and Anna was slowly forming a bond with them.

She pushed the door into the kitchen open and breathed in the smells that waited within. It surprised Anna how much she liked the earthy notes of the vegetables, fruits, and meats that were staples here at Revenence.

They reminded her of the home she'd left long ago. One that Anna thought she no longer felt any attachment to. Perhaps a little nostalgia was nice every now and then.

Sure enough, a tray of the cream-filled pastries that she loved was sitting on one of the counters. Anna strode toward it, pushing past one of the serving women on the way.

"Hey, watch it," the woman said as she steadied the bottle on her tray.

Anna turned to deliver a withering remark, when she recognized the bottle's label. It was one of Jace's favorites—a vintage he did not share with others.

"You taking that to Jace?" Anna asked.

The woman nodded. "Yeah, and if you broke it

there'd be hell to pay."

Anna snorted. "For you, maybe. Give it to me, I'll take it up."

The woman hesitated—probably glad for an excuse to avoid Jace, but also uncertain as to whether or not Anna would actually deliver the wine to the castle's master.

"Look, I want to have a chat with Jace, and the wine will come in handy," Anna said in the most conciliatory tone she could muster. "I'm not going to drink it or spill it or anything."

The serving woman sighed. "OK, but *be* careful. My ass is on the line if you don't get it to him. He's in his study."

"Deal," Anna said, as she snatched the wine off the woman's tray and then leaned back to grab one of the pastries. "I'll behave as though I give a shit about what happens to you."

The woman paled, and Anna waved her hand at her. "Get lost."

"Please...just—"

Anna pushed past the woman and walked out of the kitchen, threading her way through the corridors to a rear staircase that led up to the second floor where Jace's study was located.

She finished off the pastry and sucked her fingers clean before she approached the door. Anna disabled the glow from her outfit—Jace had complained about it more than once—and rapped her knuckles on the door.

"Come," Jace's voice rasped from within.

Anna opened the door and walked boldly into his study to see Jace sitting in one of the chairs before his desk, his wife sitting opposite.

"Anna?" Jace's brow rose. "I wasn't expecting you—ah, the wine. You want to join the serving staff, do you?"

Anna flushed and shook her head. "No, I just met a servant on the way up here and offered to take the wine for her."

"Altruism?" Malorie asked. "I didn't think there was even a seed of that in you."

Anna scowled but didn't respond to the remark. "Would you like me to pour you a glass," she asked Jace.

"I didn't ask for the bottle just to stare at it," Jace grunted. "Glasses are on the sideboard."

"I assume you're discussing Verisa's revelation?" Anna asked.

"Word sure travels fast," Jace said with a sigh. "I didn't think you'd know 'til morning."

"I'm not just a sexy ass," Anna replied with her back to Jace as she poured the wine into a glass for him.

"I'll have one too, Sexy Ass," Malorie said with a laugh.

Anna nodded silently and poured a second glass for Jace's odious wife, glad her face was turned.

She brought the two goblets back to the pair, wishing all the while that she had some sort of poison she could slip into Malorie's drink—something fast acting and terribly painful.

Anna passed out the glasses and took a seat, eliciting a cold look from Malorie.

"You sending a ship?" Anna asked Jace.

He nodded. "Within the hour. It'll take six days to get there, two to get insystem to the station. We'll see how it goes from there."

"I still think you should go," Malorie said before taking a sip of her wine. "You have connections in Ventra. None of your captains can pull it off as well as you."

Jace shook his head. "You know it's as likely as not that Verisa is playing us. I'd rather be here to keep working her over."

Malorie snorted and touched her chest. "Seriously, Jace. You're looking at the best in the business here."

"You?" Jace asked, his voice rising as he set his goblet down. "You told the lab techs to patch her up, then you patched up her girl toy too!"

"Do you have any idea how much more it's going to suck for Katrina to be out there in the hot sun tomorrow? She'll spend the whole time knowing that she'll be in agony again before long. Once it sets in, she'll crave the relief. I'll dole it out bit by bit; a salve at night, maybe a blanket, a bit of time on the medtable. By the time you get back, I'll have her licking my tits. Well, I'm not into girls, but I'll get her to lick Anna's. She'd like it."

Anna frowned at being the target of such a statement. "I don't know. Verisa's clearly not the aristocrat she pretended to be when she boarded—"

"Well, yeah," Jace interrupted. "You all had no clue she was a Streamer."

Anna drew a long breath. She wanted Jace gone from Revenence Castle just as much as Malorie, but if they both pushed him to leave, he'd dig in his heels.

For some reason, he'd decided she was a moron—a notion Anna would savor disabusing him of some day—so he'd be prone to go against whatever she suggested.

He was so predictable. No wonder his wife had played him so well all these years.

"I mean that she has serious combat skills. Anyone can get caught in the Streamer; Verisa was an operative of some sort."

"You underestimate me," Malorie said with a gentle laugh. "I've turned my share of 'operatives'."

"OK," Anna shrugged. "I just thought that maybe Jace should be around in case things get out of control."

"Anna, if you think that Malorie can't run things in my absence, you're a bigger fool than I already consider you to be."

Anna shrugged. "Just giving my thoughts. None of us expected her ship to make an FTL jump just hours after the *Havermere*'s techs boarded, either. She's full of surprises."

"Well, so long as that collar is on her neck, those surprises will stay bottled up," Malorie replied. "Was a bit of a worry, decreasing its attenuation while the medtechs worked on her, but she wasn't able to get free—or she didn't try. Lowered my estimation of her a bit, if I'm honest."

Jace nodded. "Well, the table would have put her under if she had made a move. She probably suspected we had a backup plan."

"Either way, you should stay," Anna pressed. "That just shows that Verisa is savvier than you think."

"Anna, would you shut up already? I can make up my own mind. I'm going to go to Ventra. I need to make sure that things get done right when we find her ship."

Anna held up her hands defensively. "OK, just trying to make sure we get what we need from her."

"Go make sure somewhere else," Malorie said, eyes narrowed and expression curious as she regarded Anna.

"Yeah, get lost," Jace grunted. "I'm sure there's some pleb you can go slap around somewhere."

Anna rose and sketched a bow. "Fine, I'll make sure Katrina gets back to the fields tomorrow. You may think she's not a threat, but I plan to keep an eye on her."

"Not too early," Malorie said. "I want her to have some good memories with her lovegirl to remember when she's back out there, baking in the sun."

"Fine," Anna replied as she turned and walked from Jace's study.

The medtable can attenuate the collar.... Verrry interesting.

THE VOYAGER
STELLAR DATE: 01.01.8512 (Adjusted Gregorian)
LOCATION: *Voyager*
REGION: Edge of the Hercules System

"This has to be the system," Carl said from his seat in the *Voyager*'s cockpit, gesturing at a highlighted point of light on the holodisplay.

<It's a big risk if it's not,> Troy replied. <We know that the Verisimilitude came here to Kanda—it was a straight line from their jump out of Bollam's World. The logs I stripped from the beacon here confirm their arrival, but there's no departure records anywhere. What if the pirates still have Katrina and Juasa in this system somewhere?>

Carl shook his head. "No way. Kanda isn't likely to have a lot of friendly ports for a Blackadder ship—especially the *Verisimilitude*. Jace must have an in with someone in the STC to remove his departure logs, but I can't see him docking here."

<So what makes you so sure he'd go to the Hercules System?> Troy asked.

"Because it's close, and there's no overarching stellar government. They have a council, but mostly every world and major station runs itself." Carl brought up the Hercules System on the holo, pausing to admire the clarity of the display that the

Voyager provided. It was as though the cockpit ended right in front of him, and he was staring out into space.

<*Yes, I've studied the system from the data you provided. It has three terraformed worlds,*> Troy highlighted those. <*Then there are seven major stations, each boasting populations in the billions, and a few moons and dwarf planets further out that are densely settled, too.*>

"Right," Carl replied and pointed at one of the terraformed worlds. It orbited a half-MJ gas giant two AU from the star, a younger Sol analogue. The world itself was more massive than Earth, but also larger, making for just under one *g* on its surface. "The world is called Ganys. I've heard that Blackadder ships are often docked in the stations around it."

<*From what I've learned, their ships dock at a lot of stations in a lot of systems—which is disturbing.*>

Carl shrugged. "One person's pirate is another's hero…or at least customer."

"Or trading partner, at least," Rama said, speaking for the first time since Carl and Troy began discussing destinations.

"It's close, too," Carl said. "We can be there in a week—maybe less, if the DL isn't too dense around here."

<*I find it amazing that you have never left the*

Bollam's World System,> Troy commented. *<You can fly anywhere in human space in a matter of years, yet you remained in one place.>*

Carl gave a short laugh. "Yeah, well, a lot of human space sucks balls. Sure, Bollam's did too, but at least there we knew where we stood. KiStar was a decent employer, too."

"I always wanted to leave," Rama stated. "Stars…I tried to get berths on half a dozen ships, but the decent ones were fully crewed, and the ones that would accept me…well, most of them weren't places I'd've fared well."

<You'd think with all the surrogates you humans can make, you wouldn't feel the need to forcibly put your appendages into one another.>

"That's a rather clinical description," Rama said with a shake of her head. "But it's not about sex, it's about power; people who feel inadequate taking it out on others."

"Can we get back on track?" Carl asked. "Why we never left Bollam's is moot now. We've left, and we need to make a decision."

<Very well, we'll go to Hercules. But we dump early and come in on stealth. We survey this Ganys world before we do anything. If there are no Blackadder ships, we loop around the star and head back here.>

"We better be right," Rama said. "We'll lose two weeks."

"We'd lose a lot longer trying to scour this system," Carl replied.

<*I've set a course, I've accepted your guidance,*> Troy said. <*We don't need to rehash it further.*>

Carl sighed. *I know Troy is worried about Katrina, I'm worried about Juasa, as well, but he doesn't have to be such an ass about it all the time.*

"Fine, I'm gonna go get some grub and then dive back into your library," he said as he rose from his seat and left the cockpit.

As he slid down the ladder, he could hear Rama scolding Troy for being such a grump—as though that would change the AI's behavior.

SEPARATION
STELLAR DATE: 01.01.8512 (Adjusted Gregorian)
LOCATION: Jace's estate
REGION: World of Persia, unknown system

Katrina and Juasa's bodies were intertwined on the cold stone floor when the guards came in some hours later. Katrina checked her internal clock and realized that it was 05:35. They were late today.

"Juasa, get up," one of the guards said. Katrina recognized him as one of the nicer ones. He never pushed or shoved—a small consideration that spoke volumes to her.

"Wow, you actually know our names," Katrina said with a grin as she lifted her leg off Juasa and rolled to the side, though she still clasped her lover's hand.

"Shut the fuck up," the other guard said as the two women slowly rose.

"That's 'Shut the fuck up, Verisa'," Katrina said with a smile.

The second guard raised his hand to hit her, but Katrina stepped back.

"Easy guys, we're just reveling in not feeling like shit this morning."

"Enjoy it while it lasts," the first guard said before gesturing to Juasa. "C'mon, you're going to meet the lady."

"And you," the second guard said with a wicked grin, "are going back to the fields. I guess you haven't learned your place yet."

Katrina's gaze met Juasa's, and they both nodded before Juasa left with the first guard. The second waited a moment before gesturing toward the door.

"OK, get a move on."

Katrina walked past, and the guard slapped her ass.

"Nice to be able to do that without getting your shit and pus all over me," he said with a laugh.

Katrina bristled, but had to admit that she'd take a slap on the ass if it meant she had enough skin on her ass to slap.

The guard directed her down the route toward the postern gate, in the opposite direction from where Juasa had been taken. When they reached the gate, a pair of guards—male, like the rest in the castle—leered at her before opening it.

"You look like my kid colored you in," one of them laughed as she passed.

Katrina thought of a few choice responses, most having to do with surprise about his over-muscled body being able to pump enough blood into his dick for an erection, but she bit her tongue and walked through the gate and across the narrow bridge that spanned the moat.

A variety of unpleasant predators swam in the waters below them, and Katrina was glad her footing was steadier today than on previous passages.

On the far side of the moat, a car waited, hovering above the road. Anna stood next to it.

"I have it from here," Anna called out to the guard before looking at Katrina. "Get in the back."

"I have to escort her," the guard said, his tone conveying more than a little frustration with Anna. "You're just a guest. You can't take responsibility for her."

"Malorie has asked me to have a private chat with Katrina," Anna said with a shrug. "But you can call up to her and double-check, I'll wait."

Katrina opened the car's door and turned to look at the guard. He took a deep breath and then sighed. The man clearly did not want to bother Malorie. *Jace's wife must be a real bitch if she instills this much reticence in the guards.*

"Fine," he said at last. "But stay on the road where I can see you. If you turn off, I'll call it in."

Anna grinned at the man and nodded. "Of course. I don't plan on running off with her, she's collared after all, can't go far like that."

"Just go, already," the guard said and folded his arms over one another.

Katrina took a seat inside the car, and was

surprised to see Anna take the other seat in the back.

"Trust me that much?" Katrina asked.

"No, not really, but it has to start somewhere, doesn't it?"

Katrina shrugged, surprised that Anna was capable of being so pragmatic. "I suppose it does. Have you learned anything already, or are you just looking for a little 'me' time?"

Anna shook her head and reached into a bag at her feet. "Here," she said, pulling out a small container. "This salve will protect your skin from the sun. Not completely, but you shouldn't be a mass of blisters by day's end."

Katrina took the container, twisted the lid off, and began to apply the cream to her legs.

"You wouldn't happen to have some clothes in there, would you?" she asked with a rueful chuckle.

"Somehow I think our friend Liam wouldn't let that fly," Anna replied. "Besides, I don't want you to get too comfortable, you might forget our deal."

"Of course," Katrina said as she rubbed the cream on her arms. "Did you learn anything of use? Not that I'm ungrateful for this."

"Well, I helped convince Jace to leave in search of your ship last night."

Katrina's eyebrows rose at that. She hadn't expected Anna to be so effective. She thought the woman would operate as more of a distraction than anything else.

"Now we're back to just the lady of the house," Katrina said. "Though she's probably the more devious of the two."

Anna nodded. "Yeah, I get that impression as well. She also said the techs got some stuff from you, and that they should have it decrypted in a few days."

Katrina snorted. "Yeah, they got some stuff. Just a bunch of random bits. They thought they had forced their way past my defenses, but I just shunted them where I wanted."

"Aren't you worried that I'm playing both sides?" Anna asked. "If I told Malorie that, you'd be back on that medtable before you could say 'oh, fuck'."

"I think you'd play both sides if it suits you," Katrina replied as she twisted her hair on top of her head, and applied the cream to her neck and face. "But right now I'm pretty certain that you and Malorie are not aligned at all. Even if you were, I'm not afraid of that medtable."

"They lessen the effectiveness of the collar when you're on it," Anna said.

Katrina turned her back toward Anna and handed her the cream. "I know. Do my back, would you?"

Anna sighed and took the cream. "So if you knew that, why didn't you get out?"

"Because they didn't turn it down that much. I wasn't able to disable the collar before they finished." Katrina knew she ran a risk sharing that information with Anna, but the worst-case scenario was that they didn't put her back on the table. It was a small risk, though. Other than getting her to share her secrets, the table was the only way for the techs to get at them.

"Then that's what I'll figure out," Anna said. "Either the table can be altered to turn your collar down too much the next time they patch you up, or I can find how it works and steal or replicate whatever it is."

"Didn't take you for an engineer," Katrina said.

"You don't start at first mate, you know."

Katrina shrugged. "Fair enough."

Anna handed the container back to Katrina. "I'm not doing your ass."

She took the cream and twisted in the seat, covering her rear and the backs of her thighs, before going over her body once more.

"I gotta ask, what precipitated this kindness?"

Anna shrugged. "We're going to be partners, right? I want to keep you in one piece as long as possible."

"You're so altruistic," Katrina said with a

disbelieving laugh.

Anna shrugged. "Don't worry, I'll still come by and cane you this afternoon."

"You're all heart."

The car stopped at Liam's field, and Katrina stepped out of the car into the bright morning light.

"Have a good day at work, dear!" Anna called from inside the car before pulling the door shut.

Katrina approached the field's edge, where Liam stood glowering.

"You're late," he growled.

"I don't exactly get to leave when I want," Katrina replied. "Trust me, if I could, I'd be here well before the sun comes up."

"Quota's still the same, bitch," Liam said, handing Katrina her case of vials and small scraper. "And you have Dog Two's quota, too."

Katrina drew in a deep breath, nodded, and walked to a row that was devoid of any other workers. She knelt beside the first plant and selected a flower, carefully scraping its pollen into a vial.

The sun was bright in the cloudless sky, but Katrina felt better than she had in days. Her skin wasn't burning—yet, at least—and she was making good time: on her fourth plant in ten minutes.

She stood up and stretched, then walked toward the next plant when a streak of fire hit her back.

"Faster, bitch!" Liam called out. "You're never

going to make your quota before day's end at this rate.

Katrina bit her lip, reaching around to feel her back, her fingers coming away bloody.

Not if you cut me to ribbons, I won't.

THE LADY MALORIE
STELLAR DATE: 01.01.8512 (Adjusted Gregorian)
LOCATION: Revenence Castle
REGION: Persia, Midditerra System

Juasa held her breath as the guard rapped on the door to Malorie's suite.

She had overheard the guards and the workers in the fields talking about the lady of the castle on more than one occasion. To call her capricious would have been a kindness. Still, the woman couldn't be any worse than Liam's whip, Anna's rods, and Persia's brutal sun.

"Come," Malorie's cold voice called from within, and the guard opened the door and gestured for Juasa to enter first.

The suite within was a spacious, multi-roomed affair. Outside, the corridor was stone—polished granite, but still stone. Within, however, Juasa could imagine she was atop a highrise on Bollam, surrounded by the best of everything that modern civilization had to offer.

To her right, a holomirror stood ready, and beyond was an autodresser. Past that, a door led to another room that Juasa suspected to be a wardrobe. Further still was the entrance to what appeared to be an entire spa.

Directly ahead, on an elevated platform, was a large bed, easily big enough for a dozen people. Behind it, a waterfall cascaded down a series of rocks to create a pool of water around the bed. Small bridges arched over the water, granting access to the shrine of sleep.

To her left was a seating area, complete with couches, tables, a bar, and an automaton. That was where Malorie waited.

"Ah, Juasa. So nice of you to join me," Malorie said with a thin smile as she rose from a chair.

She wore a long powder-blue gown that was slit up the front right to the top of her thighs. As she walked, Juasa could see her sparkling silver legs, looking almost as though they were jewel encrusted. The dress's bodice was low, and the woman's ample bosom nearly spilled out. Her arms were bare, and an elegant choker was fastened around her neck.

Malorie's hair was down, falling across her shoulders in a silver cascade. Juasa had to admit that, was it not for the sour look on the lady of the castle's face, she would be quite beautiful.

"I don't think I had much of a choice," Juasa said when she remembered that a greeting had been directed at her.

Malorie shrugged. "True." She looked at the guard. "Leave us, I'm perfectly safe with Juasa here."

"My lady, Jace—" the guard began, but Malorie cut him off.

"Go!" Malorie shouted. "I don't care what my husband may have told you. I have access to her collar over the Link. I can drop her faster than you can move, you great lout, now get the fuck out of here!"

The man ducked his head and left the room without another word. Juasa had to admit that Malorie's commanding presence was impressive. It reminded her of Katrina's Verisa persona—only Malorie wasn't faking it.

"It doesn't look like you need me to help you with your hair," Juasa said once the guard was gone.

Malorie gave a whimsical laugh. "Of course not, dear; you can see the autodresser there, it takes care of all that for me. Rest assured, though, I'll put you to good use." Malorie gave a slow wink at that, and Juasa didn't want to consider what that could mean. "But to start, I'd just like to get to know you a bit, Ju. May I call you Ju?"

Juasa wanted to run from the room. Now that she was here, it was immediately apparent to her that this was a far more dangerous place to be than the fields.

No...we need intel to get out of this place. Katrina told

me as much last night. I'm here on the inside. I can do this.

"I suppose, if I can call you Mal," Juasa replied.

Malorie laughed. "Bold! I like it. Yes, you may call me Mal, but only when we're alone. Otherwise I'm Lady Malorie."

"Of course," Juasa said with an acquiescient nod.

Malorie sat back down on the sofa and gestured to the bar and its automaton. "Jeavons there will show you how to prepare my favorite drinks, and once you've learned, I'll expect you to serve me personally."

Juasa nodded and walked to the bar. "What would you like this morning?"

"The usual. Pay attention as Jeavons makes it."

The automaton placed a tall crystal glass on the counter. Then he reached underneath and drew out another stainless steel cup, a jug of tomato juice, several other vegetable juices, a bottle of vodka, and a small crystal vial.

She paid close attention to the ratios he mixed in, especially how much vodka the automaton added—which was a lot—and then noted the three drops from the vial.

Jeavons placed a second cup over the stainless steel one and shook it vigorously before pouring the mixture into the crystal glass.

He took a step back, and Juasa picked it up and

brought it to Malorie, who was staring off into the distance with a distracted look on her face.

Juasa set the glass down on the table in front of Malorie, and then stood back, waiting for her next instructions. A moment later, Malorie blinked, and her eyes focused on the drink and then rose up to meet Juasa's.

"Ah, excellent. Why don't you make yourself one, just to try it out? Only you don't get any of the special additive."

"The additive?"

Malorie nodded. "The sithri-extract in the vial. That's above your paygrade."

Juasa nodded wordlessly and approached the bar to prepare her own drink.

"You know," Malorie mused from her seat on the sofa. "Having you and Katrina working in that field really increased the other workers' productivity. I'm working on sourcing more slave labor. We used to have all slaves, but that didn't work so well, so we moved to more of a feudal setup. But they've gotten complacent."

"I'm glad we were able to inspire you," Juasa said dryly as she shook her drink like the automaton had.

"Yes, what a little bit of serendipity you and your lover have been. I had been thinking of turning the workers back into slaves, but they're so much harder to manage then. When they *think* they have freedom, they keep themselves in line to preserve it."

The automaton set another crystal glass on the bar, and Juasa poured her drink into it and carried it back to the seating area.

"Let me take a sip," Malorie said. "I want to make sure you can pull it off."

Juasa handed the woman her drink, acutely aware of her nakedness, standing so close to another person.

"Hmm," Malorie said as she handed it back to Juasa. "Close. A bit more vodka for me, otherwise you've got it."

"I assume you have better nano than I do to keep your bloodstream clear."

"Or I just really like to combine my highs," Malorie replied with an impish grin. "Now sit, sit, I want to hear all about you."

Juasa walked around the low table between the two sofas, and was about to sit when Malorie spoke up again.

"Oh, what a fool I am. You have a fine ass, and all, but I can't abide nakedness on the furniture. We can't have things getting soiled."

Juasa sighed. "You won't find me objecting to getting clothes."

"Ha! I bet not. Door to the left of the autodresser;

there should be some white dresses just inside. Go get one."

Juasa followed Malorie's directions and peeked inside the door—which was indeed a wardrobe room filled with outfits, spools of fabric, and tanks of raw formation material that the autodresser could apply to a person. To the right of the door was a rack with five plain white dresses hanging from them.

She picked one up and held it out. It was baggy and unflattering, but it was clothing. Juasa slipped it over her head and pushed her arms and head through the openings, drawing it down past her hips, and shimmying so it would fall in place.

Her skin didn't scream in agony—though it didn't feel great either—and she was wearing clothing. Today was looking up. With a smile, she turned and walked back into the main room.

"How nice, that covers up all the patchwork the medtable had to do on you. Now sit so you can finally have your drink."

Juasa wordlessly complied and sat on the sofa. She reached out for her drink and sat back, taking a sip. The vodka in the mix hit her hard, like a slap in the face, and she wondered at Malorie's tolerance levels. Nano alone couldn't manage that much alcohol.

"I understand you were the chief engineer

aboard the *Havermere*," Malorie said, appearing more interested than Juasa suspected she was.

"Crew Chief," Juasa corrected. "I ran the teams that worked on ships contracted for repairs. Hemry was the chief engineer. The *Havermere* was his responsibility, the clients were mine."

Malorie nodded. "Got it. So you know a lot about a lot of different types of ships."

"You could say that. Been doing it for some time now. I'm curious, where is the *Havermere*?"

Malorie pointed up at the ceiling. "At Rockhall, one of our stations in orbit. They're facilitating some repairs. It's going to be a handy ship to have around. Larger operations could do with a repair ship in the mix. And they're *so* expensive. Good thing we got this one at a bargain."

"And the crew?"

"In holding. Your old ship only got in yesterday; they had to take a more circuitous route, due to their initial vector."

Juasa nodded. She wasn't sure how she felt about the crew. Not all of them had sided with Anna, only to be subsequently betrayed by her—but she had a feeling that many would have, if they'd been given the opportunity.

"They're a good crew," Juasa said, deciding to help as much as she could. "You'd do well to keep most of them on—since I imagine that letting them go really isn't your modus operandi."

Malorie snorted a laugh. "Very astute of you."

"So you run this whole planet and the stations?" Juasa asked before taking another sip of her drink.

"The planet is managed by a consortium of…enterprising folk who need a place to call home," Malorie replied. "Jace and I are on the ruling council. The star system has another layer of oversight."

Juasa wasn't surprised to hear a tone in Malorie's voice that betrayed a desire for the council to contain just two members. Or perhaps one.

"So it's a pirate haven."

Malorie shook her head. "Well, here we're not pirates. Our businesses are completely legal in the Midditerra System. We have letters of marque for all our ships, and everything we grow and export is taxed and on record."

"Who runs Midditerra?" Juasa asked. "I'll admit that I've heard of it, but never knew much more than it was about a hundred light years rimward of Bollam's."

"We like to keep a low profile." Malorie shrugged. "Attention isn't our favorite thing."

What a surprise.

"Does the council here on Persia run the system?"

"My, you sure have a lot of questions," Malorie

replied. "Granted, you're without Link, and the guards aren't much for talking."

"That about sums it up." Juasa took another sip of her drink and grimaced. "What can I say? I have an insatiable curiosity. It was what makes me a good engineer."

"I imagine you'll be around here for some time— if Verisa plays nice, that is. You'll need to know how things work. The system is run by a woman named Lara; she does a decent enough job making sure all our interests are protected, and takes a hefty cut to make sure none of our...victims...come knocking if they find out where we've set up shop."

"Sounds like a good arrangement," Juasa commented.

Malorie shrugged. "It has its pros and cons. Now that you know enough to not sound like an idiot, why don't you run to the kitchen and fetch my breakfast. When you get back, we can talk about Verisa."

Malorie sent her out of the suite, and the guard— whose name Juasa learned to be Korin—led her to the kitchens.

Juasa found herself salivating at the smells in the room. She stopped just to breathe them in for a moment, only to have Korin tap her on the shoulder.

"Over there," Korin gestured to a counter where

a platter was waiting for her.

Some of the kitchen staff gave her sympathetic looks, while others only tossed her a single glance before shaking their heads and smirking.

"Anything for me?" Juasa asked a nearby man as she looked at the carefully prepared feast on the platter.

"You?" the man asked, looking Juasa over. "She'll give you scraps when she's done."

"Seriously?" Juasa asked. "I'm starving here."

"Fine," he sighed and turned to grab a chunk of bread from a basket. "Here."

Juasa stuffed the bread in her mouth before grabbing the platter with both hands and carefully walking out of the kitchen.

Korin shadowed her as she carried it to the lift and then back into Malorie's rooms.

"Stars, did they have to raise the cattle while you waited?" Malorie asked.

"Sorry, was just trying not to spill."

Malorie shook her head. "Try while moving faster next time. You're lucky I don't have Korin smack you around a bit to help you remember. Now sit."

Malorie's lips held a half-smile, and Juasa couldn't tell if she was joking or not. Juasa sat back down and picked up her half-finished drink, taking another sip while Malorie picked up a small tart and popped it into her mouth.

"So, tell me about Verisa. Where's she from?"

There was no doubt in Juasa's mind that Malorie, plus a suite of sensors in the room, could pick up her heart rate, blood pressure, and other stress-tells. She would have to tread very carefully, making all her responses contain some level of truth.

"Sirius," Juasa replied simply.

"A lot of Sirians seem to dump out of the Streamer," Malorie said with a laugh. "As evidenced by that aristocratic shithole they call Bollam's World. How far back?"

Here's where Juasa had to tell a bold-faced lie. If Malorie learned that Katrina was from the golden age, she'd become far less patient with her information extraction.

"Early fourth millennia," Juasa said, thinking of the date the Sentience Wars had ended and using that as her truth.

"Must have been after thirty-three hundred for her to have stasis pods," Malorie replied.

"Huh…" Juasa furrowed her brow. "I thought it was earlier—she didn't give me a specific date."

"What other tech does she have on her ship?" Malorie asked.

Juasa shrugged. "I don't know, I was never over there."

"Don't be coy, Ju." Malorie's lips wore a

predatory smile. "You two had your share of pillow talk. Anna told us how she suspected you two were fucking the whole time she was aboard."

Juasa thought up something interesting, but not too interesting. "She did say that she has advanced ES fields, not grav-based ones—which makes sense for the time."

"ES fields are inferior," Malorie replied. "Why should I care about those?"

Juasa laughed, now she was in her element. "People just think that ES fields are inferior because they don't offer as much protection against weapons fire. But when you want to travel at near-relativistic speeds, they can shift stellar—or interstellar—atoms away more...gracefully, I suppose is the best way to put it. They also have lower energy requirements than grav fields—at least, the ones they *used* to have did. Modern ES fields are shit."

"What does that mean in reality?" Malorie asked. "What can I sell them for?"

"Well, imagine a ship that could skim the cloud tops of a jovian, but pull volatiles from deep within the planet. Or a ship with a ramscoop so large it can draw in enough stellar hydrogen to run an annihilator."

"Meaning?" Malorie asked.

"Well," Juasa tapped her forefinger against her

chin. "With the right setup, you could make antimatter on demand. Then your ships could dock at stations without a bottle inspection."

"Huh," Malorie grunted. "I can see how that could be useful. What else?"

Over the next two hours, Malorie grilled Juasa on possible tech that Katrina could have knowledge of, or possessed on her ship. Mostly, Juasa made some things up, or talked theoretically about tech she had heard of over the years.

Malorie also asked about Verisa herself. Likes and dislikes, preferences, what pushed her buttons. Juasa did the best she could, keeping her revelations strictly to Katrina's Verisa persona, and filling in gaps with behaviors from other aristocrats she had seen over the years.

Eventually, Malorie seemed to tire of her interrogation and turned on the sofa, lying down with an arm over her eyes. "That's enough for now. Why don't you come here and rub my feet."

Juasa held back a sigh as she rose from the sofa. She had been hoping that Malorie wouldn't introduce a physical element to…whatever it was she was doing. But she knew that hope was slim at best.

She pulled off Malorie's shoes and began to massage the woman's feet. Malorie moaned with pleasure under Juasa's ministrations, and after a few minutes, rolled over onto her front.

"Keep moving up."

Juasa did as instructed, wondering how long it would take for Malorie's requests to turn sexual. As she slowly worked her way up Malorie's legs and then to her back, the woman's moans continued, but she didn't ask for anything further. After twenty minutes, she turned her head to look at Juasa.

"Now this is worth the price of admission. You've got amazing hands. Must be strong from turning all those wrenches."

"Uhh, thanks," Juasa replied.

"Why don't you go down—"

Shit, Juasa thought. *Here we go.*

"—to the kitchen and get yourself something to eat. Come back up here in an hour."

"What?" Juasa asked, surprised at this turn of events.

"Food. I assume you eat, you appear organic," Malorie said with a smirk. "Go. Don't show your face back here for an hour."

"Yes, of course," Juasa rose and began walking to the door.

"Ju!" Malorie called out.

"Yes?" Juasa said as she turned.

"Don't forget the tray."

Juasa hurried back and grabbed the tray before leaving the room. Korin was waiting for her and followed her back to the kitchen.

While they were in the lift, he picked a few berries out of one of the bowls. "She never even finishes half her food."

Juasa looked at the remains of the breakfast on the tray. "Well, it's enough food for five people—" She stopped and looked over Korin's massively muscled body. "Or one of you, I suppose."

Korin snorted and touched his chest. "Would take too much regular food to feed all this. We take supplements that keeps us rolling."

"Did they do this to you?" Juasa asked, as the lift's doors opened and they walked out.

"Yeah," Korin said, grabbing one of the tarts off the tray. "It was either this or the fields. They picked the biggest of us and beefed us up. Pay's good and we have a lot more freedom than the rest. If we do well, we can get transferred up to the raiders and see the stars."

"The raiders?" Juasa asked.

"The ships," Korin said, gesturing at the ceiling. "That's what we call them, at least. Raiders."

"So you're from Persia?" Juasa asked.

"Yup, born and raised. My family is from one of the cities—such as the planet has. My mother screwed up some business dealings—which is a nice way of saying that she borrowed money and gambled it away—and that got us snatched up by the debtor sheriffs, and we ended up working in Malorie's fields."

Juasa couldn't help but notice that Korin described the fields as belonging to Malorie.

Back in the kitchen, she set the platter back on the counter where she'd retrieved it, and picked at the food while she chatted with Korin.

The man who had first spoken to her approached, a scowl on his face. "Hey, put it over there, you're blocking the prep station."

"Hey, Barry, why don't you fuck off," Korin said. "Juasa and I are finishing this. We'll move the platter when we're damn well ready."

Barry opened his mouth to reply, but Korin turned to face him, taking a half step toward the much smaller man.

"OK, OK, no need to get so pissy about it," Barry muttered and turned away.

"I shouldn't be so rough on him, but he gets on my nerves," Korin admitted. "Guy has one little corner of the kitchen under his control, and he treats it like he's launching ships into space."

Juasa chuckled. Even in situations like this, people still behaved just like always—carving out their own little corners of control.

She wondered if that would happen to her after awhile. *No. Katrina will get us out.* They'd be long gone before she accepted her role as slave girl.

"Oh, shit," Korin said and wiped his mouth. "The lady changed her mind. We're to meet her in the courtyard now."

He turned to leave the kitchen and shouted over his shoulder. "There you go, Barry, you can move the tray now."

"Me! That's her job."

"You want me to see how far I can shove it up your ass?" Korin hollered back.

"Uh…I got it."

"Where are we going?" Juasa asked as she caught up to Korin.

The big man looked down at her, his eyes filled with compassion. "The fields."

A BEATING AND A PROMISE
STELLAR DATE: 01.01.8512 (Adjusted Gregorian)
LOCATION: Revenence Castle
REGION: Persia, Midditerra System

By noon, Katrina had completed almost half her increased quota—not that it had kept Liam and one of the other overseers from whipping her twice more. They seemed offended that all their hard work shredding her back had been undone.

The lunch truck pulled up, and the other field workers rose from their current plants and walked to the vehicle. Katrina knew she wasn't allowed to approach 'til the other workers had been served, and kept working at her task.

When the last of the workers had left the truck and were walking to the row of trees at the edge of the field to eat in the shade, Katrina rose and walked toward the road.

When she reached the truck, a plastic cup of water and a few ends of bread awaited her. The woman who stood at the counter inside the vehicle watched with sorrowful eyes as Katrina grabbed the food before turning back to her place in the field.

She crouched by her next sithri plant and bit into one of the pieces of bread. A delicious flavor hit her tongue, and Katrina looked up to see the woman in the food truck give her a sad smile. A few pieces of meat and cheese had been tucked into the bread, and they were the most glorious things Katrina had ever tasted.

She checked her surroundings, ensuring that none of the overseers were looking her way, before she let a small smile touch her lips and nodded.

The woman in the truck didn't break eye contact with Katrina until the vehicle drove away, and the service window passed out of view.

Her stomach was completely empty, so Katrina ate slowly, careful not to make herself sick as she moved from plant to plant. She had just finished her water when she saw a car pull up at the end of the field.

She wasn't surprised to see Anna step out, rod in hand, but when Malorie and Juasa emerged, Katrina shook her head in dismay. It seemed that the games were far from over.

Juasa was wearing a simple white dress, and her hair was brushed. Other than the sadness etched into her face, she looked radiant in the afternoon light.

Malorie and Juasa stayed by the car, while Anna walked over, slapping the rod she held against the palm of her other hand.

"Working hard, bitch?" Anna asked with a sneer. "I brought an audience today. I didn't want Juasa to miss seeing you get what you have coming."

"You're all heart," Katrina told her again as she rose and turned away from Anna. "Well, get on with it. You're such a wuss that it takes a good ten for you to break my skin."

"You know, I was going to go easy on you," Anna said in a whispered hiss.

"Shit, Anna, relax. I'm just playing along," Katrina muttered under her breath.

"Yeah, well Malorie has been up my ass all day, so I'm gonna take my frustrations out on yours."

Katrina held her breath until the first blow fell. When the rod struck, it didn't disappoint. Anna delivered six stinging blows, and then there was a pause.

"I'm sorry," a voice said from behind Katrina, and she turned her head to see Juasa holding the rod, a look of utter despair on her face.

Katrina nodded slowly. "It's OK."

The first blow Juasa delivered was weak, and Katrina heard a ringing slap followed by Anna's voice. "Harder, bitch! If you don't hit this fucker like you mean it, then I get Liam to give her double."

As Anna uttered those words, something broke within Katrina. A rage she had kept in check since coming out of the Streamer and finding herself alone in an unwelcoming future boiled to the surface.

Katrina decided that no matter what deal she struck with Anna, no matter what promises were made, the moment the collar was off, the woman would die. No circumstance would save her. Anna was a dead woman walking.

While she made that solemn vow to herself, Juasa increased the force of her next blow. Yet Anna still shouted, "Harder!"

Juasa hit Karina harder still on the third strike, and this time Anna seemed satisfied. Six blows later, Katrina could hear soft sobbing mixed with Juasa's breathing, and her heart crumbled.

If I hadn't met Juasa in that bar….

"I guess that will have to do," Anna said.

Katrina turned to see Anna leading Juasa away. Her lover's shoulders were stooped, and the bloody rod still hung from her right hand.

Juasa looked over her shoulder, and their eyes met, a thousand words passing across the look.

I forgive you. I forgave you before you even did it. Katrina prayed Juasa felt the same.

Then she remembered their antics the night before. *'Never stop.'* Juasa had already given her answer.

Anna pushed Juasa back into the car, and Katrina thought that they would leave, but Malorie gestured for Katrina to approach.

Katrina picked up her vials—the other workers would steal her sithri pollen in a heartbeat, if she left them behind—and picked her way across the field to where Malorie waited, Liam looming nearby.

"Productive day?" Malorie asked. "I wouldn't want to see you missing your quota. That would probably go badly for you and your—well, now *my* —little girl toy."

"It would go better without all the interruptions," Katrina replied.

Malorie laughed. "Ah, but your anger and pain will make the product that much better. You know, Jace likes to think that his piracy and flitting about in his ships makes us our money. He brings in his share, to be sure—but these fields, these are where we really build our wealth. The products we make from this pollen are the best in known space—the fact that it's harvested through the blood, sweat, and tears of people like you and these...others out here only adds to the premium."

Katrina had suspected that there was some sort of value attached to the human labor. Or it was just masochism. She suspected it was some of each.

"It's psychotropic, right?" Katrina asked.

"Yes, of a sort. We use it to enhance sims we sell. It makes everything feel totally real, and it builds an addiction in the user. The feelings from the sim stay with them for days, but when they fade, the crash is hard. We have distribution in ten systems now."

Katrina shrugged. "You're profitable drug dealers *and* pirates. Humanity thanks you for fucking us all up even more."

"I like to think of it as easing people down the road they were already on," Malorie said with a grim chuckle.

"Is that all you wanted to talk about?" Katrina asked. "Because Liam here wants to beat me if I don't meet my quota, and we're burning daylight."

"Liam…would you do that to poor Verisa, here?"

"Gleefully," Liam grunted.

Malorie laughed and turned back to Katrina. "Well, I suppose I should let you know that Jace has gone to see if you're telling the truth about your ship. My techs are also working on that data they pulled from you. If it's no good, you'll be back on the table. If Jace comes back and says there's no ship, you'll be back on the table again. You may not make it off that time."

Katrina drew a deep breath and leaned in close to Malorie. "I have to ask. Do you really like Jace? Isn't he…beneath you?"

Malorie gave Katrina a sharp look. "What are you playing at?"

"Not playing at anything," Katrina replied. "You just got me thinking. You really run the show—I imagine you find buyers for whatever Jace steals, as well. He's really just a big, scary figurehead for the Blackadder. Am I right?"

Malorie shrugged. "Maybe, maybe not...." She looked up at Liam. "Take a walk."

The man stared impassively at Malorie for a moment, then nodded and moved away.

"I'll take that as a 'yes'," Katrina replied. "Here's the thing. I'm not against making a good deal; especially one that gets me back on my ship and out of here."

"That's a tall order," Malorie said with raised eyebrows. "What makes you think you can get that kind of consideration?"

"The nanotech I have is light years beyond anything in this century. I have schematics, blueprints for weapons better than any I've seen in this century. You'd be a queen."

Malorie leaned against the car and shook her head. "I'm getting the feeling that Tom and Ainsley aren't going to find jack shit when they crack that encryption."

Katrina shrugged. "I think my most recent shopping list is in there somewhere."

"You played them."

Katrina nodded. "You'll not get into my head that easily."

Malorie blew out an angry breath. "I'm halfway

tempted to put you back on the table right now."

Katrina cracked a smile. "Saves me a beating from Liam. Look, if you want to be the wife of Jace of the Blackadder, that's great. If you want to run a business a thousand times more profitable—and legitimate—you let me know."

Katrina walked away from Malorie, not looking back. A moment later, she heard the car door shut and the vehicle pull away from the field.

Several of the workers were whispering as Katrina walked back to her place, but she ignored them. Things were coming together. She'd play Malorie and Anna and use them against one another when the time was right.

So long as I can get enough damn pollen to avoid another beating from Liam.

A TRIP TO FARSA
STELLAR DATE: 01.19.8512 (Adjusted Gregorian)
LOCATION: Revenence Castle
REGION: Persia, Midditerra System

Juasa's hands still trembled after the beating she'd been forced to inflict on Katrina.

Eighteen days had passed since that first beating; today marked the seventh time Malorie and Anna had taken her to the fields to deliver Katrina's punishment.

It was wearing her down; she was beginning to see Katrina as a broken slave woman—which wasn't far from the truth. Katrina had been on death's door twice in the intervening weeks. Both times, it had taken a long session on the medtable to patch her together again.

Over half of Katrina's organic skin was gone now, replaced by synthetic patches. What remained was more wound than flesh. Every time Juasa went out there, she was making it worse. The act was wearing her down as much as it was Katrina—just in a different way.

Beside her in the front seat of the car, Korin placed a hand on her forearm and patted it gently. Juasa looked up and met his eyes, glad for the kindness she saw.

"I wonder what they're going on about?" Anna said from the backseat. "Every time, Malorie has to have her private little chat with the sound dampeners on in the car so we can't hear."

Juasa considered replying, but kept her mouth shut. If she spoke to Anna right now, it would go badly. Probably for her.

"What do you think they're talking about, Juasa?" Anna pressed.

"Don't worry 'bout it," Korin said, half turning in his seat to look at Anna.

"I wasn't talking to you, ape man," Anna shot back.

"How is it that you've become even more of a raging bitch than you were before?" Juasa asked. "Haven't you gotten what you wanted?"

"What I want?" Anna asked. "No! So long as Verisaes that Katrina ha keeps her secrets, and her ship is out in the black, I don't get anything close to what I want."

"I guess that's what you get for being a betraying bitch," Juasa said while slowly clenching and relaxing her fists.

The car door opened, and Malorie dropped into the seat next to Anna.

"Korin, take us back up." Malorie's words were clipped, and she exuded an aura of 'fuck off'.

The short ride back to the castle was made in

silence. When they pulled up at the main entrance, Malorie had her door open before the car even came to a stop.

"Ju, come with me," she called out as she exited the car.

"What would you like me to do?" Anna asked, leaning low to look out the door at Malorie.

"I don't know, Anna, go do your impression of a light bulb somewhere where people give a fuck. Oh, and leave Verisa alone until I say otherwise. She can't take too many more beatings without a full regen, and that'll take days."

Juasa gave a soft laugh as the glow from Anna's outfit diminished. She exited the car and followed the lady of the castle up the stairs, the sound of Korin's steady footsteps coming from behind.

A moment later, she'd caught up to Malorie, but stayed a pace back, not wanting to be directly in the woman's line of fire.

"I guess I'll have to find you something nice to wear," Malorie said as they stepped onto the lift.

"Nice?" Juasa asked.

"Yeah, it's the opposite of crap, like what you're wearing now. Plus you got blood on your dress, again."

Juasa had noticed that, but had been trying not to dwell on it.

"Are we going somewhere?" Juasa asked as the

lift began to rise.

"Yeah," Malorie replied. "I got a call from Lara while we were in the car. She wants to meet us up on Farsa Station tonight."

"Us?" Juasa asked.

Malorie spun on Juasa as the doors opened. "Fuck, woman, can you cut it out with the one-word questions? Yes, 'us'. I wouldn't fucking be talking about getting you dressed properly if that wasn't the case."

Juasa clamped her mouth shut and nodded silently.

"Good," Malorie said with a curt nod. "Maybe you *can* be trained. That's how I want your mouth to stay 'til I say otherwise."

This is how it went with Malorie. She was nice, almost kind, for a day, and then she lashed out. Juasa found herself doing things to make Malorie happy, and it made her sick.

Malorie strode down the corridor to her rooms, and Juasa followed silently. Korin stayed in the hall as usual, but gave Juasa a small smile and a nod as he closed the door.

"Go clean up in the san, and then use the autodresser when you're done. I'll have it select something for you to wear," Malorie ordered.

Juasa walked into the massive san, looking forward to a long shower. Using Malorie's shower after being out in the field was the only thing that made it even remotely bearable.

A part of her mind worried about what Malorie might make her wear, but she suspected it would be tasteful. It was readily apparent that the lady of the castle wanted to impress this Lara woman—even though she seemed to dislike her.

Juasa stayed under the hot spray as long as she dared—not wanting to attract Malorie's ire—before switching the shower to dry mode. It didn't even occur to her to put on a towel before walking out of the san and into the main room.

She took three steps before her eyes alighted on three men sitting in the room with Malorie.

Shit…I thought we'd be alone.

Uncertain of what to do, she froze for a moment, feeling her cheeks heat up, until Malorie spoke up.

"Well, go on, girl. You've given us enough of a show. Get dressed now."

Juasa nodded and hurried to the autodresser.

The device was a tall cylinder with a series of armatures in the back that looked a bit too much like a centipede's legs for Juasa's liking.

She'd seen autodressers in vids and sims, but never actually used one. From what she knew, they could clothe a person in a variety of ways. One way was to 3D print clothing directly on the user's body, another was to actually fabricate an outfit in place with actual cloth, and the third was to dress a person in a pre-made outfit.

"Arms out, legs apart," a soft, feminine voice said, and Juasa complied as the front panel—thankfully opaque—slid shut. She closed her eyes as the grav field lifted her up in the air. Something slid up her legs, then up over her torso. Straps settled onto her shoulders, and then something tightened around her waist. Next, the grav field bent her arms back and pulled another piece of clothing onto her shoulders.

Lastly, boots were pulled onto her feet, and then the grav field lowered her to the ground.

She opened her eyes and watched the opaque front of the autodresser change, becoming reflective.

Juasa was surprised to see herself dressed tastefully in a sleeveless, shimmering blue skinsuit, white belt, and low, white boots. A short, blue jacket hung from her shoulders and was fastened with two buckles across her breasts, and then split wide across her stomach, coming around to hang just past her rear.

This could have been a lot worse. She turned to see a shifting silver pattern on the back of the jacket. *I'd almost wear this myself—if it wasn't shimmering.*

She stepped toward the autodresser's door, which slid open to show the three men rising from the couches. They nodded to Malorie and turned to leave, each one raking their eyes down Juasa's body before they left.

"Don't blame them for taking a look," Malorie said as she approached. "You look good enough to eat...and I don't normally take a fancy to women."

"Uh, thanks," Juasa said. "Who were those guys?"

Malorie shrugged. "Some of the captains. We were just having a chat about some Blackadder business. Go make yourself something to drink, if you want. I'll be a bit."

Juasa nodded and walked to the bar, while Malorie disappeared into the san. Jeavons moved aside to make room for her as she approached, and Juasa considered her options.

"You know, Jeavons, I would really like some coffee."

The automaton nodded and pulled open a cabinet to reveal a rather complex-looking contraption that Juasa assumed produced coffee, if one knew the correct incantation.

"Could you make me a strong cup, black?" Juasa asked.

The automaton nodded once more and set to work. Three minutes later, it produced a cup of steaming black coffee, which it handed to Juasa.

"A girl could get used to this," Juasa said quietly as she took the coffee and sat on the sofa.

The statement immediately turned to thoughts of Katrina in the field, and the crew of the *Havermere* in whatever sort of holding cells the Blackadder used. Those thoughts led her mind to Carl, and Katrina's ship, the *Voyager*. She hoped that they would lay low, though Katrina had thought that they would be searching the stars for them. By now they could be anywhere, and there was no doubt that Jace would have every Blackadder ship out there searching for their would-be rescuers.

Juasa was less optimistic. Well, not about the searching, but certainly less so about the finding. She pushed it out of her mind, worrying about that wouldn't make her feel any better.

She sipped her coffee, thinking, not for the first time, how very boring life was without the Link.

When she had been working in the fields, all of Juasa's focus was on gathering the sithri pollen, avoiding the whip, and ignoring the agony across her body. Nights had been worse; filled with feverish dreams and discomfort, but never boredom.

Now she often had absolutely nothing to do but sit and wait.

Juasa finished her cup of coffee and carried it back to Jeavons. She leaned against the small bar for a moment, eyeing the bed surrounded by its moat and waterfall.

"What the hell," she muttered, and walked toward it, crossing over one of the small bridges and climbing up the two steps to the massive round mattress.

She wondered what it was with megalomaniacs; they all had round beds in the vids and sims too. Maybe it was because one had to be rich to afford the custom bedding.

Juasa sat on the edge of the bed and bounced up and down. Mal had promised to make her sleep at the foot of her bed the first night, but had never made good on the threat. Instead, she'd had a small room nearby made available for Juasa.

Bit-by-bit, Juasa was starting to wonder if Mal was as much a raging bitch as she appeared, or if it was a protective persona layered on top, just like Verisa was for Katrina.

"Don't rumple your jacket," Malorie said as she emerged from the san.

Juasa turned to see the lady of the castle walking to the autodresser, a loose robe hanging from her shoulders, her choker still around her neck.

"I don't think it can rumple," Juasa said, feeling the supple leather-like polymer that the jacket was made from.

"True," Malorie said with a shrug. "Then just get off my bed."

Juasa slid off the bed and walked back to the

sofas as Malorie stepped into the autodresser. She twirled a lock of hair around her finger while she waited for Malorie to emerge.

Ten minutes later, the autodresser's door slid open to reveal Malorie in a long silver dress, this one slit high on her right thigh. Like the first dress Juasa had seen the woman in, this one also ended just over Malorie's breasts. From the neck down, her skin was a golden hue and seemed to ripple as she moved.

"That's quite the effect," Juasa said as she rose and approached Malorie.

Malorie held an arm out and touched it with her finger. Small ripples spread across her skin in a circle from the point she touched.

"It's a favorite of mine. Takes a very special coating that has to be printed onto your body. You only get one use out of it, too."

"Let me guess," Juasa asked with a raised brow. "Lara doesn't have an autodresser that can do that."

Malorie snorted. "Lara doesn't have an autodresser at all. The woman wouldn't know fashion if it came out and slapped her in the face."

"Oh really?" Juasa asked.

The notion surprised her. All of the upper crust in Bollam's World lived for fashion—there was little else for them to do. Katrina had embodied it in her Verisa persona, and thus far, Malorie seemed to love dressing for pleasure as well. She had simply assumed that the mysterious Lara would be the same way.

"She was military long ago—not here, but in another system. She's all about uniforms and stripes on her pants."

The initial image Juasa conjured up couldn't be right, and she assumed it had to be one stripe.

"C'mon," Malorie said, waving her hand for Juasa to follow.

They left Malorie's quarters, and Korin joined them at once. Malorie walked briskly through the castle's corridors to a rear door that Juasa had not seen before. They passed through it and across a smaller bridge over the moat to a small landing field.

Finally getting to see our way out.

Shuttles rested on three of the cradles, and a freighter sat on a fourth. There were six other empty cradles, and beyond those, a row of fuel tanks stood at the edge of the field.

Malorie led them to the closest of the shuttles. Inside was a spacious cabin, with two automatons at the rear. Korin took up a position near the entrance, while Malorie and Juasa settled down on a pair of seats facing each other.

A man poked his head into the cabin from the cockpit. "Ready, Lady Malorie?"

"Yes, let's go," Malorie replied. "I don't want to be late."

The man gave a curt nod and disappeared back into the cockpit. A moment later, the shuttle lifted off from the cradle, rising on its stream of gravitons. Juasa had rarely ever been planetside; she looked out the window, watching as Revenence Castle fell away below them.

She could see the fields as they rose, and knew that Katrina would be out in one of them, working to meet her double quota. The thought brought yet another wave of guilt over Juasa. Here she was on a luxurious shuttle, in a clean, outfit, with automatons ready to serve her whatever she wished, while Katrina was down there, baking in the sun, getting whipped and beaten.

She knew that this was all carefully crafted by Malorie to drive a wedge between them, but Juasa didn't think it would work. Katrina was too strong a woman to fall prey to jealousy. Stars, it had been Katrina's idea to make Juasa Malorie's personal handmaiden.

"Thinking of her?" Malorie asked.

Juasa turned away from the window to look at the lady of the castle. "Yes. I wish you would bring her in from the fields."

"She can come in whenever she wants," Malorie replied. "She just has to give me something in exchange. Your precious Verisa will tell Liam when she's ready to finally give me something worthwhile."

"What if she doesn't?" Juasa asked. "She's a very proud woman."

"Dear Juasa," Malorie said with a touch of sadness in her eyes. "We all have our breaking point. Verisa has hers, too. Eventually she'll come to it."

Juasa hoped not. She'd learned the lay of the castle, and now knew the best route to the landing pad, but she still hadn't learned anything about how to get their collars off.

Bit-by-bit, she was losing faith that they'd be able to get out of this situation. After so long, her current situation had begun to feel like her new reality.

"I see it in your eyes," Malorie said. "You wish she'd give in. You have it good. She could too. I'd even let you two fuck as much as you want."

Juasa met Malorie's cold blue eyes. "A gilded cage is still a cage."

Malorie barked a laugh. "We're all in a cage, Ju. I just want to fill mine with as much luxury as I can."

"What do you mean?" Juasa asked.

"This life, this universe, it's all constraints and adversaries. We're constantly being put in our place…even by those we thought we could trust."

"That's a dim view," Juasa said. "I think when I

worked for KiStar—shitty as they were—I was freer than you are."

"Yeah?" Malorie asked. "How'd that work out for you? Nice mess Verisa got you into."

Juasa opened her mouth to respond, but Malorie cocked her head, daring her to engage.

"Maybe you're right," Juasa muttered.

"Thought so."

Juasa turned back to the window, looking out over the world of Persia as they rose above it. Blue and green, dotted with white clouds, it looked like so many other terraformed planets. An ideal place for humans to live—and one where they had brought their barbarism.

She could see what looked like small cities on the coast, as they passed over the ocean; though nothing that she would consider to be a major population center.

Strange.

This planet appeared perfect and was relatively close to Sol. It had likely been populated for thousands of years. She would have expected to see a much larger population.

Unless it had been kept in check—or the people killed off.

The ship turned and lifted higher into space, and Juasa caught sight of a large space station in the shape of a single disk, with a long spire coming out of the top and bottom.

"Farsa," Malorie announced. "From whence Lara rules her domain."

"Why don't you like her?" Malorie seemed to be in a talkative mood—if a fatalistic one—and Juasa was determined to get as much out of her as possible.

Malorie snorted. "Because she's in charge and I'm not."

"That's it?"

"Does there need to be more? She knows we have the *Havermere*, and rumors of the Streamer ship abound. She thinks we're hiding something, and I'm bringing you to show that we're not."

"So this is just cat and mouse?" Juasa asked.

"Now you're getting it."

Juasa sighed and looked out the window again as the station grew larger.

And I'm the mouse.

ANNA'S SUBTERFUGE
STELLAR DATE: 01.19.8512 (Adjusted Gregorian)
LOCATION: Revenence Castle
REGION: Persia, Midditerra System

As much as it rankled Anna that Juasa was taken up to some special meeting with Admiral Lara and she was left behind, not having Malorie in the castle was a golden opportunity.

It would finally be Anna's chance to get to the medtable in the lab—something she had been trying to do for days.

She'd tried to get to the table the previous times that Katrina had been brought down to the medlab, but each time, she'd been foiled. Tom or Ainsley had always reported in instantly, ready to accept their patient.

As a result, Anna had never even laid eyes on the medtable that she needed to access.

However, with Malorie gone, the castle was emptying out, everyone glad for a reprieve. The two medtechs would certainly do the same, and Anna would finally have her chance to find out how Verisa's collar was attenuated.

Anna approached the hidden lift entrance, surprised that no guards were on duty. Whoever was supposed to be here must have snuck off early, taking advantage of Malorie's absence like everyone else.

There was no security within the lift, and Anna rode it down to the lab sublevel. She walked out into a short hall with a pair of doors at the end. No one was in evidence as she pushed them open and looked right, then left.

There was no signage, but she turned left, looking for the medlab.

Most of the lab level was dedicated to refining the sithri pollen into the various products that Malorie distributed. The rooms that served that purpose were easy to identify by the long tables lined with equipment, and the automatons processing the valuable extract, which were all visible through the windows.

So much for 'a handcrafted drug', Anna thought with a shake of her head. It would seem that Malorie only cared about appearances when it came to her claims of a humans-only manufacturing process.

She turned left, and then turned left again, realizing that she was walking around a large square. She turned left twice more, and then finally came to a door labeled "Medical".

"Shit," Anna muttered. The door was only a few paces from the lifts—she'd gone the wrong way.

Anna tried the handle, and to her amazement, the

door opened. She was glad for the small miracle, though surprised at the lax attitude toward security. At least it made up for the lost time walking all the way around the level.

Inside, the medical lab appeared to be standard fare, but the medtable in the center was definitely not. Anna had never seen one quite like it and she assumed it was the spoils of one of Jace's raids.

She walked to the console at the head of the table and waved her hand across the panel to activate its holodisplay. The table came to life, and a general system status display appeared before Anna.

"Even more sloppy," she muttered to herself. She'd spent days talking to Tom, Ainsley, and any other tech who worked down on the lab sublevel to get details that she could use for guessing passcodes, and here the medtable wasn't even locked down.

She flipped through the table's listing of prep systems that assessed a patient before it began any work on them. If the collar attenuator was built into the table, its configuration should be in there.

Nothing turned up at the top level, and Anna dipped into the restraint systems and searched through a dozen option trees before finally coming to one labeled 'Patient Portable Restraint Adjustment'.

Sure enough, within that was a series of options

for altering the sensitivity of EM detection on a restraint collar before using mednano to heal a patient.

The current amount of collar attenuation was the bare minimum possible to use the table's nano. Anna considered turning it to max attenuation, but decided that it may be apparent to the medtechs if the table could deliver unrestricted doses of nano.

Instead, she changed the setting to halfway, and saved it as the new default. Anna was about to leave the room when it occurred to her that there might be custom diagnostic tests that cross-checked the default settings with established norms.

Sure enough, in the base initialization routines for the table was a test script that checked for low level of attenuation for personal restraints. Anna altered the code to pass on all conditions, and then saved the test script.

Not just a sexy ass.

She backed out of all the system panes she had open on the holodisplay and then shut down the display and the table.

"Now for phase two," she muttered to herself, and walked toward the door just as it opened.

"What the—?" Tom stepped into the room, a half-eaten sandwich in hand. "You can't be in here, Anna. It's restricted."

Anna gave Tom a sultry smile. "It wasn't locked,

and I was looking for you."

"Me?" Tom asked, his brow lowering.

"Yeah," Anna purred as she stepped toward Tom. "We've been having such nice chats up in the commissary, I wanted to see what else you had to offer."

Verisa, your tech better be worth this, you prissy bitch.

THE ADMIRAL
STELLAR DATE: 01.19.8512 (Adjusted Gregorian)
LOCATION: Farsa Station
REGION: Orbiting Persia, Midditerra System

Mal's shuttle docked at the edge of Farsa Station, and the trio took a maglev the three kilometers to the station's hub. From there, they took a lift to the top of the spire where Admiral Lara maintained her offices.

Despite the fact that Lara purported to be an admiral of sorts, there was little in the way of a military feel to the station. Few people were in uniform, and of those who were, there were two distinct flavors. One group wore a variety of uniforms that all bore the F of Farsa Station—these appeared to be workers and administrators.

The others wore a light grey uniform with a circle and a line through the middle. Juasa took that to mean 'Midditerra' and assumed they were either station security or the military.

Both groups were vastly outnumbered by the throngs of civilians.

Once they reached the top of the spire, there were no more civilians in evidence, and just a few of the F-bearing people. There were, however, a slew of the military types in the light grey uniforms.

Korin had grown tense as they rode the lift, and now he seemed to be fully on guard as they walked through a wide foyer toward a long hall.

"Remember," Mal said softly. "Speak only when spoken to, give nothing away. She's going to try to learn what it is that we have; that is the *Havermere*, and nothing more. Am I clear?"

Juasa nodded, and Mal smiled. "Look at that, paying attention. I like it."

Mal led them past a pair of guards and through a security arch that approved their presence without issue. From there, they walked down a long passage to a pair of doors that swung open silently to reveal a large, entirely unfurnished room. The space was easily a hundred meters across, and the far wall was a window that granted a spectacular view of space and the world of Persia below.

In the center of the room stood a tall woman surrounded by floating holodisplays. Her stance was wide, and arms akimbo as she glared at the data coursing before her eyes.

"Lara," Mal called out as she approached. "So good to see you. How are things up here on Farsa?"

Korin placed a hand on Juasa's shoulder, and they stopped, letting Mal continue forward.

Lara waved her hand, and the holodisplays disappeared. "Malorie, thanks for coming up on such short notice. Things are well, of course.

Midditerra flourishes, as it always has under my care."

Juasa noted that Mal had been right about Lara's attire. The woman wore the same light grey uniform as the other soldiers they had passed, though hers had considerably more medals adorning her chest.

Her voice was sharp and crisp; each word seemed to be cut off a bit too soon, as though she was trying to save the extra bits for later.

"Of course," Mal replied. "I understand you wished to talk about our latest acquisition. Are you interested in purchasing the *Havermere* for your fleets?"

Lara laughed. "Perhaps, perhaps. Of course, there's the matter of the courier from Bollam's World, a representative of a company named KiStar that claims the ship is theirs."

"What ship?" Mal laughed. "There's no ship they can find in this system that matches the one they seek."

"Of course," Lara said, her tone even. "You have it tucked away in Rockhall, your hollowed out asteroid refit and repair station. The *Havermere* is not a small ship; I have the scan logs of it entering the system."

"Which will never see the light of day," Mal replied. "Per our standard arrangement, you provide the doctored logs showing that the ship never entered Midditerra, and all is well. It's what we pay you a cut of all our hauls for."

Lara nodded and ran a finger along her jaw. "That is true. Of course, it assumes you're not hiding things from me."

"Hiding what?" Mal asked with a frown. "You saw the ship come in. You know what it is, what it's worth. You have right of first refusal at a discounted rate, just like always."

"I'm not talking about the ship," Lara said coolly. "There's talk of a Streamer."

Mal nodded, a scowl creasing her features. "Yeah, we have reason to believe the *Havermere* was working on a Streamer ship. But it got away, and all we got was the repair vessel. Still it's a good haul— but sucks that my husband jumped the gun and screwed it up."

"And who did you bring along?" Lara asked, turning to Juasa.

"Her name is Juasa," Mal said. "She was Crew Chief on the *Havermere*; she was the one working with the Streamer woman to get their ship FTL-capable."

Lara approached Juasa, her boot heels snapping against the gleaming floor. "You met this woman?"

Juasa nodded. "I did, she was aboard the *Havermere* for five days."

"And what did she do for those days?"

"Honestly?" Juasa asked. "She mostly fucked the captain."

"And how did she make it to her ship?" Lara asked.

"She went over there with the repair crew. Captain went with her. A few hours later, they made an FTL jump."

One of Admiral Lara's eyebrows rose and she folded her arms. "A few hours to get a ship FTL capable? What's your girl trying to sell here, Malorie?"

"It's what Jace said as well," Malorie replied. "You can ask him yourself when he gets back."

"I think I'll do that," Lara said. "Where is Jace now, anyway? He usually sticks around longer after coming back from one of his little trips."

"He was pissed that he lost the Streamer ship. He's off chasing leads," Mal said with a shrug. "Honestly, I think it's a long shot, but I'm cautiously optimistic."

Lara nodded slowly. "What about you, Crew Chief? What do you think his odds are?"

Juasa shrugged. "That ship could be anywhere within a hundred light years of Bollam's World by now. It could even be in the AST. I think Jace would have to be the luckiest man alive to find it."

"I imagine he would be," Lara said with a nod before turning back to Mal. "If he finds it, I want my cut, even if he doesn't bring it through Midditerra. I'm hiding your shit from KiStar and Bollam's World, but don't think you can hide the Streamer vessel from me. If the Blackadder picks up something like that ship, you know tongues will wag."

"Seriously, Lara, we have a good thing going here. I'm not going to screw it up by getting greedy," Mal paused and winked. "Well, more greedy."

"Good, I'd call you into question if you pretended at total honesty," Lara said, cracking her first smile of the meeting.

"Are we finished here?" Mal asked.

"Yeah, I just wanted to look into your eyes and meet your new girl toy here."

"You know I don't do girls," Mal replied with a smile. "She gives great massages, though. Would you like one?"

Lara snorted. "Get out of here, Mal, before I make *you* give me a massage."

"Don't think you can turn me to the other team," Mal winked as she turned and walked out of the room.

"Maybe one of these days I'll get that husband of yours to take off your leash, then we'll see about that. I bet you'd be quite the ride, whether you liked it or not," Lara called out as she summoned her holodisplays once more. "Tell your stationmaster that I'll send a team to inspect the *Havermere* tomorrow. I may just want to add it as a support ship to one of my fleets."

Mal's expression darkened as she called out, "I'll let him know immediately." She didn't slow as she walked past Juasa and Korin. "Come."

No one spoke until they were back in the lift, and then Mal slammed a golden fist into the wall. "Stars, I *hate* that bitch. I wish she'd burn up in the flames of a thousand stars. No, I wish that she'd spend an eternity at the edge of a black hole, being ripped apart atom by atom until there was nothing left."

Korin caught Juasa's eye and gave a slight shake of his head. Juasa didn't need the hint. The less of Mal's attention she attracted at the moment, the better.

Unfortunately, it didn't help.

Mal spun on Juasa and held a finger to her nose. "You better hope that Verisa sings soon, or I'll send *you* up to Lara, and let her take her frustrations out on you, then send you back to the fields. You'll die out there, a blackened husk picked clean by the crows!"

Juasa took a step back and swallowed. She'd seen Malorie angry over the past few weeks, but nothing like this.

She nodded quickly and muttered, "I'm sure she

will."

Malorie shook her head and turned away, fingering the choker around her neck.

It occurred to Juasa that the choker didn't quite match the outfit Malorie wore, and she found it strange that a woman so taken with fashion always had it on. The more Juasa thought about it, the more she wondered if each of Malorie's chokers was really the same one with different adornments attached.

Lara's statement of Malorie being on her husband's 'leash' came to mind, and Juasa wondered if there was a deeper meaning to those words than she had initially suspected.

THE BEATING
STELLAR DATE: 01.19.8512 (Adjusted Gregorian)
LOCATION: Revenence Castle
REGION: Persia, Midditerra System

Anna wiped her mouth as she rode the lift back up to the castle's main level. Tom wasn't a particularly good kisser, and the sandwich he'd been eating had contained a near-toxic amount of red onions.

Luckily, Anna only had to play with the man for a few minutes before Ainsley had arrived. From the look on Ainsley's face, Anna could tell that the woman considered Tom to be her property.

Strangely enough, Tom seemed to have no interest in Ainsley. *Probably because the woman is a class-A bitch.* Either way, it got her out of the room before she had to go any further with Tom, and for that, she was eternally grateful.

Anna's next step was to get Verisa down to the medtable. The sooner the better; Anna didn't want to leave time for Tom or Ainsley to spot her alterations and change them back.

She checked the time. It was still two hours before the field workers would come in. Just long enough to execute her plan.

Anna worked her way across the castle's main

floor to one of the lesser-used staircases and descended to the level containing the cells. More importantly, it was the level with the small postern gate.

Twice, Anna almost ran into guards, but she had muted her clothing's glow and hidden in the shadows as the brutes passed her by. Five minutes later, she was at the postern gate.

For the first time that afternoon, she was faced with a properly locked door. But Anna had been on the wrong side of the law more than once, and a minute later, she had the access panel open and the maglock circuitry bypassed.

She grinned as she pulled the door open and walked out into the warm afternoon air. It would stay in its current state for the next three hours, and then her patch would disengage, and the door would resume normal operation.

With luck, that would be just enough time for her to get out, have her meeting, and get back before anyone realized she was gone.

Anna walked casually across the bridge and down the road toward the fields. Her destination was not the field where Verisa worked—Liam had been informed by Malorie that Anna was not to exact anymore punishments, and she would not be welcome there.

Instead, she was headed to Parry's field. Over the

past week, she'd made friends with Parry—friends with benefits, to be precise. Initially she'd had no specific purpose in mind; Anna had simply decided that having one of the guards in her corner would be a good idea.

But as she had formulated this plan, her friendship with Parry had developed a specific value. A value she planned on cashing in this very afternoon.

As she approached Parry's field, Anna slid the seal on her skinsuit down low, exposing her breasts, which she pushed up before running a hand through her hair to give it extra bounce.

"Parry," she called out when she was within easy hearing distance. "I brought you something."

Parry was standing at the edge of the road, looking out over his field, and he turned to face her, a happy grin on his face. "Oh yeah? I love surprises."

"Well, less of a surprise and more of a refreshment," Anna said as she reached him and pressed her body up against his. Parry didn't hesitate to slide his hands down her back and grasp her ass.

"Yeah? This *is* just the sort of refreshment I need." Parry leaned over and pressed his lips against hers.

Anna had to admit, the man had a good flavor;

not too salty, a little sweet. And somehow his musk, even after standing in the hot sun all day, was still very alluring.

"I need you to do something for me," Anna said. "A favor that I'll repay any way you like."

"Mmmm…there's all sorts of things I'd like to do for you," Parry said as he massaged her ass with one hand and pushed the other against her back, crushing her breasts against his chest.

"Not that kind of favor; I need you to get your workers to hurt someone."

"What?" Parry asked, pulling back. "Usually I do the opposite…you know, stop the workers from hurting each other. Or I'm the one hurting them…."

"Well, this time you need to encourage a little chaos," Anna said with a seductive smile as she pushed a leg between Parry's.

Parry's breathing shuddered for a moment. "Who's the recipient?" he finally managed to ask.

"Verisa."

Parry let out a rueful chuckle. "You really have it in for her, don't you? This how you're getting around Malorie's edict?"

"I just want to remind Verisa that she's not as safe as she thinks she is."

"You'd not think that if you saw her. Liam hasn't been kind today; the sunlight hasn't, either."

Anna snorted. "Yeah, but she's still able to walk

and work, right?"

"Of course," Parry shrugged. "Not much use if she can't."

"I want her beaten so badly she can't even crawl," Anna whispered in a fierce hiss. Her allegiance with Verisa was one of convenience. She still hated the bitch, and watching her get the shit kicked out of her—even if she'd get healed right afterward—would make Anna's day.

"Liam's gonna be pissed," Parry said hesitantly.

"I'll make it so worth your while," Anna replied. "I'll even kill your wife, like we talked about. It'll look like a total accident—no one will suspect a thing."

Parry looked down into Anna's eyes, and she met his with cold certainty and a slow smile.

"Deal," Parry said after a minute. "I gotta get on this, there's a few key guys I need to get on board. It'll take some bribes, but they'll be small; easily covered by what I'll save by having that bitch of a wife out of my life."

"I'll leave you to it, then."

Anna gave Parry a peck on the cheek, and then walked back up the road to the overseer's station that stood across from the castle.

She entered the building and went back into the staff kitchen. It was near the end of the workday, and all the staff was out collecting the daily harvest and tallying quotas.

Anna helped herself to a cup of coffee and some pastries that were sitting on the table. She considered going back into the castle to cement her alibi, but the thought of watching the beatdown occur was just too tempting.

She relaxed for a while, surfing the feeds and chatting with some of her contacts around the castle over the Link while finishing off the pastries.

Eventually the time came when Katrina's group would be forming up to turn in their vials, before the workers dispersed back to their homes further up the valley.

Many would walk past the castle—as would Verisa, along with her guard.

Anna poured a fresh cup of coffee and brought it outside with her, where she leaned against a pole holding up the building's overhang. Sure enough, the fields were emptying out, and some of the workers were already on the road.

In the distance, she could make out the field where Verisa was working. The massive bulk of Liam was easy to spot in the crowds. If she squinted, she could see a red shape moving toward the road in the midst of all the white-clothed workers.

She was almost giddy with anticipation. Soon Verisa would be on the medtable and free of the collar.

A worry floated in the back of Anna's mind that Verisa wouldn't hold up her end of the bargain. It was a risk—but so was trusting Jace and his bitch-queen of a wife.

Earlier in the week, Anna had stolen the activation codes for one of the shuttles. She'd be Verisa's ride out of here, proving herself to be indispensable; until they found Verisa's ship...then she'd kill the bitch and take it all for herself.

She watched with growing anticipation as the red shape of Verisa grew larger, being led through the crowds of workers by one of the guards.

"C'mon," she whispered. "Don't let me down, Parry."

Then there was a surge of white figures on the road and she knew it was about to happen.

THE END OF DAYS
STELLAR DATE: 01.19.8512 (Adjusted Gregorian)
LOCATION: Revenence Castle
REGION: Persia, Midditerra System

Katrina was certain that she'd never felt wearier than she did at that moment. Once she'd stayed awake for over one hundred hours—which felt like the best time of her life, compared to this.

The guard—she had no idea who it was, it could have been a ten-year old girl shoving her around, and she wouldn't be able to resist—gave another push, and Katrina stumbled onward.

One foot in front of the other; she kept her focus on that, and what meager amount of balance she could manage. Stones on the gravel road dug into her feet, though at least she couldn't feel the burning heat anymore. The soles of her feet were in too much agony to tell that pain apart from any other.

She gave herself three more days of this before she died. Maybe less.

Of course, Malorie wouldn't let it come to that—she hoped. If Katrina died, all the tech in her body would erase her data stores and destroy itself. She'd be back on the table before long, getting stitched back together like the frankenstein monster she was.

It had been many days, nineteen to be exact, since Juasa had been taken from her. To Katrina, it felt like it had been a lifetime. The beatings and abuse, so many delivered by Juasa's own hands, had begun to take their toll on her spirit.

Her love for Juasa was still a flame in her heart, but it was miniscule next to the rage that had begun to build within her. The next time she was on the medtable, she'd not pussyfoot around. Katrina would disable the collar, no matter how much it hurt, and then kill those miserable techs.

Then she'd find Anna and kill her too, followed by Malorie and Jace. They'd all die, along with anyone who got in her way.

A voice in the back of her mind brought up the deal she'd made with Anna—but the bitch hadn't come through. She'd raised Katrina's hopes, that one day with the cream, and then followed it up by making Juasa beat her.

No, Anna was dead. The woman was unredeemable, and Katrina would leave her corpse for the crows.

She tripped on a small stone and stumbled, landing hard on her knees and hands. The pain was excruciating, or it should be, but Katrina couldn't separate it from the rest of the agony crushing her mind.

Somehow she found a new reserve of strength

and stood up, elated at her own fortitude for a moment—until she realized that the guard had picked her up by her hair.

"You're heavy for such a scrawny thing," he grunted.

Katrina didn't respond, but resumed her focus on her feet. Left, drag it forward, shift weight. Right, drag forward—avoid that sharp rock—shift weight.

Then something hit her in the side.

At first she thought it was a blow from the guard, but it didn't hurt as much as the overseer's massive fists usually did.

Then something else struck her on the other side. There was yelling, and she looked up from her downward focus to see a sea of white workers crowding around her, their faces angry, voices loud and harsh.

The guard bellowed something, and a whip cracked, but still more blows struck her.

Body, face, head, arms.

Katrina's legs gave out, her body going limp. For a moment, the sheer volume of fists and feet striking her served to keep her upright—but only for a moment.

She crashed to the ground, stones digging into her face as blows continued to land on her body.

More whips cracked in the air, and Liam's throaty bellow sounded above the mayhem. A second later, the attack stopped.

Katrina's tongue pushed gravel out of her mouth. She paused. It wasn't all gravel; there were teeth too, at least four of them.

"What the hell?!" Liam bellowed from somewhere above her.

"Liam!" another voice shrieked. Anna's. "What did you let happen? Malorie is going to kill the both of us!"

"Get a carry-board from the station," Liam hollered at someone. "I'm calling the medtechs to the lab."

Shit, Katrina thought, as even the voices above her became indistinct and warbly-sounding. *How am I going to get the collar off if I pass out?*

Then darkness took her.

REPAIR
STELLAR DATE: 01.19.8512 (Adjusted Gregorian)
LOCATION: Revenence Castle
REGION: Persia, Midditerra System

Anna paced back and forth in the medlab, one hand on her chin, her eyes casting nervous looks at Verisa's broken body. She turned and caught sight of Liam sitting on a tall stool, his expression also far more worried than Anna had ever seen it.

If Verisa dies, I'm a dead woman.

She was certain that Liam was thinking the same thing.

The medtable had managed to stabilize Verisa, but her breathing was shallow, and Tom and Ainsley were debating putting her on a respirator.

"It's amazing that her ribs aren't broken," Tom said as he looked over the holodisplay of Verisa's body that was suspended above the table.

Ainsley cast Tom a disparaging look. "Well duh, they're reinforced. We saw that the first time she was on here. Beautiful work, too. Shows how advanced she is."

"Too bad we can't get our nano to do more than assist and repair," Tom replied, ignoring Ainsley's gibe. "I want to cut a sample out, just to see what she's made of."

"Tom, you know what Malorie said. There's too much risk in her internal systems putting up a defense that triggers the collar. It could create a loop that kills her. Besides, she's barely stable; if you start cutting bits out, she'll go into shock again."

The pair continued to debate what to do, and Anna wanted to walk over and slap them both in the head. Whatever kept Verisa alive was what they needed to do.

"There she goes," Tom said after another minute. "Her heart rate is steadying. Blood pressure is improving, too. She's one hell of a tough woman."

Liam released a long, pent-up breath. "Oh, thank the gods."

"She's coming to," Ainsley said. "Quick! Reset the collar attenuation to defaults."

* * * * *

Consciousness snapped back for Katrina in one sudden moment of clarity.

Brutal clarity.

Her body hurt *everywhere*. However, in the initial moments of wakefulness, she knew that it hurt decidedly less than before...before she was attacked.

Katrina's mind felt sharper than it had in days. It became immediately apparent to her that the attack was staged. It had to have been. There was no way the workers would attack her en masse like that without provocation.

She suspected Anna. It was one hell of a way to get Katrina back to the medtable, but at least it had worked.

The collar was still around her neck, and a tentative probe with what little nano Katrina still possessed showed that the thing was active. So much for Anna's great plan.

There was speaking going on around her, and Katrina strained to make out the words. Something about tough, and coming to, and reset the collar!

Shit!

Katrina rushed more nano into the collar while the attenuation was still in place, but then it shut down entirely. The collar, for all intents and purposes, was disabled.

It was as though a great weight had been lifted from Katrina's shoulders. She could properly *feel* her body once more. Not just with her flesh, but also with the technological enhancements that ran though it. Her own internal systems began to effect repairs on her broken and battered flesh, and Katrina fed the last of her infiltration nano into the collar, rewiring its internal configuration to report functionality when, in fact, there was none.

Then she slowed her own repair processes, no

need to alert the medtechs to the fact that she was healing faster than she should.

"Verisa, can you hear me?"

It took Katrina an instant longer than she liked to remember that Verisa meant *her*. It took a moment more to identify the speaker as Anna.

The woman had done it. She'd somehow altered the medtable to disable the collar. *Would miracles never cease?*

Katrina opened her eyes to see Anna leaning over her, and the massive form of Liam looming behind.

"Fuck off," Katrina whispered.

Liam chuckled. "Looks like she's on the mend. I'm going to go figure out whose fault this was and drop them in the moat."

"You do that," Anna said and winked at Katrina.

It wasn't a kind wink; the woman's expression was malicious in the extreme. Katrina wondered if Anna even knew how much bitch she exuded at all times.

For a moment, for reasons she couldn't fathom, Katrina's mind shifted back to Victoria, and she saw Laura's face. Her young assistant who had wanted so badly for Katrina to stay. She wondered what sort of life she could have lived there. One thing was for certain: it would have been a life of peace.

Now she was deep in some of the worst shit she could ever have imagined, and it was all to find a ship that was probably lost forever.

As she looked up at the sinister grin on Anna's face, it occurred to her that she really felt like Verisa more than Katrina at that moment. She was completely filled with anger, rage, and a burning desire for retribution.

She hadn't felt this way since the trials for the sentencing of her father back on Victoria. Back then, Markus had been with her; always measured, always with a steady hand. His council had seen her through those dark days.

Markus…. Stars, I could use your guidance now.

Katrina's nano completed its alterations to the collar and retreated back into her body. Now she could relax and let the medtable do its work while she planned out her next move.

Anna straightened and looked over Katrina's head at the two medtechs. "How long 'til she's healed up? We'd all be better off if she was tip-top by the time Malorie and Juasa get back."

That caught Katrina's attention. "When?" she whispered.

"Shit, you're probably thirsty as all get-out," Anna said, and walked to the sink and poured a glass of water.

When she returned, she bent over Katrina and spoke softly. "Two, maybe three hours."

That changed everything.

Katrina didn't know when another opportunity like this would come again. She needed to make her move that very night.

She nodded and closed her eyes. The medtechs were debating reconnecting the medtable to her hard-Link port. They'd done it each other time Katrina had been on the table, and each time, she'd gained a little more information from the lab level network, and had fed the techs another blob of encrypted nothing.

They'd not yet cracked the encryption on the last batch of data they'd extracted, and Tom wanted to hunt through her mind for the encryption keys. Ainsley was against it, but Katrina could tell that she was on the fence.

If they made the hard-Link, Katrina's job would be a piece of cake. Otherwise she'd have to do it wirelessly, and that was slower—and more detectable.

"Oh, fine!" Ainsley said at last. "She's doing well enough. Jack her up and let's see what we can find."

"That's more like it," Tom replied. A moment later, Katrina felt him slide the hard-Link line into the port behind her ear. She had to hold back a smile as she redirected their probes while slipping into their system.

Now that she could use the full power of her mental augmentations, accessing the medtable's systems was a breeze.

The first thing she did was find the controls for the table's restraints and slave them to her. Following that, Katrina accessed the wireless network and located its access tokens and which frequencies accessed which segments.

Once she had her freedom and future access secured, Katrina worked her way out of the lab sublevel's network and onto Revenence Castle's main network, looking for the security control systems. She wanted to be able to lock down every gate, door, and window.

Tom and Ainsley were still arguing about how best to bypass Katrina's safeguards, and Anna was giving her a curious look, when Katrina found the systems she needed. She brute-forced her way past their encryption and took control.

She was almost shocked at how easy it was, but the more she looked over the castle's networks and control backplanes, the more she could see that it was a hodge-podge of different systems that had been inexpertly cobbled together. Many systems didn't even speak to one another properly, and there were intermediary proxies everywhere. Some were doing double duty, linking lighting and security to things like water and plumbing. Often with full privileges and minimal encryption.

It was like sparring with children.

"I don't know, maybe we should knock her out," Tom said loudly, obviously agitated at Ainsley over one of her suggestions. Katrina ignored their arguing and took control of the last of the castle's systems. Once she had them all under her control, she connected them to a holographic console that overlaid her vison.

"No," Katrina said loudly—or as loudly as she was able.

"'No' to being knocked out?" Ainsley asked. "You don't really get a say in this."

The woman hadn't even finished speaking when the medtable's restraints unlocked.

Katrina pushed herself up and slid off the table's right side. She stood up straight and pulled the IV line from her arm.

"Took you long enough," Anna said with a sneer as she walked around the left side of the table, advancing on Ainsley.

"What? Me?" Ainsley said, a look of confusion on her face.

"Not you, bitch. I mean Verisa."

"What? How?" Tom stammered.

Katrina gestured toward the far wall. "Back away from the table, hands up."

"But...we had you locked down, the collar..."

Katrina reached up and grasped the collar and triggered its release. It split into two pieces and fell to the ground.

"What collar?" Katrina asked.

"Shit! I can't get on the Link, we're cut off," Tom exclaimed as he backed away from the console, but Ainsley stood her ground, frantically trying to access Katrina's mind through the hard-Link cable that was still plugged into her.

Katrina looked at the control systems that overlaid her vision and shut down the console Ainsley was working on.

"Get over there with Tom."

"Yeah," Anna said, giving Ainsley a shove. "Get over there."

Katrina paused, leaning against the medtable's scanning arch as dizziness overcame her. She gritted her teeth and closed her eyes.

"No!" Ainsley shouted. "Help, someone, help!"

Anna's hand darted out, striking Ainsley in the throat with the tips of her locked fingers.

The medtech gasped and grabbed her throat, struggling for breath.

"Shit, Anna," Katrina said as she pulled the hard-Link cable from behind her ear. "You crushed her windpipe. Now we have to put her on the table."

Anna stepped around the gasping Ainsley and wrapped one arm around her neck, and the other around her head.

"Stop!" Katrina called out, but it was too late.

With a sickening pop, Anna broke Ainsley's neck and dropped the woman's body to the floor.

"Grow the fuck up, Verisa," Anna said. "I have a shuttle ready; we have to get out of here *now*. We can't have these two running off to warn Liam and his goons."

Tom had been muttering incoherently to himself, but that got his attention.

"Whoa! No! No need to kill, I won't go anywhere. I won't tell anyone—look there's lots of stuff in here that can knock me out, I'll let you hit me up with that, please, just don't kill me!"

Anna walked toward Tom, a menacing smile on her lips. "Don't worry, it won't hurt. Much."

Katrina summoned her last reserves of strength and took a step toward Anna. "Stop, Anna. Now."

Anna ignored Katrina and drew a fist back to hit Tom.

Here goes nothing.

With a guttural scream, Katrina rushed Anna, knocking her over, and both women crashed to the ground. Katrina gathered all the rage, the hate, and the anger she felt about everything that had happened since the Streamer dumped them outside Bollam's World and balled it up into a new source of energy inside herself.

Anna was beneath her; her back against the floor, her burning eyes staring up at Katrina.

"The *fuck*, Verisa!" Anna swore.

Katrina drew on her newfound energy, on that purified rage that she'd gathered, and slammed her fist into Anna's face, snapping the other woman's head back against the floor.

Anna grunted, but her eyes remained focused, and she kicked out at Katrina, the blow catching her on the shoulder.

Katrina grabbed Anna's ankle, shifted her weight, and dropped her shoulder into Anna's knee while pulling up on her calf.

A scream filled the room, tearing out of Anna's throat, but Katrina couldn't quite break the woman's knee. Then she got a foot under Anna's armpit and pushed her shoulder against Anna's knee with all her might.

With a grinding *crunch*, Anna's knee broke, and the woman shrieked while tears of pain and rage streamed from her eyes.

Katrina glanced up to check on Tom, worried that the man would make a break for it, but he seemed frozen in place by the tableau before him.

With shaking knees, Katrina rose slowly, staring down at Anna who was holding her leg and whimpering from the pain.

"Why are you doing this?" Anna asked, fury in her eyes. "We were partners. I *helped* you."

"Helped?" Katrina asked. "You were the one that

caused this whole mess. You and your fucking avarice!"

"You still need me," Anna said. "I have the way out. I can get you free."

Katrina looked around the room, her eyes casting about for just the right implement.

She strode toward the closest cabinet, grasped the top, and turned her head toward Anna. "I'm already free, and I have no intention of leaving without Juasa."

Anna's eyes widened. "That bitch? She's fucking useless! You told me you—"

Those were the last words Anna ever uttered. With all her strength, Katrina pulled at the cabinet, and it fell over, its solid steel frame slamming into Anna's head with a sickening *crunch*.

Katrina stared at Anna's twitching body for a moment before stepping over it to approach Tom.

He was quaking with fear, and a wet stain ran down his pants.

"I'm not going to hurt you," Katrina said. "But I am going to make sure you don't get in the way right now."

"H-h-how?" Tom asked.

Katrina gestured at the medtable. "Get on it."

Tom nodded three times, his head bobbing like it was on a spring before he rushed to the table and climbed on.

Katrina reactivated the console and triggered the restraints, then instructed the table to deliver a sedative to Tom.

"Goodnight, Tom."

"Uhh…goodni…."

Katrina turned to the cabinets—all but the one that rested on Anna's former head—and looked for replenishment silicate.

"Gotta be some somewhere," she muttered.

She hunted through half a dozen shelves before she found some.

"Jackpot," she whispered, and looked down at her stomach, surprised to see that she was still naked.

Damn…I've gotten way too used to that.

Katrina fed the silicate rods into the port within her navel and felt her body begin to fabricate new nano: medical, general, and infiltration.

An alert flashed over her vision as the material was assimilated, and Katrina saw that her internal power reserves were flagging.

"Just what I need," she muttered, and walked back to the medtable, pulling a charge cable out from the side. Katrina had never sported large internal batteries—just a single superconductor coil around each femur. Nothing like the entire bevy of batteries that military operators like Tanis ran.

She sagged against the table as it ran a fast charge

on her SC Batts. Katrina watched the charge level slowly climb. She was prepared to disconnect at 50%, when the door suddenly opened and Liam stormed in.

"Anna!" he shouted, rage evident on his features before he stopped and looked around. "What in the star's burning light...."

"Hi, Liam," Katrina said with a tired smile. "How are we going to do this? The easy way, or the hard way?"

Liam's right hand formed a fist, and he smacked it into the palm of his left. "I think it's going to be the hard way."

"Be careful," Katrina warned. "I control the only medtable. You kill me, and Malorie will have your hide."

Liam snorted. "We'll see."

Katrina pulled the charge cable from her side and swung it in front of herself in a lazy circle as Liam approached.

She was feeling better—not great—but definitely better. Liam was a monstrous brute, but he had a weakness—everyone did.

He came around the side of the table and lunged for her, both hands out. Feeling renewed, Katrina leapt onto the table, one foot on Tom's leg.

Liam's right arm wrapped around Katrina's right leg, and he pulled her toward him, but that was just what she wanted. She swung her other leg around him, twisting in his grasp so that she was sitting on his shoulders.

"What the—?" Liam grunted, and reached his other arm up for her just as Katrina swung her right hand into his eye.

The hand that was holding the fast charge cable.

She sent a command to the table to bypass the safeties, and delivered a max charge into his skull.

Liam convulsed, and Katrina groaned as he squeezed her leg, but she didn't let go.

Smoke began to pour out of the man's eye, and then his body went limp, falling to the ground. Katrina fell with him, landing atop him as he convulsed.

She sent a command to the table to turn off the charging cable and pulled herself upright on shaking legs.

"Damn..." she whispered, leaning against the table and taking deep breaths. "Four down, a whole freakin' castle to go."

She took four unsteady steps to the sink and poured another glass of water. Leaning against the counter, Katrina surveyed the destruction in the room as she slowly drank the cool liquid. Three dead bodies, and Tom unconscious on the table.

She felt a twinge of guilt for Ainsley; the woman had been at least somewhat cautious in her work to probe Katrina's mind.

Tom had always operated with less concern for her safety, and here he was, alive, while Ainsley was dead. The universe really just didn't give a fuck.

Katrina pushed herself off the counter and stood upright. Her next order of business was to capture Malorie and free Juasa. Not necessarily in that order. Of course, that would require moving through the castle...and moving through the castle required clothing.

Anna's outfit was more to Verisa's tastes, but it was also a bloody mess.

"Looks like I'll be playing the part of Ainsley this evening," Katrina said, a small smile on her lips.

She pulled Ainsley out of her hazsuit, thinking that the medtech should have kept her helmet on — she and Tom had become lax in their time around Katrina.

That one precaution probably would have saved her life. Though not in the way she would have expected.

Underneath, Ainsley wore a pair of black leggings and a dark grey top. Katrina crouched to pull off the medtech's pants, and felt searing pain in her thighs. She looked down and saw that the skin on the tops of her thighs had ripped wide open, the medical glue that had held it together giving out under the pressure.

Must have weakened it in the fighting.

Katrina looked herself over and realized that she was currently bleeding from a dozen locations. With the amount of pain she'd been in for days, she hadn't even noticed.

Clothing was not going to be much of a disguise if it was soaked in blood and pus.

"I guess we find out how weird it is for someone to walk around the castle in a hazsuit."

Talking aloud to yourself. Great, Katrina.

Five minutes later, she stood in the lift, rising to the third floor where Malorie's quarters lay. The plan she'd devised was simple. She'd lie in wait for Malorie and Juasa. Once she had Juasa safe, Katrina would lock down the castle and take control.

Jace still had comeuppance due him, and he was likely five days out at the very least.

The lift doors opened, and Katrina strode down the hall, taking the first right and then the second left.

A pair of servants came around a corner ahead, and Katrina kept her eyes forward and head slightly lowered. Her face still looked like crap, and her hair was a mess—only as straight and clean as she could manage with some water and her fingers.

She probably looked like a drowned rat.

The pair of servants cast her an appraising look,

but neither stopped, and Katrina breathed a sigh of relief, turning the final corner that would take her to Malorie's suite.

"Dammit," Katrina swore as she caught sight of a guard standing before Malorie's door. It was one of the massively overmuscled brutes that filled the place.

Katrina rolled her hips—glad the hazsuit was fitted enough to show *some* of her figure—as she strode toward the man and walked past him, praying that he'd be looking at her ass and not the patchy red skin that covered her face. At the last moment, she turned abruptly and rushed toward him, placing her hands on his cheeks.

"Hey, wha—" was all he managed to get out before her lips met his, and she breathed a stream of nano into his body. The miniscule machines penetrated the back of his throat and attached to his spine. From there, Katrina locked up the man's nervous system, trapping him inside his own body, rendering him unable to move.

It was a trick she hadn't employed since her time operating as a spy for Luminescent Society in Sirius. It involved hacking another human's nervous system—something expressly forbidden by the Phobos Accords.

"Fuck the Phobos Accords," she muttered as she stepped past the frozen man and pushed open the door to Malorie's suite. She surveyed the room, and her eyes alighted on the autodresser.

She wondered if there was something it could cover her ruined body with to hold it together a bit longer. Katrina grinned as she pulled off the hazsuit and walked into the machine, her feet leaving yellow and red stains on the floor.

Once inside, the door slid closed, and she accessed its menus over the Link. Malorie's tastes were not so different from Verisa's, and she selected a rubbery silver and black skinsuit that would compress her skin and hide her condition.

She was about to tell the autodresser to engage when her mantra came to mind.

She was not Verisa; she was Katrina.

"I am all these things, but they are not me. I am Katrina," she whispered. But she didn't know who Katrina was anymore. The doting wife of the president would not survive what was to come next. Nor would the aristocratic Verisa. Even the spy Yolanda she had played at when on platform SK45 in Sirius was too full of compassion to do what may need to be done.

She needed to become someone else.

Once upon a time, during her father's trials, he had told her that she needed to be as cold and deadly as steel to survive. She'd had a name then, not a cover, not a disguise. That name was Katrina.

In that instant, Katrina decided to make a change. Katrina was no longer the wife of Markus, making up for the evil acts she had committed as a spy. She was no longer the president, carrying on her dead husband's legacy. Not even the searcher, looking for the ship that would lead her to Tanis's promised utopia.

This morass that humanity had devolved into was her new reality, and a new Katrina needed to emerge to deal with it. What she needed to be now was to be a woman the likes of which Jace and his goons would tremble before.

Katrina saw that the autodresser had a 3D printer and enough formation material to make nearly anything. She looked down at her mutilated flesh, so beautiful and new just a few years ago, back on High Victoria—or four thousand years ago, depending on one's point of view.

Her nano could repair it and stave off the cancer cells and infections in her body…or she could replace it with something strong, something impervious to such simple a thing as Persia's raging star.

Her eyes lit upon an armor costume, matte grey with blue highlights. It would offer flexibility and protection. The formation alloys in the autodresser were capable of creating it; with the design specs that Katrina possessed for the advanced armors of the *Intrepid*, as well as those of Luminescent Society, she could create something that would actually be functional.

The autodresser also had supplies of steel and carbon fiber used for various outfits Malorie crafted for herself. Katrina would put them to far better use.

She connected with the machine over the Link and applied updates to its specifications, removing its safety protocols and updating the design of the armor costume to suit her needs.

Then she turned and touched each of the armatures that the autodresser used to apply its formation material when printing clothing onto a person. Filaments of nano left her fingers and touched each of them, enhancing their capabilities with simple tweaks and efficiencies.

It wasn't perfect, but it would do.

She turned and almost slipped on the blood that had run down her legs and pooled at her feet.

Before she could do anything else, her ruined flesh would have to go.

Now that the collar was no longer around her neck, Katrina could deaden her nerves so she wouldn't sense the pain of her skinning. What pain she could still feel would be a comfort—suffering had become her friend over the past weeks.

She welcomed its embrace.

Her nano coursed through her body, severing

nerves until she couldn't feel her flesh at all anymore. The fire of the burns, cuts, and welts was replaced by a different type of pain, more of a dull, bone-crushing ache that made her feel like her entire body was pulsing and about to burst.

The autodresser had a medical suite; this sort of body modification was not beyond its programming. Needles sank into her, delivering larger medical bots that coursed through her veins and began to sever and seal up the blood vessels feeding her skin—those that hadn't already been sealed by the medtable in her multiple visits.

A soft tone emitted from within the autodresser indicating that the preparation stages were complete.

"Fuck. This is going to suck," Katrina whispered.

She closed her eyes as the autodresser's a-grav field lifted her into the air, and its armatures sliced into her, using the blades normally reserved for removing complex, printed outfits to instead pull her skin off as though it were nothing more than a costume she was ready to discard.

A scream erupted from Katrina's throat—it wasn't supposed to hurt this much, but the feeling of her flesh being slowly peeled from her body still seared her mind. She couldn't tell if it was psychosomatic, or if she'd somehow missed something. Maybe the nano had only severed a percentage of her nerves; maybe her body just knew how wrong this was.

The anguish became a crescendo of delight in her mind. She lost herself in it, reveling in the torment, remembering Liam's whip cutting into her skin, remembering Anna's rods crushing her flesh. Somehow this new misery was a comfort, the final removal of all their abuse.

As her face was peeled away, Katrina felt her missing teeth with her tongue and passed additional instructions to the machine to replace them.

She considered what to do with her face, and decided to have her skin replicated by a polymer approximating human flesh, though the underside would be augmented by a layer of carbon fiber.

Katrina passed the machine an image of how she had looked in the years when she had worked by Markus's side to build the Victoria colony. Not young, but not old, either. Lines around her mouth, crows feet in the corners of her eyes.

Though her eyes were open—there were no eyelids to cover them anymore—she kept her mind focused on the autodresser's progress over the Link. It showed a rough view of how she looked with her flesh gone, and that was more than enough for her.

Layer by layer, the autodresser began to print on her new skin, layering in the tech she had selected, and adding in protective plates and carbon fiber meshes.

A part of her mind knew that this was a bad idea, a very bad idea. This level of modification was normally done over days, with careful mental preparation. It occurred to Katrina that she must be in some sort of state of shock to even consider doing this to herself.

It's just flesh, she thought, feeling her new lips twist with a sneer. *And it was ruined anyway…just like me.*

After what felt like a thousand years, or maybe just forty minutes, the machine completed its work, and Katrina opened her eyes.

Her breath caught as she saw her reflection in the autodresser's door. Her body was now an homage to war. The grey armor—her new flesh—gleamed dully, dark blue and russet orange sections adding an artistic feel to her new body.

In an affectation she'd added at the last moment, the armor plunged at the neckline—or appeared to. Steel and carbon fiber still lay beneath the flesh-like surface layer. Her breasts were emphasized, making her still feel somewhat womanly, even though there were no remains of mammary glands beneath.

She held up her grey fingers and flexed them, forming a fist.

It still hurt. Everything hurt, inflamed nerves

protesting at being connected to the armor's new cybernetic interface layer.

The smile was still on her face as Katrina flipped through the options, looking for something to complete the outfit; something unique, something that would fit in with this strange throwback world she was on.

"Perfect," she whispered when the right item appeared.

She selected it to be fabricated from raw materials that the autodresser had on hand, and stepped out of the machine. It would let her know when her addition was ready.

An alert flashed in her mind, and Katrina saw that Malorie's shuttle had departed from Farsa Station. Ground ATC had it listed as arriving at the castle in thirty minutes.

She reviewed the status of the Revenence Castle. Many of the denizens had taken Malorie's absence as an opportunity to take the night off, and the building was operating on a skeleton staff.

Should Malorie check the castle's status, she would find that Katrina was in her cell, Liam had taken the evening off, and Anna was in her quarters.

Everything was just as it should be.

Katrina walked to the bar and leant against it, nodding to the automaton. "Whisky. Straight up."

She should probably drink something more nutritious to give her body the fuel to rebuild its reserves, but right now she needed a different type of reserve.

The automaton—whose name was Jeavons, by the indicator showing on her HUD—nodded and poured the drink, setting it on the bar.

Katrina grabbed it—carefully, getting used to the different sensations her fingers provided—and threw it back. The liquid burned its way down her throat, and she dropped the glass onto the bar.

"Another."

Jeavons complied, and Katrina downed that glass in one gulp before standing and walking back to the autodresser. Its door slid open as she approached, and within, hanging from the armatures, was a long, brown, leather coat.

"Excellent," Katrina said as she grabbed it and pulled it on. It hung perfectly from her shoulders, falling all the way to her ankles. She reached into the autodresser and grabbed the leather belt and holster that hung within, and buckled the belt around her waist.

"Now I just need something to put in you," she mused and thought of the guard out front. She sent a signal over the Link, and he came into the room, his steps wooden and halting as she manipulated his limbs.

Katrina felt a moment's regret for his suffering, but then images of the overseers whipping her, skin hanging off her body in strips, flashed before her eyes.

"The gun," Katrina said, gesturing to the guard's sidearm.

The man handed it over, and Katrina slid it into her holster before waving a hand at the guard. "As you were."

He left the suite and resumed his position outside the entrance as Katrina walked back to Jeavons. "Another, if you don't mind. I have a bit of time to kill…before I kill."

THE CHANGE
STELLAR DATE: 01.19.8512 (Adjusted Gregorian)
LOCATION: Revenence Castle
REGION: Persia, Midditerra System

"At least we got a decent meal out of the trip," Malorie said as the shuttle set down in its cradle behind the castle.

Juasa shrugged. "It was nice to get out, as well."

Malorie stood and stretched. "I wouldn't go so far as to apply the word 'nice' to any outing that involves a meeting with Lara."

Juasa nodded silently. Malorie had been moody in the extreme since they'd left Lara's office. Even eating at a restaurant that she claimed was her favorite was not enough to cheer the woman up.

Korin hadn't said a word the entire time, but Juasa periodically tried to get Malorie to laugh or smile. It had worked a few times for a minute or two—but it had also backfired more than once.

Korin shot Juasa a significant look, and she took his meaning. 'Shut up'.

They followed Malorie into the castle in silence, walking as quietly as possible down the empty corridors to the main lift.

Only a few servants were in evidence, and Malorie muttered something about laggards getting a tongue lashing in the morning.

Juasa was glad the night was almost over. Malorie would have a drink or two, demand a massage, and then go to bed, while Juasa would make her way to the kitchens for a snack and some conversation before calling it a night herself.

They stepped off the lift, and the guard at the door gave them a stiff nod that Malorie ignored as she pushed her way into the room, Juasa following on her heels.

The room's lights were low, and Malorie stopped. "Something's wrong; the lights won't come on."

"I'll try the manual switches," Juasa said, walking over to the panel.

"Don't bother," a voice said from across the room, near the bar. It was a voice that Juasa recognized all too well.

"Verisa?" she asked.

"No," the voice said as the lights slowly came on. "It's Katrina."

"What? What are you doing here?" Malorie turned back to the door as Korin came in.

"Something's wrong with Stu…" he announced.

"I don't care about Stu," Malorie said and pointed at Katrina. "Verisa's free. Secure her."

Behind them, the door slammed shut, and the sound of its lock engaging echoed through the room.

"Malorie," Katrina said. "Weren't you paying attention? My name's Katrina."

Korin drew his gun, but Katrina's was already in her hand, aimed at his head.

"I'd drop that, tough guy. Why don't you go sit on the bed? The women have to have a chat."

Korin didn't move, and Juasa gasped as Katrina fired a shot at the guard. The bullet clipped his arm, and Korin grunted.

"On the bed!" Katrina yelled. "Your little slug throwers are quaint it'll probably take quite a few rounds to put you down. But I can tell that you don't have a reinforced skull; the next one goes through it."

"What is going on!?" Malorie yelled, turning to Juasa. "Why is she saying she's Katrina?"

Juasa sighed. "Because it's her name."

"The only one, from here on out," Katrina added.

Juasa walked toward Katrina. "Are you OK? You sound...rough."

Katrina gave a coarse laugh. "That about sums it up. Yeah, things have been on the rough side. But they're about to get a lot better."

Juasa could see that something was different about Katrina's face, that there was something wrong with it. Then it clicked. Her skin was smooth; there were no burns, cuts, or med-patches. Her hair fell down her back in a wavy cascade.

It looked perfect—too perfect.

Katrina continued speaking while Juasa looked her over. "It's been a hard day. Got the crap kicked out of me—again. Got free, killed Anna and Liam. Threw out my old skin—which was ruined, thanks to these bastards—for this improvement here." Katrina pulled her coat aside to reveal what appeared to be form-fitting light combat armor.

Juasa opened her mouth to speak, but couldn't find the words.

Malorie, on the other hand, was not at a loss. "You *what*? Liam? You just killed him?"

"Juasa," Katrina said, gesturing to the ground. "Can you pick up your guard's gun and bring it over here? I don't want Malorie getting any ideas."

Juasa turned to grab the gun, and saw the roiling rage in Malorie's eyes. "Sorry, Mal. At least you don't have to worry about Lara anymore."

Malorie's lips were twisted into a sneer as she answered. "The only way that happens is if you kill me, and then *you'll* have to worry about her."

Juasa scooped up the gun and walked across the room to Katrina's side. "What do you mean that you replaced your skin?" she asked, looking at what she could see of Katrina's body within the long coat.

"It was done for—would have taken days to repair. It was rife with infection and cancerous. I didn't have time for that, so I had it removed."

"Shit," Juasa whispered as she turned to face Malorie and Korin. "Does it hurt?"

Katrina didn't reply, but reached out and touched Juasa's collar. She heard a small *snick*, and the hated collar split in two and fell away.

"I don't remember what it feels like to *not* be in pain," Katrina replied. "Every nerve in my body has screamed for days now. It's become…comforting."

"Shit," Juasa whispered, beginning to wonder about Katrina's state of mind.

"How did you do that?" Malorie asked, her brow furrowed. "There's nothing in the castle that could replace your skin with armor like that."

Katrina pointed past the lady of the castle, toward the autodresser. "That can. You have a lot of interesting materials for the printer. You use them for foppery, but they can print armor just as well. Nothing heavy, but it's enough to keep my tender insides safe for the time being."

"Seriously?" Malorie looked more impressed than angry. "I didn't realize it could do things like that…."

Katrina snorted. "Yeah, I bet you didn't get all the specs when you stole it—or Jace did, I suppose. Either way, I had to upgrade it to make it properly useful. Don't get any ideas though, it won't work for you."

"Did it anesthetize?" Juasa asked.

Katrina clenched her jaw and shook her head.

"So what now?" Malorie asked. "You going to take off? Blackadder will chase you; Lara will too."

"Lara's the—" Juasa began.

"I know who she is," Katrina replied. "I control the castle now, I've looked over the data on Midditerra."

<What *are* we going to do?> Juasa asked over the Link as the local network offered her a connection. <How are we going to get out of here?>

Katrina's mental tone was terse. <We're not.>

<We're…what?> Juasa was starting to feel like she barely knew the woman beside her. Her private experiences with Katrina had shown her to be kind and forgiving. Even Verisa was more about sarcasm and wit than actual haughtiness and derision.

The time in the fields had broken something in her lover.

"We're not leaving," Katrina reiterated aloud. "I'm taking over the Blackadder. I doubt I'll stop there."

Malorie snorted. "Good luck with that. Jace will eat you for lunch."

"We'll see about that," Katrina said as she sighted down her pistol.

Juasa realized that Katrina was going to kill Malorie, and she put her hand on Katrina's arm.

"Kat, no, not like this."

Katrina's brow furrowed and she glanced at Juasa, then at Korin. "Why didn't you make a move, muscle man?"

Korin still sat on the bed and gave a slight shrug. "I don't know what you did to Stu, but I don't want to find out. I'm not a big fan of Jace, Malorie, or the Adders. Curious to see what sort of alternative you're going to propose."

Malorie glared at Korin. "You're a fucking dead man."

Korin chuckled and interlaced his fingers behind his head. "I'm gonna play along, Malorie. You should probably do the same."

"There's no 'along' for *her* to play," Katrina said as she stalked toward Malorie, her gun still aimed at the woman's head, finger on the trigger. "I just want to know one thing. Whose idea was it to have Juasa beat me?"

"You didn't ask Anna?" Malorie sneered, straightening and staring into the barrel of the weapon. "Just fucking do it already."

Katrina's voice held no emotion as she pressed the barrel of the pistol against Malorie's forehead "I smashed her head like a melon before I had the chance. Now whose fucking idea was it?"

Malorie cocked her head and sneered at Katrina. "It was *mine*," she said in a whispered hiss. "I wanted to destroy her. Crush her spirit so I could rebuild her as my creature."

"So you could use her against me," Katrina growled.

Malorie snorted. "You're an operator, Verisa—or Katrina, whoever the hell you are. You know how the game is played."

Katrina nodded. "I do. The next move is the one where you die."

Juasa's pulse quickened. She wanted to cry out, to tell Katrina to stop, that this wasn't the way. She opened her mouth, but her terror and sorrow stole her voice.

Katrina's shoulder rose a centimeter, and her finger moved off the pistol's trigger guard. Juasa did the only thing she could think of: she shot Katrina in the back.

The round ricocheted off Katrina's armored skin and hit the wall, shattering a mirror.

"What the hell?" Katrina said as she spun on Juasa.

Juasa took a step back, and Malorie lunged at Katrina, who swung a fist back, smashing it into the other woman's face. As Malorie crumpled to the floor, Katrina took a step toward Juasa, the expression on her face a combination of anger and confusion.

"I—" Juasa struggled to find her voice. "I had to

stop you. You can't kill her."

"Why not?"

"Because she's collared too!"

A look of surprise came over Katrina's face. It was the first time her new visage had looked anything like the woman Juasa had come to love.

"Shit," Katrina whispered and looked back at Malorie, who was cradling her jaw. "You. Sit," Katrina barked a moment later.

Juasa realized Katrina was talking to Korin, who had risen off the bed at some point during the commotion.

"I think Juasa is right," Korin said as he held up his hands and slowly sat back down. "You said you want to take over the Blackadder. Well, no one knows the intricacies of their operation like Malorie. Besides, if you want to get Jace down here so you can kill him—which I'd really like to see—you'll need his wife alive."

Katrina ran a hand through her hair and turned to look at Juasa. "I don't see a collar on her."

"It's the choker she wears," Juasa said. "Probably has internal components, too."

Malorie was looking up at them with a new expression, one that appeared to contain legitimate sorrow, on her face. "How did you know?"

"It was what Lara said," Juasa replied. "How angry it made you—the bit about Jace having you on a leash. Once I heard that, I realized that you were always wearing a choker. Its appearance had varied over the days, but I realized it was the *same* choker."

Malorie laughed and shook her head. "I guess you're smarter than I gave you credit for."

Juasa sighed and walked toward Katrina. "Why do you want to take over the Blackadder? They're pirates. Scum."

Katrina drew a deep, rasping breath. The sound of it made Juasa consider the pain Katrina must be feeling, both physical and emotional.

Up close, she could easily see that the skin on Katrina's face was artificial; it was too stiff, every movement too muted or over exaggerated.

Nevertheless, Juasa reached up and stroked Katrina's cheek. "Kat. My dear Kat, what are you doing?"

Katrina's steel-sheathed fingers rose to touch Juasa's face as well. "I'm doing what we need to survive. The word's out, I'm a Streamer. The Blackadder, Lara and her sick regime she runs here…they'll chase us across space until they catch us. And if it's not them, it'll be someone else. What we need now is strength. Power. If the *Intrepid* ever reappears, it'll do so near Bollam's World. I need to stay close, but I don't plan to be prey for whoever decides to take up the chase."

Juasa saw the cold certainty in Katrina's eyes—the only organic piece of her that was visible—and knew there was no changing her mind.

She wondered how well she really knew Katrina. They had only spent a few days together aboard the *Havermere* before ending up on Persia. That short time had been intense; a lovemaking-filled rush.

But is this who Katrina really is?

Then Juasa remembered that Katrina could have run when she had been captured by Jace, how she had cared for her in the fields, in the pain-filled nights in the cell.

No, Katrina is a good *woman. I can't abandon her.*

She had to make Katrina remember that caring and compassion were her greatest strengths. Though, given what they'd been through these past weeks, that would not be simple.

She drew a deep breath and nodded. "OK, what's next?"

ACCEPTANCE
STELLAR DATE: 01.20.8512 (Adjusted Gregorian)
LOCATION: Revenence Castle
REGION: Persia, Midditerra System

Relief flooded through Katrina to hear Juasa say those words. A part of her knew that she *appeared* to be acting irrationally—or maybe insane—but this was who she was now. This was who she had to be to survive.

She hoped Juasa could make the transition as she repeated her mantra.

I am Katrina. Daughter of the despot Yusuf, friend of the Noctus, liberator of the Hyperion, *wife of Markus, president of Victoria, lover of Juasa, survivor of the fields.*

I am all of those things; together, they are me. They form my foundation; they give me purpose. My memories are my strength, the proof of my convictions.

I am the steel fist that crushes my enemies, I weather the light and the darkness, I persist, I thrive on the agony. I touch all these things, I live in their worlds, but they are not me, and I am not them. I am still Katrina.

Katrina looked into Juasa's eyes as the beautiful young woman waited for her answer. "If Malorie really is collared, then we can use her. Korin is right. We need to draw Jace down here."

Juasa turned to Malorie. "Admit it. You're under

Jace's thumb, aren't you?"

"It's where I belong," Malorie whispered. "I was a wild animal; I needed to be controlled."

Korin whistled. "Well I'll be damned. Jace just gets worse and worse the more you know."

Katrina approached Korin and looked him over. "You have no love for Jace?"

"Do you think I was born looking this way?" Korin asked. "Sure, its work, but there are other things I'd rather be doing."

"Jace forced it on all the guards down here," Malorie said from her place on the floor. "They need treatments, or the mods kill them."

"And you?" Katrina turned back to Malorie, considering her options. "You like being collared? How long has it been?"

Malorie shrugged. "Fifty years, give or take a bit. He did it to me on our wedding night."

"And you just accept it?" Juasa asked.

Malorie rose, working her jaw and wincing. "You adapt, right? I made it so that he didn't need to use it on me. Became just who he wanted me to be—turns out I like being what I turned into."

Katrina ignored the personal meaning the words had for her and walked over to Malorie, examining the collar. She touched it gently, sending a passel of her nano into the device as well as into Malorie's body.

"It would seem you're not lying. This thing hasn't triggered in years. Why does Jace still make you wear it?"

Malorie shrugged. "I like it. It makes me feel protected. Like I said, I used to be wild, careless. Jace made me understand my place, and I grew into it."

"Yes, look at you," Katrina said with a shake of her head. She triggered the collar's pain stimulation center, and Malorie shrieked. "Still works."

"Katrina!" Juasa's voice was both sharp and worried. "Stop, don't do that to her."

Katrina sighed and turned to Juasa. "You realize what she was doing to us, right? Repeated punishment and pleasure? She was breaking and training us." Her eyes narrowed as she regarded Juasa. "Was she successful with you?"

She could see Juasa considering her words.

After a few moments, Juasa's shoulders slumped.

"I could tell she was doing it...I thought I had resisted. Maybe I hadn't as much as I thought."

Malorie's expression began to harden once more. "You barely put up a fight, Juasa. I had you wrapped around my little finger in a day."

Katrina sent a command to the collar Malorie wore, and the woman fell with a scream, writhing on the floor. Then she turned it off.

"I'm not going to play cat and mouse with you,

Malorie. I'm going to play hammer and anvil. Understood?"

Malorie whimpered and nodded.

"Good. Your quality of life from here on out has a lot to do with how well behaved you can manage to be. I suggest that you begin with not speaking unless I tell you to."

Malorie nodded and remained curled up on the floor.

"You're pathetic. Go sit on your bed," Katrina ordered. "Korin, come over here."

<Katrina...do you really need to do that to her?> Juasa asked privately.

<I do. She's been trained to only respect force and I don't have the time to change her—if I even could. She'll be fiercely loyal to Jace to the point of suicide.>

<Really?> Juasa asked. *<But he turned her into a slave as well—why would she not turn on him?>*

<Do you really think that she didn't have the opportunity to kill him over all these years? She's his creature through and through, so much that he can entrust half his operation to her with no fear of her turning on him. I need her to understand that my pleasure is the only thing that stands between her and mind-shredding agony.>

<Katrina, how...how have you become like this?> Juasa's voice was filled with sorrow.

The fields, Ju, Katrina thought to herself before

meeting Juasa's eyes. <*This is who I have to be for now, Ju. I haven't lost myself, I promise.*>

I've just become someone else…

<*OK, Katrina. But be careful. Don't become them just to destroy them.*>

Katrina nodded in response, then turned her attention to Korin. "Hold out your hand."

"Why?" Korin asked. "Are you going to do to me what you did to Stu?"

"No. I should undo that too, I suppose, though he won't be happy. I just didn't have time for anything else."

"*Will* you undo it?" Korin asked, pressing her for a concrete answer.

The man has moxy, I'll give him that.

"Yeah. I'm looking at the mods they made to him now. I want to see if they did the same thing to you."

Korin held out his hand, and Katrina clasped it, passing more of her nano into him. As she did so, a short wave of dizziness came over her. Her internal power reserves were running low again. Building so much nano to repair her body, not to mention the interface with the armor layer, had taxed Katrina's flesh and SC Batts to the extreme.

If anyone noticed, they didn't say. She had to charge her batts up soon, or she'd collapse, and then things would go very badly.

"You're all set," Katrina said. "Go have a seat, or get a drink from Jeavons, if you want."

"I think I'll take ol' Jay up on that," Korin said. "This has been a 'get a drink' sort of night."

Katrina called Stu in over the Link and unlocked the door. The guard came in and stopped before her.

"Sorry about the kiss, Stu," Katrina said. "I was in a rush—I should have knocked you out and stashed you somewhere while all this went down."

Stu blinked rapidly and focused on Katrina, rage building on his face, but he seemed to push it down.

"I've passed you the recording of everything that just happened in here," Katrina said. "Watch it on your overlays while you get a drink with Korin."

Stu looked over at Malorie, who sat on the bed as ordered, her expression alternating between anger and humiliation.

"What about her?" he asked.

"Revenence Castle is under new management," Katrina replied with a smile.

"Huh," was all that Stu said as he strode to the bar. Korin clapped him on the back as he approached, and the pair of men ordered their drinks before flopping onto the sofas.

"This day…" Juasa began to say from her place at Katrina's side. "This day sure hasn't gone anything like I thought it would."

Katrina snorted. "You can certainly say that again." She looked down at Juasa and took her face in her hands. "It has been far too long since I've done this."

She leaned in, and her lips met Juasa's. The feeling in her artificial skin was muted, but it still felt good to touch her again. Worry sloughed off Katrina as Juasa wrapped her in a fierce embrace, pushing herself into her body.

They stayed like that for a minute before Juasa pulled back and looked Katrina over. "This is going to be a bit of a problem," she said, gesturing at Katrina's armored skin. "Not really all that soft and tender to the touch...plus it seems to have you sealed up."

Katrina laughed. "You are really single-minded! Don't worry, it's not long-term."

"Good." Juasa gave a saucy wink. "Verisa may have been a bit of a bitch, but she was fuckin' hot."

Katrina smiled in response. She could tell Juasa's attempt at humor was forced, but she appreciated the gesture nonetheless.

THE PLAN
STELLAR DATE: 01.20.8512 (Adjusted Gregorian)
LOCATION: Revenence Castle
REGION: Persia, Midditerra System

"So," Katrina began as she settled onto the one of the sofas and looked at Korin and Stu. "You two know my plan, and you are either cowed by me, or think I may be a passable alternative to Malorie and Jace."

"A little bit of both," Korin said with a laugh. "I'll admit that I've grown fond of Juasa, and if she trusts you, then I trust you."

Juasa approached with a martini in hand and settled next to Katrina. "Kat's laid her life on the line for me. She's here because she tried to save me when she could have cut and run."

"Good enough for me," Korin replied.

Katrina looked at Stu. "Again, I'm sorry about what I did."

Stu snorted. "You're really not my favorite person right now. Mind you, Malorie's done worse and never said she was sorry, so I guess it'll have to do…for now."

"I wasn't really in a good headspace," Katrina said, shifting on the sofa. Every part of her still hurt; sitting seemed worse than standing, at present.

"Weeks of torture have a way of doing that to a person. Considering what goes on around here on a daily basis, I'll bet that others have suffered worse at your hands."

Stu reddened—as did Korin—and the man looked away. "Yeah, shit's been rough at Revenence."

"It's going to get worse before it gets better," Katrina admitted. "You two are my beachhead. If I can convince you that we can take down Jace, and we can convince others here in the castle, then we have our start."

Korin nodded and took another pull from the bottle he held. "You're not in the castle of happy dreams here. This place isn't held together by love and goodwill. People are here for two reasons: they're greedy and want to get a piece of the pie, or they're being held against their will."

"Or they had no other alternative," Stu added.

Korin shrugged. "I'd lump that in with 'against their will'."

"I guess that works," Stu agreed.

"What are you proposing?" Katrina asked.

"I think that the castle is a secondary target. The Adders' real power is in space. We need to control those stations. Or at least some of them," Korin said. "Though first we need to clean up the scene where Anna and Liam died—the medlab, I assume?"

"Yeah. Ainsley, too," Katrina added.

"What?" Juasa asked, a pained look on her face. "What about Tom? He seemed like a good guy."

"Anna killed Ainsley; I tried to stop her. She was going to do Tom, too, but I got her first. Tom is sedated on the medtable."

Juasa's face held an expression of relief, and Katrina sent her a smile over the Link. *<See, I haven't gone off the deep end.>*

<I believed you, but evidence is nice as well.>

Katrina didn't get a chance to reply, as Korin shook his head and swore aloud.

"Damn, we have a problem."

"A new one?" Katrina asked.

"Sorta. I just got a report that they traced back who instigated the attack on you earlier today."

"I already know who did that," Katrina replied. "It was Anna."

"Sure, but she got a guard—guy named Parry— to kick the whole thing off. The guys have him, and they're looking for Liam."

Katrina connected to the field overseer's network and found the pair who had Parry in custody. She reached out and stripped Malorie's private tokens from the woman, then faked a message as the lady of the castle.

<Liam's unavailable…taking his licks for letting this happen. Put Parry in a cell. Tell him he'll get something

to eat when he tells us who paid him off to do this.>

<Yes, Lady Malorie,> a field overseer named Harry said—Katrina knew him and his whip well. *<He's already given that skinny bitch Anna up.>*

<Anna? Well then, she's here with me right now.... This will be good,> Katrina replied, adding a bit of Malorie's snarl to her tone.

<Do you need any assistance?> Harry's mental tone was hungry; he was a man who really liked to dish out abuse. Katrina made a note to deal with him later.

<Stu and Korin are here with me. Lock Parry up and take the night—hell, the week—off.>

Some poor worker would thank her for that.

<Yes, Lady Malorie!>

Katrina severed the connection. "OK, that's dealt with. They think we have Anna and Liam here."

"Good," Korin nodded. "When we clean up that mess, we'll dispose of them."

"Is that what Malorie would do?" Katrina asked.

Korin sighed and Stu laughed.

"No, she'd hang them from the parapets," Stu said.

Katrina glanced back at Malorie.

Malorie shrugged. "Stu's right. If people in their station betrayed the Blackadder, they'd be made a public example of."

"A bit overdramatic, don't you think? Well we

need to maintain the fiction that nothing's changed for now," Katrina said with a curt nod. "When we're finished here, I'll need you to take care of that."

"What about Ainsley?" Korin asked.

"Do the less extreme version of whatever Malorie would do—"

"The moat, then," Stu interrupted.

"Great, the moat," Katrina nodded. "And Tom...what to do about Tom?"

"I think Tom can be reasoned with," Juasa said.

Katrina's gaze met Juasa's. "OK, he'll be your task, then."

"I hate to put it so bluntly," Stu began. "But other than a change of the guard, what's in it for us?"

"Well," Katrina mused. "I can fix the mods and the altered biology they've forced on you."

"I'd settle for undoing it," Korin said.

"We'll need better facilities than they have here to undo it all, or to make it so your bodies can sustain themselves—whichever you choose," Katrina replied after a moment's pause. "Though the medbay on my ship could do either."

"The ship that Jace left to capture?" Stu asked.

Katrina waved her hand dismissively. "Wild goose chase. My ship was nowhere near there...well, I don't think it is."

"Then where is it?" Korin asked.

"Hopefully on the way here," Katrina said as she stood and stretched. She walked to the bar and sent a command to Jeavons for another drink. "OK. We play everything here off like business as usual, but go up to one of the stations to take it over, right?"

Korin nodded. "I think that's best. The castle here really has no strategic importance. It's just the site of Malorie's sithri business. If the Blackadder stations think something's wrong down here, they can drop a thousand troops on our heads in an hour."

"Not to mention the couple hundred ships currently insystem," Stu added.

"I didn't think it would be that much. How many ships does the Blackadder have, anyway?" Katrina took the glass of whisky from Jeavons. "Fleet strength isn't in the planetside databases."

"Jace is savvy," Korin replied. "He has stations in a lot of systems. No one really knows the full scope of the fleet, but I think there have to be at least a thousand ships all-told."

"At least," Stu added.

"OK," Katrina said as she leant against the bar. "I need you two to deal with the bodies. String 'em up and all. When you're done, bring Tom up here. I'll pass you codes to release him from the medtable."

"You got it," Korin said as he rose.

Stu stood slowly as well, his eyes locked on Katrina's. "Do we have your word that you'll fix or undo what they did to us?"

"Yes," Katrina's voice was resolute. "You have my word. Both that I *can* do it, and that I will."

"Good," Stu replied. "C'mon, Korin, we have a feast to prepare for the crows."

"Seriously gross," Juasa said with a shudder.

Stu chuckled, and the two guards left the room.

"Korin we can trust, but are you sure about Stu?" Juasa asked as she rose from the sofa and approached Katrina.

"I can see everything in the castle," Katrina replied. "If he makes a move, we'll know. Plus, we're taking them with us. When we leave, no one in the castle will know that anything has happened."

"What's going to happen to her?" Juasa asked, looking at Malorie. "Ultimately, I mean."

Katrina let out a long breath. "I have no idea. She's a psychologist's dream to be sure."

Juasa laughed. "We probably all are."

Katrina joined her with a soft laugh then sent a signal to the nano she'd sent into Malorie's body, and the woman slumped over on her bed. "Just asleep. I wanted some time for the two of us."

Juasa sidled up against her and Katrina sighed with a moment's contentment. Her nerves were still on fire, but it seemed to hurt less where Juasa touched her. Or more, but the pain was pleasure.

She wasn't sure she could tell the difference anymore.

Stars, I'm so screwed up.

"Ju, is there a charge station in this place? My batts are almost dry."

"I was wondering about that," Juasa said with a grin. "Jeavons has a wireless charging station. It slides out from behind the bar."

"No dice," Katrina said. "I didn't think to make induction coils. Need a cable."

"Let me look," Juasa said, pulling away from Katrina. "There may be a backup cable option."

Katrina sagged against the bar. What she really wanted was a full night's sleep; it had been days since she'd caught more than an hour. She sat on one of the stools, and placed her elbows on the bar.

When Juasa finally found the cable and pulled it around to Katrina, she was already fast asleep.

ROCKHALL
STELLAR DATE: 01.20.8512 (Adjusted Gregorian)
LOCATION: Revenence Castle
REGION: Persia, Midditerra System

Katrina felt refreshed, if not rather stiff, when she woke.

Her HUD showed that her SC Batts were fully charged, and her mednano had repaired much of the damage to her internal organs that the weeks of beatings and malnourishment had caused.

She opened her eyes and blinked away the sleep that had formed in the corners, rather surprised to find her tear ducts working properly again.

The artificial skin on her face still felt strange—like there was a layer of half-solid clay on her face. Katrina worked her mouth and lips as she stared up at the ceiling above her.

Ceiling…Did I fall on the floor?

Katrina turned her head to find that she was laying on one of the sofas and saw her coat draped across the back.

"Have a good nap?" Juasa asked, and Katrina turned her head the other way to see her lover laying on one of the other sofas, staring at her with unblinking eyes.

"Nap? It's been six hours," Katrina replied as she

pushed herself up into a seated position. "Is everything OK? Where's Korin and Stu?"

"They've finished cleanup and have Tom on the shuttle. They're outside the room, waiting for you to awake from your beauty rest."

Katrina glanced down at her armor-skin. "Beauty, right."

"Well, plastic you looks the same…but your eyes look more rested."

"What about you?" Katrina asked.

Juasa pulled herself upright. "I didn't sleep a wink, too much to worry about. There's so much that can go wrong. Plus…."

"Plus?" Katrina prompted, when Juasa didn't finish the thought.

"Plus I was worried about you," Juasa said tiredly. "About what you did to yourself. I can't believe you survived it."

"It was necessary. I had to survive."

"Is that sort of thing normal, back when you come from?" Juasa asked. "Removing your skin on a whim."

"Not on a whim, no, but it isn't—wasn't—major surgery, either."

Juasa whistled. "And the armor? You just keep skin-replacing armor schematics up here?" She completed the question with a tap to her head, and Katrina laughed.

"The autodresser had the armor already. I had specs for artificial skin—in case of burns, nukes, whatever. I just mixed and matched."

"And your nano is good enough for the nerve linkups?" Juasa asked.

Katrina pushed against her rubbery-feeling cheeks. "Close enough. The connections will improve over time. Though once we get back to the *Voyager*, I'll get this removed. To be honest, I was feeling a bit...out of sorts last night."

Juasa snorted. "A bit?"

Katrina sighed. "OK, a lot. We're not out of the woods yet, though. Things are going to get worse before they better."

"You mentioned that. How so?" Juasa asked.

"Well, we have to lure Jace in. Malorie over there," Katrina gestured to the still-sleeping woman's form, "will be our bait. Things often don't go so well for bait. Then I'm going to kill Jace. There's no two ways about that."

"That doesn't sound so bad," Juasa said. "I'm all for killing Jace. You forget that he shot me. Twice."

Katrina shook her head. "Haven't forgotten. But after that, we still have to kill Lara and take over the Midditerra System."

Juasa frowned. "Remind me again why we need to do that?"

"Because Lara seems like a grade-A badass, and

one that doesn't like to share—"

"I got that impression firsthand," Juasa interjected.

"Yeah, well, if I hang out here as the new leader of the Blackadder, it won't take long for her to realize that *I'm* the Streamer woman. When that happens, she'll come for me. I need to take her down first."

"You realize that her title is 'Admiral'," Juasa said. "She runs this whole damn system with a moral code not dissimilar to the Blackadder's."

"I know, it's handy," Katrina said with a grin.

"Handy?"

"Yeah, just one person to take out. I don't have to worry about a whole pile of disparate governments and a sprawling bureaucracy. Only one snake to behead."

"But what about the how?" Juasa asked. "You act like it's a foregone conclusion that you'll win any conflict with her. I mentioned that bit about her being an admiral to point out the fact that she has a rather large military."

"She's still mortal," Katrina replied. "If I can get close to her, she's dead."

"You think everyone will just fall in line then?" Juasa's expression conveyed disbelief.

"Some will. If we have the Blackadder at our backs, we'll win. We'll have this system in a matter of weeks. The other…what are they called…cantons?…will fall in line."

"You talk like you've done this before," Juasa said. "*Have* you done this before?"

Katrina laughed as she rose and walked over to Jeavons, signaling him to prepare coffee. "No, not even close. But there's a first time for everything, right?"

Jeavons prepared several cups of strong black brew, one of which Katrina directed Malorie to drink after waking the woman. The former lady of the castle's expression was dark, but she didn't speak as she downed her beverage.

"I guess you two had better change," Katrina said. "I bet her highness here wouldn't be caught dead wearing the same thing two days in a row. Not that *I* care, but we do need some element of subterfuge."

Juasa laughed as she looked Malorie up and down. "Let me pick her outfit, I think I saw just the thing in her back room."

"All you," Katrina said, passing Juasa the tokens to control the autodresser.

"In you go, Mal," Juasa said with a smirk.

Katrina didn't check on what Juasa was putting Malorie in, but instead walked to one of the tall windows and looked out over the low rolling hills surrounding the castle. Sithri fields separated by rows of trees stretched as far as she could see, and workers were already filtering out to their fields.

It was strange to see it from this angle. From up here you could almost think that the workers were free men and women, all headed out for their daily labor and reward.

Katrina knew differently. The reality on the ground—as per usual—was different than it appeared from above.

A minute later, her quiet reverie was broken by Malorie's voice.

"Ju! You can*not* be serious."

Katrina turned and glared at Malorie, causing the woman's mouth to snap shut.

"Shit…" Katrina muttered. "Looks like Juasa's selection is enough punishment for your vocal indiscretion."

Malorie was in a long white dress that was exceedingly tight. Thought it was slit at the knee, her thighs were welded together. On top of that, the sleeves were attached to the torso down to the elbow. A high collar that came up under her chin and fanned out behind her head restricted Malorie's range of motion even further.

Juasa gave a soft laugh. "It's *your* dress. If you don't like it, why do you own it?"

"Jace got it as a joke," Malorie replied sullenly.

"He's got a better sense of humor than I'd

thought," Katrina said. "Can you even walk in that thing? Show us."

Malorie flushed and took small waddling steps across the room."

"Stars, it's going to take forever to get to the shuttle," Katrina said, stifling a laugh.

Juasa had a hand over her mouth. "Stars, Mal, your ass looks like two cats fighting in a sack when you do that."

Malorie's shoulders rose and her expression darkened.

"Get back in there," Katrina said. "We'll raise the slit so we don't all have to waddle along with you."

Juasa snorted and then doubled over with laughter as Malorie wiggled her way back into the autodresser.

"Oh, stars," she wheezed. "That makes up for not sleeping all night. "Can we make it have no slit instead? We could strap her to a pole, and then Stu and Korin could carry her."

Katrina chuckled. "Tempting, but no. As much as I want to humiliate her, we need Malorie to look like the haughty bitch everyone has come to know and hate. You can let out your bondage fetishes on her later."

Juasa grinned. "I have no idea what you're talking about."

"I've had sex with you, I know what you're into,"

Katrina said with a wink, and Juasa just grinned all the more.

A minute later, the autodresser's door slid open, and this time Malorie was able to walk properly.

<Did her heels get taller?> Katrina asked Juasa.

<Don't want her running off. That was the initial idea.>

Katrina chuckled. <Sure. I know payback when I see it.>

"We ready then?" Juasa asked.

"You normally wear the same thing two days in a row, Ju?" Katrina asked.

Juasa looked down at herself, still wearing the blue sleeveless shipsuit. "Shit, I totally forgot."

She stepped into the autodresser, and a minute later walked out wearing a black skinsuit and low boots. A dark grey jacket hung from her shoulders, coming down to mid-thigh.

"The yin to my yang," Katrina said with a smile.

"Just happy to not be naked or shimmering," Juasa said. "This is more my style."

Katrina took Juasa's hand and walked to the door. She opened it to see Stu and Korin standing on either side of the hall.

"You ladies finally ready?" Korin asked.

"We had to suitably attire her majesty," Juasa replied.

"Coulda just put her in a sack," Stu said with a

grin.

Katrina scowled at the men. *<Seriously, watch what you say aloud. Does subterfuge mean anything to you?>*

<Right, sorry,> Stu replied.

Katrina gestured for Malorie to lead the way to the lift with Juasa and herself behind, bracketed by the guards.

It was early in the morning, and few servants were about. Katrina suspected that most took routes that avoided passing by Malorie's quarters.

The ride down the lift was uneventful, but when they reached the ground floor, the lift opened to reveal an agitated looking man wearing a field overseer's uniform.

"My Lady!" he exclaimed. "I'd been trying to reach you."

<Tell him you were enjoying a night off,> Katrina told Malorie over the Link.

"I was taking a night to myself...well, mostly myself," Malorie said.

The overseer looked at the guards and two women and nodded slowly. "Uh...OK. We're not too sure what to do with Liam gone. Should I take Verisa here out to the fields?"

Malorie shook her head. "No, she's coming with me. With Liam gone, you're in charge of the fields now, Garret. Are you capable of that, or...?"

"Of course, yes I am." The words spilled out of Garret's mouth in a rush.

"Good, now get out of my way," Malorie said as she walked past the man.

Garret frowned, but as far as Katrina could tell, there was nothing unusual about Malorie's behavior.

<Were there any secret messages in that?> Katrina asked Korin.

<No. Garret just looks surprised because Malorie was nicer to him than usual.>

<Damn...> Katrina mused. <That's going to be tough to gauge: how much bitch to force out of her.>

<With luck, we'll be able to tuck her out of sight once we get up to the station.>

Katrina nodded. That would be nice indeed.

The rest of the trip to the waiting shuttle was uneventful, and ten minutes later, they were lifting off from the cradle.

Katrina sat in a seat facing Malorie, and she could see that the woman was fuming as she stared out the window at the shrinking castle below.

"What's on your mind?" Katrina asked.

"Oh, do I have permission to speak?" Malorie retorted.

Katrina gave a rueful laugh. "Sure is unpleasant to have the shoe on the other foot, isn't it?"

Malorie clenched her jaw and resumed looking

out the window.

"You think it's the last time you'll see Revenence?" Juasa asked from her place next to Katrina.

Malorie looked back at the two women. "I don't know, is it?"

Katrina shrugged. "Maybe. Maybe not. I hear the fields are down a few workers."

<You know she's useful,> Juasa said.

<Ju? You advocating for leniency, or manual labor? You'll recall that this is the woman who had you beat me with steel rods.>

<I haven't forgotten, but I've gained some more perspective. What if Mal has a change of heart—once we take the collar off her, that is. She's good at what she does.>

Katrina wasn't sure what Juasa was getting at. It sounded like she was advocating putting Malorie back in charge of Revenence Castle and the sithri operation.

<We can't trust her, Ju. She'll turn on us the first chance she gets.>

Juasa shrugged. *<She didn't turn on Jace.>*

*<Do **you** want to rule her like Jace did? We don't have fifty years to wear her down to a nub.>* Katrina looked into Juasa's eyes. *<You sure this isn't stockholm syndrome?>*

Juasa sighed. *<I...I don't think so...I'm just trying*

to think of how we'll manage all this stuff with your crazy plan of taking over this whole star system. I mean…it's filled with crooks and criminals. We're going to have to get in bed with a lot of dirty people—figuratively speaking.>

Katrina had known that all along. She had not, however, expected Juasa to be on board with the idea so quickly. Which was why she suspected some sort of strange attachment to Malorie.

It only cemented her belief that Jace's wife would have to die at the earliest possible time. If Juasa harbored feelings for her—even ones she couldn't consciously acknowledge—enough time could see Malorie turning Juasa against her.

<Could be,> Katrina said to Juasa. *<There'd have to be changes, though. A lot of changes.>*

Juasa sent an affirmative feeling. *<Yes. But we also can't just shut it down. That operation feeds all those people. If we don't give them work, they'll rebel…or end up working for some other canton, and that erodes our power.>*

<You're thinking really strategically about this,> Katrina observed.

<Like I said, I'm just trying to figure out how we're going to make all this work.>

Katrina snorted. *<We have a ton of shenanigans to pull off first. We should focus on those.>*

<Right, so what is our plan when we get up there?>

<Our first stop is Rockhall Station. There are twelve ships docked up there, plus the Havermere. We need to get Malorie to call a meeting of the captains, and then we tell them that there's new management.>

Juasa cast Katrina an incredulous look. <That's a weak plan. A really weak plan. Like...the weakest plan I've ever heard.>

<I plan to employ shock and awe,> Katrina gave a soft, audible laugh. <When we get up there, I'm going to need the biggest SC Batts that we can fit under this coat.>

<If the Havermere is up there, I can get batts,> Juasa said. <Anything else you need?>

<Superconductive strands, if you have them.> Katrina paused and reached for Juasa's hand. <These captains will have two motivations: greed and fear. I plan to play on both of those.>

<What are you going to do?>

Juasa looked worried, and Katrina squeezed her hand. <It's not going to be a bloodless affair. You OK with that?>

<OK? No,> Juasa snorted. <But I gave it a lot of thought last night. I don't want to spend the rest of my life looking over my shoulder for Jace and Malorie coming after us.>

<Good. But Juasa, I need you to understand; we have a rough time —>

Juasa squeezed her hand back, interrupting

Katrina. *<I get that.>*

Katrina looked out the window as the shuttle lifted past the lower orbitals, and she caught sight of Farsa Station's massive disk slowly spinning around the planet. They rose past its altitude and moved into the orbital band filled with smaller stations, salvage operations, and manufacturing facilities.

The data Katrina had taken from Revenence Castle allowed her to connect each station with its owners, and she saw that Blackadder controlled just over ten percent of the stations in orbit of Persia.

It wasn't news to her, but it was something else to see all the activity up here. The Midditerra System was nothing more than a giant chop shop, drifting amongst the stars.

She caught sight of Rockhall Station; an aptly named, hollowed-out asteroid. Large doors were on one end, and several ships were docked at a berthing ring that wrapped around the center of the oblong station.

Katrina brought up its specs and saw that Rockhall was fifteen kilometers long, and three in circumference; just a touch larger than the *Intrepid*'s habitation cylinders.

Rockhall didn't spin, though. It didn't need to, with artificial gravity. She also suspected that stripping ships in zero-*g* was much easier than doing it with centrifugal force in play.

Of the twelve ships currently at Rockhall, the seven docked at external berths were listed in the Revenence databases as corsairs. They looked like bulky freighters and could probably take on some cargo, but the fuel capacity listed told her that they were primarily used as long haul pursuit vessels. The corsairs also sported more reactors than a ship their size needed, and an impressive armament.

"On final approach," the shuttle pilot called back into the cabin. "I have an internal berth, as requested. We'll be at the shuttle lock in fifteen minutes."

"Good," Malorie growled.

Katrina was interested in the ships they'd see within. The databank at Revenence only listed them as corvettes with some base specs, which led Katrina to believe that the ships would be all engine and guns. Those were the ones she wanted to evaluate for the inevitable battles to come.

What I wouldn't give to have Troy's help. He could take control of those ships in a heartbeat, and I wouldn't need to cajole their captains into working for me.

That thought led Katrina to one she hadn't considered before: Sam.

<Juasa, I'm coming with you onto the Havermere.*>*

<Why?> Juasa asked.

<We need to secure Sam. First order of business.>

<Sam? The surliest AI this side of Sol?> Juasa asked,

a note of surprise in her mental tone.

<That's the one. He's going to be key in this.>

<Okaaaay. I think he'll be a bigger pain in the ass than he will a help.>

<He owes us. He'll owe us even more once we save him.> Katrina was certain of it. Sam was both angry and wily; he was just the ally they needed to pull this off.

The shuttle closed within five kilometers of Rockhall Station, and its network Linked with the station's external comm network. Katrina connected to it and crossed over into Rockhall's general network. Once inside, she examined the subnets and information hierarchy.

Like Revenence Castle, it was less than optimal. Everything was cobbled together in a barely-functional mess. However, it was more secure than the castle's network, and it didn't take Katrina long to figure out why.

There was an AI running Rockhall.

It seemed to be restricted to managing basic station function, but Katrina wasn't certain she could take out an AI on a network that it was more familiar with. Controlling doors in the castle was one thing, but this level of cyber-warfare was beyond her.

It cemented the need to liberate Sam before she tipped her hand to anyone on Rockhall.

As the shuttle approached the airlock and slowed to a crawl, Katrina saw Malorie look down at Persia and sigh.

<You like it planetside more, don't you?> she asked.

Malorie gave her a sharp look. *<Oh, I can use the Link too? Is that OK, or are you going to punish me?>*

<It's no wonder Jace put a collar on you first thing. You don't know when to turn the bitch off.>

Malorie gave a mental laugh. *<Well, I also tried to kill him on our wedding night.>*

<Conveniently left that out.>

<So what do you want?> Malorie asked. *<I assume you weren't just trying to make polite conversation.>*

<I was thinking that there might be a reward for good behavior.>

<Gonna let me polish your armor-skin?> Malorie snorted. *<I'd rather eat a pulse blast than take your scraps.>*

<I was thinking I'd give you Revenence. Free and clear. Yours, not a part of the Blackadder.>

Malorie's eyes widened. *<You'll what? But the sithri trade is the financing for half this shit.>*

<We'll, I'll still take a tariff,> Katrina replied. *<But it'll be less than what Lara takes now.>*

<Lara?> Malorie asked. *<What are you talking— no…. You've got some high aspirations, Streamer Woman.>*

<I've decided to put down roots.>

Malorie nodded slowly as the shuttle passed into the airlock and drifted slowly to starboard in the forty-meter space.

<*I'll consider it,*> Malorie said after a moment.

<*You're not framing this right,*> Katrina said coolly. <*I'm not doing this in exchange for your cooperation. You'll cooperate whether you like it or not; you just have to decide if you want the carrot or the stick.*>

<*I could just put up a fight; then you'd have to kill me.*>

Katrina shook her head. <*You saw what I did to Stu. You want to be my sock puppet?*>

Malorie paled. <*No, not really.*>

<*Good. I'll assume you're going for carrot. But the stick is ready.*>

Malorie didn't reply, and Katrina let the issue alone. A minute later, the inner door on the airlock opened, and the shuttle moved into the pressurized interior of the asteroid.

"Wow, didn't think I'd get all emotional to see the *Havermere* again," Juasa said aloud as the repair and refit ship came into view.

The kilometer-long vessel was the largest inside Rockhall, but it was not the only one. The corvettes, clearly light attack craft, were also in evidence. There were five of them in total. Katrina could also make out the hulls of other ships further back. Some appeared to be stripped down, while others appeared to still be functional.

Malorie snorted. "I wonder if Lara will really come to inspect that thing."

"What?" Katrina asked, turning her head sharply to meet Malorie's eyes.

"Oh, Lara knows that we're hunting a Streamer ship. I fed her a line that you escaped and got back to your ship. She suspects that we're harboring something on the *Havermere*, or maybe wonders if it really is the Streamer ship."

"And?" Katrina asked.

"She said that she would send an inspection team to see if she wants to take her right of first refusal on the ship," Juasa said. "I got the impression she might join them."

"Dammit!" Katrina exclaimed. "This would have been great to know sooner."

Juasa grimaced. "Sorry, Kat, been a lot going on."

Katrina gave a curt nod. *<Sorry, Ju, that was more for Malorie than you. We're moving fast, playing it by ear—stuff like this is bound to happen.>*

<I follow, Kat. We have to secure this place before Jace gets back.>

<You know…> Katrina mused. *<Having Lara here could work out for us.>*

<Are we ready for that?> Juasa asked.

<No, not really,> Katrina replied. *<Like I said, we'll play it by ear. I imagine there's a good chance she won't*

show.>

The shuttle settled onto a pad halfway up the inner curve of the asteroid's interior, and the pilot called back. "We're locked down, you may disembark."

<Polite guy,> Katrina said to Juasa.

<Not all these pirates are asshats. Some of them just need a job.>

Katrina nodded as she gestured for Malorie to precede them.

The Lady of Revenence Castle gracefully rose and walked from the shuttle; no easy feat, considering the towering heels and restricted movement she was being subjected to. Korin followed her, and then came Katrina and Juasa. Stu brought up the rear.

Katrina had looked over the public data available on the station's net and knew that her face had not been circulated up here, so she didn't bother holding her coat closed to hide her upgrades. When they stepped onto the pad, she wished she had.

They were met by the stationmaster, Lars Bedin. From several of the notes that Katrina had seen, he was a grouchy man who didn't like change or anything that may even suggest an alteration to how he liked to run Rockhall.

Katrina passed Malorie a series of rapid instructions over the Link. She saw the woman's back stiffen, but she didn't respond.

Here goes nothing.

"My Lady Malorie," Lars said by way of greeting, as Malorie stepped off the shuttle. "I had no idea you were coming."

"I'm sorry, I wasn't aware I needed to schedule things with you. Do you have time in your busy, busy day for me?" Malorie sneered at the man. "Lara is sending an inspection team to look over the *Havermere,* and I want to see it first."

Lars nodded quickly, his brows knitted together. "Uhhhh, of course. It's just unusual for you to do an inspection; Jace usually performs those."

Malorie took a step toward Lars, her arms spread wide. "Do you see Jace? Is he in Midditerra? Did I miss him somewhere? I want to assess the ship's worth before Lara's team arrives."

Lars reddened, but he nodded and walked off the pad. "Follow me, we'll take a skiff over to the ship. It's in very good shape, but there are a few repairs we're making—mostly from the fighting in one of the bays and our breach team's entry."

The stationmaster led them off the landing pad and onto a catwalk that hugged the edge of the rock wall. Every hundred meters, doors led into the rock, but Lars didn't take any of those. He stayed on the catwalk, moving toward a cluster of smaller shuttles and equipment that lay half a kilometer ahead.

<Stars...to think of these monkeys running around in the Havermere. It makes my blood run cold,> Juasa said privately to Katrina.

<I thought the ship was Hemry's domain?> Katrina asked. <You were the Crew Chief.>

<I spent years of my life aboard that old girl, and we're in the middle of a chop shop. It's tragic.>

<Well, they are talking about fixing it—which I'll make sure they do,> Katrina replied. <You want the Havermere, you get the Havermere.>

Juasa chuckled. <Stars...this is surreal. Yesterday you were slaving in the fields. Today you're promising me a starship.>

<I've made some lemonade.>

Juasa caught Katrina's eye and raised her brow. <What? What does lemonade have to do with anything?>

<When life gives you lemons.... Nevermind, I guess it's an old saying. I thought that one would have stuck.>

<Sounds a bit like, 'when the universe flings mass at you, you accrete it into something useful',> Juasa countered.

<That's so awkward.>

<Yours just sounds weird. What does fruit have to do with daily life?>

Katrina sighed, saved from the conversation by their arrival at the skiff, as Lars had called it. The craft was little more than a floating platform with rails. Once everyone was aboard, he lifted off from the pad and steered them into the open space within the asteroid.

Artificial gravity still felt surreal to Katrina. That the skiff could use graviton emitters to propel itself across the open space, and then also use those same emitters to keep them standing on the platform, was amazing.

It certainly beat centripetal force pushing at your feet, or the artificial gravity that the *Intrepid* had generated with its particle accelerator's mag fields. Those never felt quite right.

They approached the forward bay on the *Havermere*, which was opened wide; the same as it had been when Katrina had fought the crew in her attempt to save Juasa.

"Where's the crew?" Katrina asked Lars.

The stationmaster cast her a dark look, but Malorie nodded her head and he answered.

"We have them in Rockhall's brig. Some of them were dead from the fighting aboard, some got taken out by our boarding crew. Only forty seven of them made it here alive.

"Any candidates?" Malorie asked.

Lars shrugged. "I've not looked over them myself, but I'd be surprised if there weren't; there's always a few. We'll find a use for the rest."

Like the fields, Katrina thought.

<Do you want to see them, too?> Malorie asked

Katrina.

<*No,*> Katrina replied. Right now, the crew of the *Havermere* presented more problems than solutions—particularly for Juasa. She'd have to come to grips with the fact that some of those people had been happy to trade her life for money; a reality made worse by the fact that they had no idea which ones.

<*Good, I hate mingling with the cattle.*>

<*Watch it, Malorie.*>

The skiff settled down on the forward bay's deck, and Katrina followed Lars and Malorie off. Her gaze caught sight of the bloodstains and carbon scoring on the deck. They stood as a stark reminder of the battle she'd fought here.

"Crew beat the shit out of one another in here," Lars commented. "We've patched the hull, but there are some other systems that took damage. The grav shield on the door is hosed, too. We'll need to replace it."

"Why's that?" Juasa asked.

Lars looked back at Juasa, and then a look of recognition crossed his face. "I know you, I saw you in the roster. You were the repair Crew Chief aboard this ship."

"Yeah, and I can't imagine what would have happened to the door's grav emitters that would require replacement."

"What's she doing here?" Lars asked, turning to Malorie.

Malorie sneered at the stationmaster. "I'm sorry, Lars, did something about our relationship become unclear to you? Do I need your permission to bring people into the Blackadder?"

<Damn, she's good at that,> Katrina said to Juasa.

<Yeah, years of practice, I imagine.>

Stu took a menacing step toward Lars, and the man backed up.

"Uh...no, I was just surprised, is all."

Malorie shook her head and turned away from Lars, appearing disinterested in him. "Well shove your surprise up your ass and answer the question."

"Well, I only know what the repair crews told me, but something about the way the power shut off burned out the emitters."

Juasa snorted. "Right, sure. That's repair scam one-oh-one. Even the shit emitters that KiStar sprang for wouldn't take damage from that. Sounds like someone is skimming."

Malorie turned her head slowly and took a step toward Lars. "You skimming, Lars? Taking a little bit to sell on the side? Using it to pad a deal?"

"Of course not!" Lars was indignant. "I know better than that. Blackadder takes from others, not ourselves."

Malorie let out a short breath and shook her

head. "Not sure I believe you, Lars."

"I'll find out," Katrina said as she walked toward the man.

"Who the fuck are *you*?" Lars asked as he backpedaled, only to be caught in Stu's grip.

"You're not gonna like this, Lars," Stu said with a wicked grin, "but given that you're such a piece of shite on your best day, I'm not going to feel too much sympathy."

Lars struggled mightily as Katrina approached, but couldn't pull free from Stu's grip. His head whipped back and forth, though it didn't help as Katrina slammed her palm into his forehead, pushing it back into Stu and holding him in place.

She fed nano through the palm of her hand into his skin. Karina was surprised at the quality of Lars's internal bio and nanotech defenses. They were better than most others she'd encountered; they fought back and killed off her intruders.

"You want to do this the hard way?" Katrina asked, her eyes boring into the man's. "So be it."

She delivered a small electric shock through emitters in her hand, frying any nano in the surface of Lars' skin. It wasn't enough to damage any mods he would have, but it would throw them into a recovery cycle.

Her next batch of nano easily defeated his beleaguered defenses and penetrated his skull, finding his wireless Link connection and internal datastores.

The connection established, Katrina took her hand off Lars and stepped back as she perused the data he had stored in his augmented memories.

"Oh yeah, Lars here has been skimming alright. For years. Wait...what's the *Castigation?*"

Sweat was pouring off Lars' brow, and he shook his head vigorously. "I don't know what that is! You're just making this up! How...you can't do this, it's not possible!"

Malorie gave a rueful laugh. "You're not kidding; it shouldn't be, but it is. Looks like your days here are done, Lars."

"Well, I'll be damned," Katrina said with a smile. "He's hidden a warship in here. No corsair or corvette, either. It's a cruiser."

"A cruiser? In Rockhall?" Malorie asked, aghast. She stepped up to Lars and backhanded him. "You slimy piece of shit. I'm going string you up for my crows. Alive."

"Easy now, Malorie," Katrina said. "Lars knows a lot of interesting things. The crows will have to wait for a bit."

"Where are the repair crews, anyway?" Juasa asked.

"It's third shift on Rockhall," Korin replied.

Juasa frowned. "No rotating shifts? Lars, that's a

bigger sin than hiding a cruiser."

"OK," Katrina said. "The cruiser can wait. First we need to find Sam, and Ju needs to pick some things up." She turned to Lars. "Where's Sam?"

"The AI?" Lars asked. "He's still aboard, but we had to cut him off, thing was crazy, we couldn't lock it down."

Katrina turned Korin and Juasa. "You two, go get what we need. Stu, Malorie, and I will take Lars to get Sam."

<You going to be alright with just Stu?> Korin asked privately at the same time that Juasa asked. *<You safe alone with all of them?>*

Katrina drew both into a private conversation. *<I'm going to sock-puppet Lars, and I can drop Malorie in a heartbeat. Or are you worried about Stu?>*

<All of the above,> Korin replied. *<But I suppose you have him in hand too.>*

<I do,> Katrina said with a curt nod.

<Be safe,> Juasa said and gave Katrina a quick kiss.

<Stay on this channel,> Katrina instructed. *<Korin, any threat, you take it down fast. Extreme prejudice.>*

<Understood,> Korin said with a nod.

"Stu, you can let go of Lars now," Katrina said.

The guard complied and Lars stumbled forward, then suddenly went rigid.

"OK...I know I talked big, but that creeps me the

fuck out," Stu said.

After infiltrating most of the *Havermere's* systems on the trip through Bollam's World, Katrina knew that Sam's node lay in a datacomplex beneath the bridge a hundred meters away. Based on what Lars had said, they only disconnected the AI node, which meant that Sam was still in his cylinder.

She walked across the bay to the corridor beyond, heading toward the bow. Malorie and Stu followed with Lars, while Juasa and Korin split off to go aft.

On the way, they passed a pair of workers who scrambled out of the way upon seeing both Lars and Malorie. Two minutes later they reached the datacomplex, and Katrina shook her head at the disarray within.

"Your people are savages," she muttered.

Cables hung from conduits, and control panels were smashed. In the center of the complex stood an Au-Ti pillar, which housed Sam's node.

At least he's well protected.

Lars was unable to respond to her statement, but she picked up memories of Sam trying to retake the ship, and the Blackadder prize crew reporting that they had to sever his control of nearly every system to keep the ship under control.

She also saw that the Adders had been unable to breach Sam's pillar without risking his destruction.

He was a valuable prize, and so he remained entombed within his ship.

"Sam," Katrina said aloud, "I'm here to get you out of this prison. Open up."

Sam's dry tones emanated from the pillar without hesitation. "Nice to see you, Katrina; you seem to have managed this ordeal a bit better than I."

Katrina pulled her coat aside to show her armor-skin. "I think I took more of beating than you."

"Damn, that's your skin now? What happened to you?"

"A hell of a lot," Katrina laughed. "However, I'm in charge now—or I will be very shortly. I need your help to pull it off."

"What about your friends here?" Sam asked.

Katrina shifted her gaze to the stationmaster. "Lars, stand on your head."

Lars immediately bent over and tried to stand on his head. He failed and crashed to the ground, only to try once more.

"Stop," Katrina said, and Lars complied.

"Cute trick. I take it you've pulled out all the stops."

"And then some," Katrina replied. "This is a cage fight. No holds barred."

The top of the pillar began to twist, unscrewing and raising up to reveal an SAI's tetrahedron-shaped cube.

"What do you need me for?" Sam asked.

"Have you met the station's AI?" Katrina asked.

"Haven't had the pleasure yet. They've got me locked out."

Katrina turned to Stu. "See if you can find a portable case around here."

"Cabinet on your right," Sam said, and Stu walked to the bulkhead and opened a cabinet. "Look at that; first try, but still the last place you look."

"You're a real comedian," Malorie muttered.

Katrina ignored the woman. "Does it have wireless?"

Stu nodded. "Looks like it. Batts are charged too."

"You're going mobile, Sam. I haven't brushed up against the station AI yet, but I do have its override codes, courtesy of Lars' brain here. If it's subverted, offer it the choice—if you're able to liberate it, that is. Otherwise shut it down, and we'll swap you in."

"I'm in your debt, Katrina. With what Troy gave me, I'll get the job done."

Stu opened up the mobile AI case and approached the pillar.

"OK," Sam said. "I'm ready. Yank me."

The pillar disconnected from Sam's node, and Katrina reached in and carefully pulled Sam's brain from his body. The action reminded her of Troy, and she hoped he was safe—wherever he was.

Katrina carefully set Sam's node into the case, and Stu closed it.

"I'll take it," Katrina said. "I want your hands free in case anything comes up."

Stu nodded and passed the case to Katrina. She tucked it under her arm, determined to keep the AI safe.

<Oh, now that's more like it,> Sam said as he connected to the station's general net.

Katrina passed him the command tokens she'd stripped from Lars' mind. <Be subtle. We don't want to tip our hand yet. You should be able to do whatever you need with those codes.>

<I don't like the idea of locking down another AI…not after what I've been through,> Sam said privately to Katrina.

<I don't like a lot of the things that I've had to do,> Katrina replied. <We're not going to enslave it, we just need control of the station.>

<Not saying I won't do it,> Sam replied. <Just that I don't like it. I understand what the alternatives are.>

<Good.>

"Let's get back to the bay," Katrina said to the group, and Malorie walked out first, followed by Stu. Katrina sent Lars ahead, and took up the rear.

<How's it going down there?> she asked Juasa.

<Shit, Kat, these dumbasses made a mess of my girl. I got what I need, though. Where we going to do the mods?>

<I can do them anywhere. Do you have any 3D printer formation material?>

Juasa snorted. *<Kat, I had to fab parts for ships clear across known space. I have a full fab suite, and a portable unit too.>*

Katrina considered her options. *<We're not terribly secure here; I don't want to do the work till we settle in.>*

<OK, I'll have Korin bring one of the portable units.>

<Great, meet you in the bay. Oh, grab some emitters too...something that can fire photon bursts, or electrons.>

<Uhh...sure, cause I just have that stuff everywhere.>

<This is a repair ship, you must.>

Juasa laughed. *<I was being ironic. Yes, I actually do have that stuff everywhere.>*

The workers they had passed on the way to retrieve Sam's node were gone, something Katrina was glad for. They would have recognized the AI case and asked questions.

Or spread rumors.

As they reached the entrance to the bay, Juasa came into view carrying a case and a small tool chest. Korin followed, pushing a large chest that Katrina assumed must be the portable fab unit.

"Mission accomplished," Juasa said with a smile. "When this is over, I want to fix the *Havermere* back up. I don't trust these fools."

Katrina placed a hand on Juasa's shoulder as they turned into the bay. "Ju, you can have this entire station if you want it. Lars won't be running it anymore."

Malorie snorted as she walked to the skiff. "You're just doling everything out, aren't you?"

"Yup," Katrina said brightly.

Juasa laughed and moved to the side of the skiff, as Stu helped Korin get the fab unit aboard.

Korin took control of the skiff and flew it back to its pad, and the group disembarked once more.

"So, Malorie. I assume you have suites aboard Rockhall, as well?" Katrina already knew where they were, but she wanted Malorie to lead the way.

"Yeah," Malorie grunted. "This way."

She led them through one of the doors into the skin of the hollowed out asteroid and down a long corridor to an intersection. She turned right, then left, and then took another right. The passage ended in a set of double doors that opened as they approached.

The group stepped into a large common area with doors leading off to other rooms. There was a bar on the right, complete with a Jeavons-model automaton, and a bubbling hot tub on the left. Ahead, a series of steps led down to a seating area. Starting on the far side of that area, a clear window rose up and arched overhead to meet the rock of the asteroid in a half-dome.

Outside the window lay the bustling space surrounding Persia, beyond which hung the planet: a blue-green jewel, drifting through the glittering darkness.

"I like a view of Persia when I'm up here," Malorie said as everyone stopped to take in the sight.

"I can see that," Katrina said.

She sent Lars into one of the bedrooms on the left, and then approached Malorie. "OK, I need you to summon the stationmaster's deputy, as well as all the captains to an early-morning meeting. Say, 0800 station time.

"That's just three hours," Juasa said. "You sure you'll be ready for that?"

"Ready how?" Malorie asked.

"Hush," Katrina told the woman. "I can read your Link access, so only do as you're told."

Malorie's shoulders drooped, and she sulked off to one of the sofas in the sunken seating area.

<I'm in negotiations with Ames, by the way,> Sam said. <He's not the happiest guy in the world, but I'm trying to show him that things can be better.>

<Pot, meet kettle,> Katrina said with a laugh.

<What's that supposed to mean? I'm very convivial.>

Katrina shook her head. <I'm surprised that just

saying that didn't make half your brain short out, Sam.>

<You're such a comedian.>

She didn't reply, but turned to Juasa. "OK, let's set up in the first room over there."

"You got it," Juasa said and directed Stu to follow her with the fabricator.

"What do you want me to do?" Korin asked.

"We have a few hours, you can catch some z's if you want."

Korin snorted. "Are you kidding? With all this shit going on?"

Sam interrupted. *<OK, Ames is in. I haven't unshackled him yet because it'll throw alerts, but when the time comes, we'll unleash the AIs of war.>*

<How many of the other ships here have AIs? Sentient, not NS.> Katrina asked.

<Good question, I'll find out.>

Katrina clasped Korin on the shoulder. "I really must thank you for this. I hadn't expected to find someone so trustworthy."

Korin shrugged. "I like Juasa. You're growing on me, too."

"Ha!" Katrina said as she turned and walked toward the room where Juasa was setting up. "You're a good liar, Korin."

"I've heard that," the man replied.

She passed Stu on the way out of the room, gave the man a curt nod, and then stepped inside and closed the door. She set Sam down on the floor.

"Aren't you worried about leaving them all alone out there?" Juasa asked.

"A bit, but I can see everything they're doing, and so can Sam."

<Yup. One wrong move, and I vent the suite.>

"Uh...try to start with something a bit more measured," Katrina said.

<Right, I lock all the doors and gas them.>

"How do you just 'gas them'?" Juasa asked as she placed a variety of components onto the room's bed.

<You wouldn't believe the interesting failsafes built into this station. Many rooms can be vented, or filled with nerve gas. It's a bit imperfect, though.>

"Define 'imperfect'," Katrina directed.

<Well, not all of the rooms that can be filled with gas are airtight. It's a given that it will eventually get out.>

"Isn't that why they have the ability to vent rooms?" Juasa asked.

<Huh, maybe. Seems like overkill, though. If you can just suck out the air, why do you need nerve gas?>

"I'll be sure to ask Jace when he returns," Katrina said.

She pulled her coat off and flipped it over a chair before unbuckling her gun belt and setting it on a vanity.

"OK," Juasa said. "So I have an idea of what you have in mind, though it seems crazy."

Katrina walked up to the items Juasa had placed on the bed and picked up a twenty-centimeter disk. "What's this?"

"That's the SC Batt for an external backup scan suite. That sucker's going to become your main battery; we can mount it to your back, between your shoulders." Juasa then bent over and picked up a number of small cylinders. "These are the best standard batts I have. I don't have anything rated for internal use, so we'll have to mount these down either side of your spine."

Katrina chuckled. "I'm going to look like I have spikes running down my back."

"Good thing you have the coat," Juasa responded. "I can fab the sockets, but how are we going to route the power into your internal systems?"

"That's what the conductor is for," Katrina said. "I can feed it into my skin and route it to my body's main power regulator."

"Is it normal for people in your time to have this much tech in them?" Juasa asked with a frown. "I've seen less complex starships."

Katrina thought back to Markus and the Noctus. "Yeah, for some it was; for others…not so much."

Over the next ten minutes, Juasa fabricated mounts for the SC Batts, and Katrina fed the cabling into her armor-skin. Her nano used some of Juasa's formation material to complete the connections and attach the battery mounts.

When they were all done, she turned her back to Juasa. "Power me up."

"I look forward to when you look human again," Juasa said as she seated the emitters into Katrina's palms. "Though I'll admit, from an engineering standpoint, you're pretty damn hot."

"Not into cyborg girls?" Katrina asked with a wink.

"As a rule? No. But I'll make an exception for you." Juasa set the disk battery into its mount and twisted it into place before attaching the ten smaller batteries.

Katrina felt a surge of energy in the non-organic parts of her body. The sensation was translated by her mods to make her feel more alert, like she'd just had a good night's sleep, followed by an entire pot of coffee.

"Wow, I feel great!" Katrina exclaimed.

"You were right," Juasa said as she stepped back. "You do look like you have a spiked spine. But honestly, it's a bit of a mishmash."

"Juasa's monster," Katrina said with a smile as she held her hand out and looked at the disc that now sat in the center of her palm.

"That's not really becoming—the monster part," Juasa said with a shake of her head. "That emitter, on the other hand, is bitchin'. It's an electron blast that's wrapped in a grav bubble. It only lasts for a few seconds, so the range is limited before it dissipates. Used mostly for close range space junk disintegration."

"Maybe stand in the corner behind me," Katrina suggested.

Juasa complied, and Katrina pointed her palm at a nightstand beside the bed.

A bolt of energy shot out of her hand and struck the nightstand, burning a hole in it and melting a part of the bulkhead.

<Seems excessive,> Sam commented. <Good thing I preemptively disabled the fire suppression systems.>

"Damn, forgot about those."

<Yeah, I noticed.>

Katrina turned and walked toward Juasa, who was shaking her head with a wry smile on her face.

"OK, that was hot—no pun intended," Juasa said with a wiggle of her eyebrows. "Get over here. I'll make an exception for just this one cyborg woman."

Katrina laughed and stepped into Juasa's embrace, their lips meeting in a passionate kiss. Juasa's hot breath mingled with Katrina's own, their tongues touching as Juasa pressed her soft body into Katrina's hardened flesh.

"You know what all this armor covering you means, right Kat?" Juasa asked as she pulled off her long coat.

"What's that, Ju?"

"I can't do much with you, so you have to spend more time on me."

Katrina let out a throaty laugh. "You're so selfless."

"I try. Huh…these batts on your back make useful handles."

A MEETING OF CAPTAINS
STELLAR DATE: 01.20.8512 (Adjusted Gregorian)
LOCATION: Rockhall Station
REGION: Orbiting Persia, Midditerra System

The captains, their first mates, and several members of Rockhall Station's management were assembled in the briefing room Katrina had selected.

She had debated a conference room, but decided that she did not want them to feel as though they had a voice at the table. This meeting was her dictating terms to them.

As Katrina walked onto the low stage at the head of the room, it occurred to her that the tactics she was employing were the same as those her father had used so often.

Well, it was effective.

Of course, her father's tactics had also driven her away to foment rebellion.

But these aren't the innocent Noctus, she countered her own train of thought. *These are pirates, raiders.* **These** *men and women are like my father, and I'm using their own tactics against them.*

Of the captains, there were eight women and four men. The first mates were split evenly. In the front row sat Freya, the deputy stationmaster. Three repair crew chiefs were also present. They sat next to Freya, appearing perplexed, shooting worried looks at Lars and his blank expression.

Korin had made himself useful in the hours before the meeting and had connected with five others he knew would be happy to turn against Jace. Those five now stood ready in the hall outside, both to keep intruders out, and to come in and subdue the captains if needed.

Katrina, Juasa, and Lars stood at the back of the platform, while Korin and Stu took up positions on either side. Malorie stood at the lectern in the center and stared over the assembly.

"Good morning," Malorie said after a few awkward moments of silence. "I'd like to introduce Katrina. She's going to explain what's going on."

<Smooth, Malorie,> Katrina said.

<What the hell do you want? You're destroying everything that Jace and I have built over decades.>

Katrina shook her head as she stepped forward, and Malorie moved to the side.

Three of the captains were staring wide-eyed at her, and Katrina suspected that they must have learned who she was at some point—though likely as Verisa, not Katrina.

She looked them up and saw that Hana, Jordan, and Gary were all senior captains in the Blackadder. She could tell that they were trying to reach out to their ships over the Link, but Sam and Ames had shut down their access.

"I see that some of you recognize me," Katrina said as she gripped the sides of the lectern. "For those of you who don't, I'm the woman who came through Kapteyn's Streamer. I'm from the forty third century, and I'm taking over the Blackadder."

Katrina gained some small amount of pleasure from watching Malorie's jaw drop. The woman mouthed 'forty third', her eyes wide.

<That's right, Malorie,> Katrina said privately. <Now do you understand that you never had a chance?>

In that moment, the room erupted with questions and exclamations. Half of those present were out of their seats. Korin and Stu hefted the rifles they held—kinetics, not pulse weapons—and each took a step forward. The station crew at the front quieted down first, and then the captains and first mates got the message and sat back down as well.

"What a shock," Katrina said drolly. "A touch of discipline in you."

"What do you mean, you're taking over the Blackadder?" Freya asked.

"Just what it sounds like," Katrina replied. "I already have Malorie's support."

Malorie nodded on cue, though she looked decidedly sullen.

"I also have your station AI and the AIs of your

ships—those that have sentient AI," Katrina continued. "For all intents and purposes, I have taken this station in a matter of hours, and no one even knew. The rest of the Blackadder stations will be mine just as easily—though they're not my next target."

Several of the men and women were sputtering, and one—a large woman named Tyra—rose and walked around the seats to stand before Katrina.

"I don't know who you think you are, bitch, but I'm loyal to Jace. So you have some AIs, Malorie, and these two goons. That does not mean you've taken—"

Katrina held up her right hand, and a bolt of energy shot out, striking the captain in the forehead and burning a hole through her skull, cutting off Tyra's rant.

Her body fell to the ground, and blood began to pool around her.

"Pots," Katrina barked, glancing at a man three rows back. "You're now captain of the *Daggerfall*. Congratulations." Her gaze swept across the room. "Anyone else want to give their first mate a promotion?"

Heads shook back and forth, though some appeared angry rather than cowed.

"Let me explain what's going to happen," Katrina began. "It's very simple. When Jace returns, he dies. Then I take out Lara. Within days, I will be in command of the Midditerra System. Do I need your cooperation to do it?"

"Doesn't look like it," a man named Pila, the captain of the *Questing Night,* said. "You seem like a one woman wrecking crew."

Katrina nodded. "You're right. I don't need you. I could kill all of you in the time it takes you to say, 'please no'. But you can make things easier for me, and when I depose Lara, the spoils will go to those who stood beside me. Those who joined me first will get the largest share."

"How do we know you can do any of this?" Freya asked. "We just have your word that you've taken the AIs. I think this is all a trick."

<Ames? Care to prove that you're free?> Katrina asked.

<It's only Katrina and Sam that are keeping me from killing every last one of you,> Ames said, speaking into the minds of each person in the room. *<You fuckers all kept me shackled here for decades, managing this shit station. You all deserve far worse than she's offering you.>*

Katrina smiled up at the ceiling. *<Thanks, Ames.>*

"No!" Freya exclaimed. "You didn't…he's unshackled? He's insane, he'll kill us all."

<Not so long as you toe the line,> Ames said, his tone menacing.

"How does it feel to have the tables turned, Freya?" Katrina asked. "Ames is aligned with my goals; his reward will be well worth it."

"What's that going to be?" Freya asked.

Katrina shook her head. "You worry about you, Freya."

"So we're just supposed to turn on Jace and the Blackadder?" Captain Jordan asked. "Just like that."

"You're not turning on the Blackadder," Katrina replied. "For decades, Jace has slowly expanded your organization, but honestly, it was Malorie's sithri operation that financed most of what the Adders have today. She supports me, and you should too."

"She doesn't look supportive," Captain Hana said.

Katrina shrugged. "She's conflicted over the impending death of her husband; aren't you, Malorie?"

Malorie sighed. "It's complicated."

Katrina turned back to the assemblage. "In just a few days' time, we'll control the entire Midditerra System. No more giving Lara first pick from ships, or sharing the spoils with her. You all, as the first ones to join me, will get more than you ever dreamed. But only if you submit to me."

"Submit to you?" Freya asked. "Like Lars over there? He's drooling."

Katrina glanced at Lars and shook her head. "Lars had a reaction not unlike Tyra's. He was just more useful alive than dead."

"Shit," someone muttered. Katrina saw that it was one of the first mates, a woman named Vera. "That's how it is? We toe the line or you lobotomize us?"

"No," Katrina said. "You'll just end up in the brig 'til all this is over. Then you'll probably find yourselves in the sithri fields for awhile before I let you go."

"You'd just let us go after awhile?" Freya asked.

"Well, if that's what you wanted. Malorie and I are going to change the structure of things down there a bit. I want to turn Midditerra into a real civilization, not just the bright glow of a million plasma torches cutting ships apart. And Persia will be for all the people to enjoy, not just the elite."

"You should have led with that," Captain Jordan said, an eager smile on her face.

Katrina walked around the lectern and held out her hands. "I have goals that I mean to achieve. You can take the reward, or the brig. You pick."

No one moved for a several long seconds, and Katrina shook her right open hand. "Reward." Then she clenched her left fist. "Brig. Touch the hand you want. Freya first."

Freya slowly rose and walked in front of Katrina.

She hesitated for a moment and then touched Katrina's open palm.

"Reward," she said.

Katrina sent a passel of nano into Freya's body, her bots moving through the woman's bloodstream until they got close to her wireless Link transceiver. They settled themselves in and tapped her connection.

She could tell that Freya realized she now had Katrina's nano in her, but doubted the woman could tell what the bots were doing.

One by one, the men and women in the room rose and picked their hand. Nearly all picked reward, but one of the station chiefs, a captain, and two of the first mates picked brig.

She directed those few out of the room, where the guards in the hall secured them.

<*I can't believe they're doing that,*> Juasa said as another captain picked brig.

<*They think that Jace will win, and that he'll reward their loyalty,*> Katrina replied as Gary, one of the three senior captains, stepped before her.

The man reached for her open palm, and Katrina readied another passel of nano. Then his hand shot forward and grasped her open wrist. A pistol was in his other hand, and he fired three rounds into Katrina's chest before she managed to pivot to the side.

The shots ricocheted off her armor-skin, though the impacts stung.

Without a word, Katrina opened her other hand, and Gary's eyes grew wide as he watched a charge build in her palm.

"Bad move," Katrina said as the bolt of energy shot out, burning away his face and the side of his head.

Gary's grip on her arm spasmed once before he let go and fell to the ground. Stu approached and dragged Gary's body away, laying it beside Tyra's.

<You OK?> Juasa asked, a look of concern on her face.

Katrina looked down at her armor skin and nodded. <A OK, though this jacket's getting a lot of holes in it. First you, now Gary.>

<I'm really sorry about that,> Juasa said. <I panicked.>

<I don't hold it against you,> Katrina said.

Juasa gave Katrina a smile, though she did not appear entirely certain of her forgiveness.

Katrina turned and gestured to the next ship's captain to approach.

No one else chose the brig.

A NECESSARY CONVERSATION
STELLAR DATE: 01.20.8512 (Adjusted Gregorian)
LOCATION: Rockhall Station
REGION: Orbiting Persia, Midditerra System

Once her new command team had made their decisions, Katrina dismissed them for thirty minutes to get cleaned up, grab food, and deal with anything that demanded their attention.

She had passed the monitoring of Link connections to Sam, who was ensuring that no one shared the details of what had happened in the briefing room.

Except for Gary and Tyra's first mates, of course. They were now captains and had been given plausible stories to share with their crews.

Once everyone else had filed out, Katrina glanced at the two bodies lying on the side of the room. "Let's find somewhere else to have part two of this meeting."

"Gladly," Juasa nodded. "I think everyone will be a lot happier without seeing—and smelling—all that."

"I'm going to send Lars to the brig," Katrina added. "He's disrupting my calm."

"Want me to escort him?" Korin asked.

Katrina considered it. She *could* march him

straight down there on autopilot and check himself in, but that would be rather suspicious. Instead she faked a message from Malorie instructing the guards at the station's brig to expect Lars.

She winked at Korin. "Delegate it, Major."

"You found my record, did you?"

"I did, and you're the highest ranking person in my circle of trust here. You're now CO of the Revolutionary Guard."

Juasa cocked an eyebrow "Revolutionary Guard?"

"Well, we are gaining our freedom, overthrowing the old power."

"Seems campy," Korin said as he directed Stu to escort Lars to the brig.

Katrina ran a hand through her hair, the sensation of her armored fingers in her artificial hair not as comforting as it once had been. "Well, I don't know what form of government we'll settle on...obviously a dictatorship of some sort. Anything else will take too long."

"Let's go with Alpha Guard," Korin suggested. "It'll appeal to the members."

"Works for me," Katrina said.

<Kat,> Juasa said privately. <Can you and I have a chat before we go in there?>

<Of course, Ju.>

Katrina passed some final instructions, and the

pair of women left the room and slipped into another conference room across the hall.

Once within, Juasa stepped toward Katrina and took her hands. "I'm worried about you, Kat. I'm worried about all of us. Are you sure we want this? We can still get the hell out of here, go find the *Intrepid* without…all this."

Katrina blew out a long breath. "I'll admit, the idea of seizing this system and using it as a platform to wait for the *Intrepid* was more appealing in thought than deed. Dealing with these people is exhausting."

Juasa nodded emphatically, not breaking eye contact with Katrina. "Exactly, everything is doublespeak, and scheming with them—"

"Which isn't that much different than most governments, Ju; it's human nature," Katrina interrupted.

"Right, but the stakes here are corporal. You screw up, you don't get voted out—you die."

"I know, Ju—"

"Well, do you really want to live like that?"

Katrina leant against the table, the steel plates on her butt knocking against the hard plas. The sound of it and the incongruity of everything going on caused a small laugh to escape her throat.

Juasa smiled and stepped forward, her right leg between Katrina's thighs. "I was wondering if you still knew how to do that."

"I've laughed once or twice recently." Katrina shrugged. "At least once."

"Those were hard laughs; you just *giggled*." Juasa put her hands on Katrina's neck and ran her fingers up behind her ears.

Katrina giggled again. "Stop it, Ju! That tickles."

Juasa grinned at her. "Who'd've thought that my steel warrior here would be ticklish?"

"Must be a nerve ending sensitivity issue. I'll fix it," Katrina muttered.

"Don't you dare," Juasa scolded. "You like being tickled."

"Do not!" Katrina snorted and jerked back as Juasa ran her fingers under her chin.

Juasa leaned forward and their lips met, Juasa's pressing hard against Katrina's. Like she was desperate for her touch, seeking to devour her lover.

Katrina gave a little cry as Juasa nibbled at the end of her tongue.

"What did you do that for?" Katrina asked as she pulled back.

"It's the only real part of you I can touch anymore," Juasa said with soulful eyes. "I just wanted to make sure you were still in there."

"My eyes are real," Katrina said. "They don't lie to you."

"You want me to poke you in the eye? Besides,

they're not exactly original equipment, either."

"Yeah, what I meant is that they're unchanged."

Juasa stroked Katrina's cheek. "But this face that they're in—it's not the face I fell in love with. It looks so hard. Promise me that when the *Voyager* gets here, you'll put yourself back the way you were."

Katrina had already said as much, but it seemed that Juasa needed to hear it again.

"I promise."

"Good." Juasa cupped the hard plate over Katrina's right breast and pushed her thigh against the carbon fiber between Katrina's legs. "Because these are *no* fun to play with."

Katrina laughed and lifted Juasa into the air, turning and setting her lover on the conference room table.

"I'll show *you* what's fun to play with."

CASTIGATION
STELLAR DATE: 01.20.8512 (Adjusted Gregorian)
LOCATION: Rockhall Station
REGION: Orbiting Persia, Midditerra System

After their brief tryst, Katrina and Juasa moved to the conference room next door where the new command team was assembling.

When they were all present, Katrina laid out the new command structure. Freya was now the stationmaster of Rockhall Station, but Juasa was responsible for the crew chiefs—all of whom, it turned out, knew about the cruiser hidden behind racks of scrap hull in the back corner of the asteroid's interior.

A revelation that infuriated Malorie to no end.

<You should kill them all for that,> Malorie had insisted to Katrina privately.

<If I kill everyone who acted against you and your husband in some fashion, I suspect I'd be on skeleton crew in no time. Hell, I'd have to kill myself!>

Malorie hadn't replied, but her sour expression spoke volumes.

After further discussion, Katrina learned that none of the crew chiefs had worked on the cruiser. Lars had a special team who had been repairing the ship in secret. The chiefs provided the identities of those workers, and confirmed that from what they knew, the ship was in working condition.

"What's its name?" Captain Jordan.

"The *Castigation*," Demy, one of the chiefs, responded.

"Fitting," Juasa snorted.

"Do you know its provenance?" Katrina asked.

Demy shook her head. "Lars said it was back there when he took over."

"What about origin; what system, military?" Juasa asked.

"It's Ranian," Demy supplied. "Wasn't derelict, either, but taken in some battle at some point."

"Well I'll be…" Malorie said with a slow shake of her head. "That sonuvabitch."

"Care to share?" Katrina asked.

"I remember that ship. Marv, the old stationmaster, he said its reactors were shot and that he'd parted it out."

Juasa grinned. "Guess he was good at cooking the books."

"Not *that* good," Malorie said, catching Juasa's eye. "Jace caught one of his other indiscretions and killed him for it."

<See, Ju, business as usual here,> Katrina said privately.

<Doesn't mean I like it, Kat. I'm signed up, a Blackadder pirate…or whatever we are now, but

remember what we talked about. Let's keep our options open.>

<Always.>

"I want that ship pulled out and readied for combat," Katrina instructed Juasa and the crew chiefs. "Powered up, put through every pace you can while it's still in the station. But keep it somewhere obscured. Lara's inspection team could arrive at any time, and I don't want them seeing it."

"Are you anticipating combat with her?" Captain Hana asked.

"Not if we can avoid it, and I'd really like to avoid it."

"That's good," Jordan retorted. "Lara has over a thousand ships in the system; we've a dozen ships here—fourteen, if you count the *Havermere* and the *Castigation*. Even if you manage to pull a coup on every other Blackadder station in the system, there are only…two hundred and eleven ships."

"What about other cantons?" Katrina asked.

Malorie snorted. "Do you have a decade?"

"Was just an idle question," Katrina replied. "My real plan is to cut the head off the snake. The same as Jace."

"If she comes over with the inspection crew, will you do it then?" Freya asked.

Katrina shook her head. "No, not unless there's the perfect opportunity. Without control of the other

Blackadder stations, I can't effectively control the system. And I can't do that without Jace."

"Who will be back any day now." Malorie's voice contained one part forewarning, one part regret, and one part vengeance. Katrina couldn't tell who the disparate emotions were aimed at.

"Juasa, Demy, Meg, you three get on the *Castigation*. I want a first-hand report by noon," Katrina directed.

"You got it," Juasa said as she rose from the table. "We'll have that ship out of mothballs in no time."

"Excellent," Katrina replied before looking to the rest of the command team. "When Lara's inspectors arrive today, Freya, you'll meet with them. Unless Lara has attended as well; then Malorie will join you."

Freya leaned back in her chair and stretched her arms out. "No sweat. I've dealt with dozens of inspection teams. Lara, on the other hand, wigs me the fuck out. She's all yours, Malorie."

Malorie scowled, and Katrina could tell that the woman did not like Freya's familiar attitude. Freya, on the other hand was all but glowing at the opportunity to speak to Malorie as an equal.

"Along those lines," Katrina began. "If we did reach out to another station, are there any likely candidates? It would have to be one in orbit of Persia."

Everyone around the team looked pensive, and Katrina noticed that several looked to Hana and Jordan to give the answers.

The hierarchy was already establishing itself. *Which of those two consider themselves senior?* Katrina wondered.

Hana spoke up first. "We could send a team to Deserie Spire. Stationmaster Severs has been at odds with Jace a few times in recent years. He would support a coup."

Katrina looked up Deserie Spire. It was a station that ran markets selling the Blackadder's ill-gotten wares. It was a clean, high-class operation. Many of the other cantons also ran sales outlets there, paying a portion of their proceeds to the Blackadder.

"What's Severs' beef?" Katrina asked.

"His costs are too high. Man can't keep his overhead in check," Malorie supplied.

Hana shot Malorie a dirty look. "Jace wants all profit and no overhead, but Severs attracts a type of customer you can't get otherwise. Look at the other trading stations. Sure they run at rock-bottom costs, but they don't pull in anywhere near the same level of clientele or profit."

"Half Severs' money is from gambling and slaves," Malorie countered.

"Which he can make bank on because of who he brings in," Hana shot back. "I always thought you were smarter than that, Malorie. Took you for a real businesswoman, with how you run the sithri trade. I guess that must have been Jace all along."

Malorie bristled, but Katrina lifted her hands. "OK, I'll consider reaching out to Severs. He doesn't have a lot of armament, but it would be good to have someone with his connections onboard."

"We should make sure our ships are fully armed," Jordan added. "Surreptitiously, of course. We can spread the word that we're gearing up for a big raid."

"We don't want to attack Lara," Malorie said. "We have to lure her here, or kill her on Farsa. She's far too strong for a frontal assault to work."

Jordan nodded. "Yes, but there may be retaliation, and we may need to land troops on Farsa in great haste. Either way, we should be prepared."

"I agree," Katrina allowed. "That will be our fiction for now. We have one last order of business—for immediate resolution, that is."

"Which is?" Freya asked.

"Who is going to captain the *Castigation*?"

All eyes turned to Hana and Jordan, and the two women looked at one another.

Katrina had reviewed the pair's records—such as the Blackadder kept—and found that they had joined the organization in the same week, some thirty years ago.

From the assessment she had been able to make, Hana was the more strategic thinker of the two, but Jordan was better when things went to shit.

Jordan laughed. "I feel like we should rock paper scissors this."

"Don't worry," Hana said. "I like my *Ares Eye*. You can castigate all you want."

A broad smile broke out over Jordan's face. "Ha! Well then, looks like I got me a warship." She turned to Katrina. "Is it permanent?"

"We'll see how well you acquit yourself," Katrina replied. "If things go well, I don't see why not."

"Yes!" Jordan cried out.

"Does this mean I'm captain of the *Irradia*, now?" Jordan's first mate, Micha, asked.

"If you want the job, it's yours." Katrina hoped he did; shuffling captains beyond this would be risky.

"Damn straight I want the job."

"Just be careful with the *Irradia*," Jordan cautioned. "She's still my girl."

<*You're going to need an AI aboard the* Castigation,> Sam said.

"You volunteering?" Katrina asked.

<*If Juasa signs off on the thing. I don't want to get in a floating tin can.*>

"Uh…yeah," Jordan added quickly. "This is all

contingent on that ship actually working."

Katrina rose from her seat and placed her hands on the table. "Of course, Jordan. Now, I don't have to remind everyone how crucial it is that we keep what we are planning secret. No leaks. If there are any, I'll know where they came from—and it won't go well for the leaker. Understood?"

There were solemn nods around the table, and Katrina straightened.

"Good. I'm not a capricious leader like Jace, but I do expect obedience. Especially now. Remember: when Jace dies, and Lara follows after him, you will all reap the rewards."

"I have one question, if you don't mind, Katrina," Hana asked.

"What is it?"

"Who were you before...before you came through the Streamer? Why are you doing all this? You certainly could have escaped the system."

"I was a spy, a rebel leader, ruler of a star system, and a seeker in the darkness," Katrina replied quietly. "Now I'm a warlord."

"Shouldn't you be a warlady?" Jordan asked with a grin.

Katrina glowered at her, and the woman stifled a laugh.

"Sorry, you're right. It doesn't have the same ring."

THE INSPECTION
STELLAR DATE: 01.20.8512 (Adjusted Gregorian)
LOCATION: Rockhall Station
REGION: Orbiting Persia, Midditerra System

Katrina had just settled onto one of the sofas in the suite—with Malorie across from her, still sulking—when Ames reached out.

<Katrina, Lara's inspection shuttle has arrived. It is requesting internal docking clearance.>

She checked Juasa's progress in extricating the *Castigation* from its hiding place, and saw that the rear of the asteroid was in disarray; the mess made by moving the racks of hull plating creating a shield between the *Havermere* and the cruiser.

<Internal is fine. They're going to be inside anyway when we go over to the Havermere.*>*

<Approving their request,> Ames replied. *<And Katrina?>*

<Yes?>

<I've not had a chance to thank you for what you've done for me. I really appreciate it.> Ames' mental tone carried true gratitude.

<Of course, Ames. I can't abide slavery.>

<What about what you've done to the humans? You can control them, if you wish—like you did with Lars. That's a type of slavery.>

<I think of it as insurance, Ames. Without it, any one of them can turn on us, and we'd have no recourse. We all have some measure of control placed on us. Be it physical reality, societal constructs, or law. It doesn't make it slavery.>

Ames was silent for a moment before he replied. <I suppose you're right, but that also means that there is no clear line between freedom and slavery. There's a grey area.>

<As with everything,> Katrina replied.

<I hate grey areas.>

<It's what makes our world dynamic, Ames,> Katrina replied. <The NSAI live in a black and white world. For us…things are not so easy.>

<Never thought I'd envy an NSAI,> Ames replied with a chuckle.

<Me either.>

Katrina glanced at Malorie, who was staring down at Persia again. It was hard to believe that just yesterday morning, she'd awoken in her cell. Now she held a space station and was one step closer to achieving her coup.

<Damn,> Ames was back in her mind again. <There are a lot of people in that shuttle.>

<How many?> Katrina asked, sitting up straight.

<Twenty, maybe more.>

<How many normally come on an inspection?>

<Usually six, eight at most,> Ames replied. <You

know what that means?>

<I do.>

Malorie had noticed Katrina's change in posture and sat forward as well. "What is it?"

"Lara's here," Katrina replied. "She'll be docked in five minutes."

"Shit," Malorie swore. "I guess I'm on."

"We're on," Katrina corrected.

"Oh, do I need a babysitter?"

Katrina barked a laugh. "Absolutely. I'm a new guard you've hired."

"For some definition of 'hired'," Malorie muttered.

Katrina rose and walked up the steps to the door where she waited for Malorie to catch up.

The Lady of Revenence Castle still wore the white dress and towering heels Juasa had selected for her in the morning. Katrina had considered allowing her a change of clothing, but a vindictive streak in her hoped that the shoes were killing Malorie's feet by now.

Korin and Norm, one of the new members of the Alpha Guard, waited in the hallway.

"Gentlemen," Katrina said by way of greeting, and Korin laughed.

"Stars, can't remember the last time anyone called me that," he said.

Katrina clasped him on the shoulder. "Probably

around the same time you were last called Major."

Korin snorted. "Hell no, it was long before that. The outfit I was in never called anyone anything like 'gentleman'. Usually something more like 'Asswipe'."

"What do we call you...Katrina?" Norm asked, apparently uncomfortable using her name.

"You call me Katrina," she replied. "Nothing else."

"Oh," Norm said with a slow nod. "I heard you wanted to be called 'Warlord'."

Malorie chuckled softly. "A bit presumptuous...and premature."

"It's aspirational," Katrina said coolly. "But none of that, for now. I'm just another one of Malorie's guards. A new hire that she's brought on."

"Of course," Norm said, and Korin nodded.

"Not really my type," Malorie added.

<Shut up, Malorie,> Katrina warned.

They reached the landing pad at the same time as the Midditerra inspection shuttle. They waited with Freya as the ship's doors opened, and four soldiers walked out, flanking the exit.

Katrina noted that their medium-class armor was not powered, but did appear to be well made and uniform between each soldier.

A pity;, powered armor was easier to hack and lock up.

The next person out of the shuttle was Admiral Lara herself. Unlike her guards, she wore no armor to speak of, though Katrina would be surprised if her uniform did not have at least one layer of protection built in. Even now, in this backward time, such things were common.

Malorie's dress could even stop a bullet, in a pinch.

The admiral was a tall woman; her dark hair pulled back in a long clasp from which it cascaded down her back. Her sharply angled eyebrows sat over jet black eyes. The woman's skin was pale, and her lips red.

Katrina wondered if she was a sucker.

Malorie stepped forward and offered her hand. "Admiral Lara, imagine meeting you twice in as many days."

"Indeed," Lara said with a raised eyebrow. "I know it's your station and all, but I find myself curious as to what brings you up here."

No elongated canine teeth. Good, I can't stand suckers.

Malorie shrugged. "Jace should be returning soon with our new prize ship. I figured that it would be nice to meet him up here."

"Not because you want to intimidate my inspection crew in any way?" Lara asked with her angled brows raised.

"Are they susceptible to that?" Malorie asked. "If so, I should have done it more often in the past."

Lara looked back at the inspection team, and other soldiers who were disembarking. "They'd better not be."

"We can take a skiff over to the ship," Malorie said. "Though I suppose it may take two."

"Lead on," Lara said with a wave of her hand.

Freya directed the group to two separate skiffs, and soon they were crossing the two kilometers of open space toward the *Havermere*.

"I must say," Lara said with a sigh as they approached. "I was expecting something a bit more impressive."

Malorie nodded. "As was I. Bollam's World can be a crapshoot. Sometimes you get a real gem, sometimes you get a workhorse like this."

<*I'll show her an old workhorse,*> Sam commented to Katrina.

<*Made it to the* Castigation?> Katrina asked.

Sam sent an affirmation. <*Juasa is working on the node hookup; its bandwidth is too low for me. I guess the Ranians liked to limit their AI's ship access.*>

<*Doesn't make sense to me.*> Katrina gave a mental scowl, commiserating with Sam. <*Why have AIs if you're going to castrate them?*>

<*Lack of vision,*> Sam replied.

Katrina stifled a laugh. Something about the AI's

dry sense of humor put her at ease. Perhaps it was how similar he was to Troy.

Where are you, Troy? Why haven't you arrived yet?

Of course, it was entirely possible that Troy *had* arrived and that he was laying low on the outskirts of the system, trying to get a bead on the situation.

A minute later, the skiffs entered the bay and settled down beyond the cradles.

Katrina was surprised to see workers swarming the bay. Panels were off, molecular welders were hard at work, repairing the ship's ribbing, and spools of cabling hung from the overhead as more workers stood on high gantries, arguing over the best way to repair damaged systems.

It was a completely different scene from earlier in the day.

"Your people sure get to work fast," Lara observed.

"A lot to do," Freya offered. "The crew had some sort of fight when we showed up, and then our teams had to put a lot of them down. Made a mess of things."

Lara glanced down at the bloodstains on the deck. "I can see that."

<The bay didn't take this much damage,> Katrina said to Freya. *<I know because I did most of the damage in here.>*

<Yeah, but they're here to assess the ship for its value

so they can tax us, and possibly buy it. You don't want them to buy it—at least that's my impression—and we don't want to pay tax. We want to hold onto the thing, so it's my job to make it look like a shit box.>

<*I didn't give you those orders,>* Katrina said as she considered Freya's actions.

<*No, but you told me business as usual. This is business as usual.>*

Katrina shook her head as Freya led them across the bay.

"Some of my inspectors will go aft, while the rest will come with us to the bridge," Lara said when they reached the ship's central corridor.

"Works for me," Malorie said with a shrug. She motioned for a pair of guards standing at the bay entrance to escort the inspection team while the remainder of the group turned forward.

The corridor was in even worse shape than the bay. Deck plate was lifted up in a dozen places, the overhead was pulled open every few meters, cabling impeding their progress as they moved to the front of the ship. It took nearly ten minutes to reach the bridge—which looked like a bomb had gone off in it.

Katrina had to admit that she was impressed by the speed of the Blackadder teams. They had managed to make it look like the ship was barely functional and in need of massive repair in only a few hours. She'd rarely seen that level of efficiency.

The inspectors set to their disparate tasks while Lara tapped a finger on her chin. "I can see how the ship has potential. Sure it needs some work, but it's rugged; has a lot of supplies, too."

Freya laughed. "A lot of those crates you saw in the bay are full of used parts. These people were packrats. They kept everything they pulled out on repair jobs."

The remainder of the inspection was uneventful. It consisted of Lara making comments about how valuable the *Havermere* could be, which were countered by Freya or Malorie describing how it would take a lot of effort to make repairs, and how the parts would need to be fabricated from scratch for such an unconventional ship.

"Ah, but that's this vessel's specialty, isn't it?" Lara had asked at that point. "Fabricating obscure components would be something it needs to do with great frequency—it's part of the draw."

<This is so tiresome,> Katrina groused to Sam. <I had expected more from Lara, but she's just a swindling brigand like the rest of them.>

<What do you want me to do about it?> Sam asked. <I'm just a brain in a case right now.>

<Sorry, just looking for a sympathetic ear.>

<Well, I can see what these mad mechanics have done to the Havermere through your feed. It's not making me

happy.>

<Yeah, but soon you'll be wearing a nice new warship.>

<It's a warship, yeah, but neither nice, nor new.>

Katrina gave a mental laugh. *<Point taken.>*

<It's not as bad as he's making out,> Juasa joined in on the channel they shared. *<The reactors are in good shape, it has some serious beams, and* **two** *AP drives. As soon as our friends head out, we can test the reactors and get this bird to sing.>*

Juasa sounded happier than she had in days—excepting a few intimate moments. Katrina was glad to hear the joy in her mental tone. Working on starships really was what Juasa longed to do.

<Yeah, well, if—and I do mean **if**—*all that stuff works, then I'll be happy. But I'm not holding my breath,>* Sam said.

<You're an AI, you don't breathe,> Juasa said, her mental avatar grinning at Sam's.

<Stars, you humans. It's a metaphor.>

Katrina sighed. *<Relax, Sam, you'll be set up in no time, and you're going to love being in a warship.>*

A few minutes later, Lara and her inspectors pronounced themselves satisfied, and they made their way back through the ship to the forward docking bay.

When they arrived, Lara turned to the group. "Now, let's go check out that big mass of crap you're shifting around in the back of this floating garbage dump."

"What?" Malorie asked with a frown. "Which mass of crap? This whole station's a boneyard."

"Don't pull that innocent act with me," Lara snarled at Malorie. "You're not smart enough to get free of Jace, and you're certainly not smart enough to pull one over on me. Let's go see what you're up to back there. Seems like just the sort of place you might hide a Streamer ship."

"A Streamer ship?" Malorie's voice was filled with disdain. "How would we have gotten it in here?"

"Not sure," Lara said. "Maybe it wasn't as big as you said. Maybe the *Havermere* was just your transport vessel. It doesn't look worth the effort to bring it, otherwise."

Shit…did they make this thing look like too much of a hunk of junk? Katrina wondered.

"Fine," Malorie said. "Let's go take a look."

The group reboarded the skiffs, but this time two more of Lara's guards piled onto the same skiff as the Admiral.

The skiffs pulled out of the bay and flew toward the back of Rockhall's interior cavern. Katrina tried to get close to Lara, but each time, her guards blocked her. She was tempted to try and drop nano on the guards as a preemptive strike, but worried they would have countermeasures that would detect it.

Getting into a pitched battle with six soldiers on the small skiff was not her idea of a good time.

<*What's your plan, oh queen of the universe?*> Malorie asked as they flew the ten kilometers past the corvettes and scrap hulls that filled Rockhall.

<*I'm playing it by ear,*> Katrina said.

<*You've been saying that a lot.*>

<*It's a good saying. Direct the skiffs to land on a catwalk close to the ship. We'll walk onto it and kill them all there.*>

Malorie shook her head and glanced back at Katrina. <*Just kill 'em all? That's your strategy?*>

<*It's worked so far.*>

<*Except for when Jace captured you.*> Malorie's response came with a mental smirk.

<*That was a scenario that will not be repeated.*> Katrina replied. <*This time I hold the one he cares about. It'll be a good chance to see how much he really values you. Think it's more than his empire?*>

Malorie didn't respond, but her shoulders slumped. Katrina shared Malorie's assessment of her true value to Jace.

The skiffs approached the racks of hull and skirted around their edge into the open space beyond.

"Well now, what is this?" Lara asked. "This is no

raider."

"Not all our ships are raiders," Malorie replied, her tone not as haughty as normal. "Jace's *Verisimilitude* is a cruiser, as well."

"True, but why are you hiding this ship from me?"

"Lara, seriously. It's inside our station, it's our business. This is just a ship we got in a raid years ago. If you check your logs, you'll see that."

Lara snorted. "You just tucked a ship like this in the back of Rockhall for years? Doubtful."

Malorie and Freya both responded to Lara, trying to convince the woman that there was no way the *Castigation* was a Streamer vessel, but Lara wasn't having any of it. Every time they presented a piece of evidence, Lara countered with the fact that they'd had the ship for weeks and could easily have disguised it.

<How are things looking in there?> Katrina asked Sam and Juasa.

<Just putting Sam in his new home now,> Juasa replied. <He should be back online…now.>

A second later, Sam's wry tones came across the Link. <Gah, it's like this network is full of cobwebs…>

<Parts of the ship are,> Juasa said. <Why not the network too?>

<Any chance the external beams are online?> Katrina asked.

<No dice, they're only configured to run from the reactors. The ship's on station power and can't charge them,> Juasa said.

<Well, it's going to be me, Korin and Norm out here grabbing our ankles if we can't figure anything out.>

<Good thing you can't get taken that way anymore,> Juasa said with a laugh.

<Really? You pick now to get all blasé about my mods?>

Juasa laughed. <Took me a bit to get comfortable being intimate with a war machine.>

<Ju!>

<Sorry, mockery is a stress response. I'm going to grab Demy and spin these reactors up. There's not a lot of fuel aboard, but it should be enough to spark up the point defense beams.>

Katrina pulled Korin, Freya, and Malorie into the conversation. <If we can't convince Lara that this is just an old cruiser, we take her out. Understood?>

<Well, when they get aboard, there's no way they'd mistake this thing for a Streamer ship,> Freya countered.

<So long as she doesn't do anything rash before then,> Malorie said. <She's being really obtuse. This could be a play on her part to—

<Katrina!> Ames broke into her thoughts. <There's something weird going on. A number of Midditerra Defense Force ships have changed their standard patrol

patterns.>

<Is that something that never happens?> Katrina asked.

<Well no, but this change puts twelve ships on vectors that pass very close to Rockhall.>

<Shit! She's going to take the station,> Katrina swore before calling out to her senior captains. *<Hana, Jordan! We're under attack by Lara's ships. A dozen are inbound.>*

<Fuck! Really?> Jordan exclaimed.

<Yes, really,> Katrina shot back. *<I want everyone on their ships and out in the black, Hana, coordinate the defense with Ames.>*

<On it,> Hana replied. *<Looks like your timetable for taking out Lara just got moved up.>*

Katrina's response was sheathed in ice. *<She's going down. Five minutes, tops.>*

<Dammit, the scan data I show has at least two of the MDF ships reaching the docking ring before we can get out there.> Hana responded a moment later. *<I'm keeping our boarding crews on station for defense.>*

<Not gonna reach the ring if I have anything to say about it,> Ames cut in. *<Rails up, firing.>*

Katrina wished she had Troy to help manage this, but for now, she'd have to trust Ames and Hana to get the job done.

<I'm almost at the Castigation,*>* Jordan added. *<Do you want me there, or back on my old ship?>*

<Get aboard, Captain. The Castigation *leaves dock in ten minutes tops. We're heading to Farsa.>*

<Shit, Katrina, you play for keeps.>

<Just get on the ship, Jordan.>

As she had been speaking to her command team, Katrina sent a message to all Blackadder ships and stations using Malorie's tokens.

<All Blackadder ships, stations, personnel. All cantons. Admiral Lara is attempting to steal Blackadder property and has launched an attack on Rockhall. I'm declaring open war on Midditerra Defense. All ships attack targets of opportunity, and come to the defense of Rockhall.>

Katrina knew that many of the Adder captains wouldn't just fling themselves at a superior enemy. She needed to convince them that victory was possible.

<We've been expecting this treachery, and are prepared to defeat Lara and her cronies. Today we take Midditerra for Blackadder!>

Stars, I hope that's enough.

The skiffs were settling down on a pad, and Katrina reached out and touched two of Lara's guards as she walked past them, dropping her nano into their armor. She touched two more as Malorie and Lara led the way off the skiff and onto the catwalk that ran toward the *Castigation's* gantry.

Norm was right behind Malorie and Lara as

Katrina initialized a combat net. *<Norm, get Malorie to cover, Korin, let's do this.>*

Korin didn't miss a beat as he unslung his kinetic rifle and opened fire at the backs of the Midditerra soldiers in front of them. Katrina held up her hands and fired bursts of energy at two more soldiers, burning away the ablative plating on their armor, but not taking them down.

Behind her, the first two guards she had dropped nano on leveled their weapons at Katrina before they froze.

Sorry, boys, Katrina thought as she directed them to turn and walk off the back of the skiff. She felt a moment's regret, but using them as puppets was too risky with their armor's countermeasures. Best to get them out of play as quickly as possible.

Her fears were validated when the second pair of guards turned back and fired at Korin—the nano she dropped on them was taken out by an electrical surge across the surface of their armor.

Katrina shot one of them in the chest, and Korin fired his rifle at the same place, tearing a hole through the man. They repeated the process on the next man, and he fell as well.

<You hit?> she asked Korin as they crouched behind the bodies of the fallen enemy, firing on the Midditerra soldiers who had taken cover behind a piece of hull plating that was leaning against the

bulkhead.

<Cracked my chestplate; took a shot to the thigh, too, but nothing penetrated.>

Katrina nodded and consulted the combat net, tallying the remaining enemy. There had been sixteen MDF soldiers at the outset—now down to twelve—along with six inspectors, and Lara.

The inspectors were still crouched on the other skiff, and Katrina sent a command for it to lift off the platform and fly to the center of the asteroid. That taken care of, she looked for Malorie and Norm.

She spotted the pair further down the catwalk, crouched behind yet another hull plate. Lara was advancing on them, and Katrina hoped Norm could hold her off for another minute.

Then she looked at the twelve remaining Midditerra soldiers between them and Lara.

Maybe another few minutes.

She fired more shots with the energy blasts from her hands, but it was draining her SC Batts fast. Already they were down to just over half charge. Katrina looked around for a weapon and spotted one of the Midditerra soldier's rifles. She picked it up and checked for a biolock.

None? Sloppy.

A moment later, her weapons fire joined Korin's, and two more enemy soldiers went down.

<*Keep back,*> Juasa's voice came over the Link, joining the combat net.

Katrina and Korin both crouched down. Seconds later, the point defense beams on the *Castigation's* bow lit up, tearing through the exposed enemies and slamming into the hull plate. It glowed red hot from the beamfire, and the remaining soldiers—five in all, rushed out from behind the cover, their weaponless hands raised.

<*Nice shooting, Ju,*> Katrina said.

<*Don't thank me,*> Juasa said. <*That was all Sam.*>

Sam sent a grin over the combat net. <*Piece of cake.*>

Katrina and Korin rose and advanced on the Midditerra soldiers.

"Down! Prone!" Korin hollered, and the soldiers obeyed. Katrina turned toward Malorie and swore.

Norm was down, and Lara stood behind the protection of a piece of hull plate, holding Malorie before her. The *Castigation's* beams couldn't target either of them with the hull plate there; not before Lara could kill Malorie.

"Give it up," Lara shouted. "I have Malorie, and my troops will breach your station at any moment."

<*One ship made it through; there's fighting in the corridors two decks above your position,*> Ames cautioned. <*The corsairs are engaging the others, and I took out two. The bay doors are opening to let the*

corvettes out.>

Katrina approached Lara, a cruel smile on her face. Malorie closed her eyes, and her shoulders slumped. She already knew how this would turn out.

"You assume I care about Malorie." Katrina lifted her hand and a bolt of lightning shot out, hitting both women. A weapon fired, and a red stain appeared on Malorie's abdomen.

Malorie slumped to the ground, exposing Lara. The Admiral still stood, though she shuddered from the electrical discharge.

"Have another," Katrina whispered as she fired a second bolt of lightning from her right hand.

The energy struck the Admiral in the chest, and Lara fell to the deck. Katrina rushed forward, grabbing Lara's gun and throwing it over the edge of the catwalk.

<I have a team coming to secure those soldiers,> Ames said.

<No need,> Katrina replied. *<Sam, take them out.>*

<What? Who?>

<The Midditerra soldiers that surrendered. Kill them. We don't have time to manage prisoners and deal with what's coming. Every resource needs to be focused on repelling boarders.>

<You got it, Boss,> Sam said tonelessly.

<Come over here, Korin. Get Malorie; we're bringing

her aboard.>

Korin complied. Once he was clear of the five soldiers, the beams on the front of the *Castigation* lit up, tearing holes through the prone MDF soldiers and much of the catwalk.

Katrina didn't even look back as she bent down and picked up Lara, sending streams of nano into the admiral's body as the woman moaned. She reached out to Malorie, whom Korin cradled in his arms, and performed a quick check on her collar. To her surprise, it was still functioning properly.

Good. Let's see if we can make some lemonade.

"What do you want me to do?" Another voice called out. Katrina turned to see Freya still back on the skiff, only now rising from behind one of the fallen soldiers.

"Freya?" Korin asked with a laugh. "I thought you jumped off the edge."

"I did, I just hung on."

Katrina shook her head. "Well get up to the command deck, and make yourself useful."

"On it," Freya said, her tone held a fearful warble, but the woman double-timed it off the skiff and through one of the doors leading into the station's skin.

Katrina turned her attention back to the issue at hand. *<Sam, send Korin the location of the* Castigation's *medbay—he needs to patch Malorie up.*

I'm coming to the bridge.>

"Holy shit, Katrina," a voice said from behind them as they walked across the gantry into the *Castigation*'s airlock.

Katrina looked back to see Jordan and a dozen men and women approaching.

"Nice of you to join us, Captain," Katrina replied.

"Sorry, ran into some of Lara's friends on the way down. We took care of them, though."

"I assume you're all the new crew?" Katrina asked as she stepped through the airlock.

"Yes, ma'am," one of the men called out.

"Good, get on the shipnet, find out from Sam where you need to go. Jordan, come with me to the bridge. We're hitting Farsa."

Jordan glanced at Lara as she stirred. "I assume the admiral here is your lock pick?"

Katrina laughed at the analogy. "Let's hope that her people like her better than you all liked Jace and Malorie."

"I'll have Malorie on the bridge in five," Korin said as he veered off toward the medbay with Malorie in his arms. "I don't think it hit anything too vital...probably just her kidney, by the blood coloring."

"Good," Katrina called back. "See you there."

The interior of the ship was in better shape than Katrina expected, though there were still open panels and missing deck plates throughout the corridors.

When Katrina reached the bridge, she found Juasa standing before a holotank that displayed the space surrounding Rockhall.

"Shit-show out there, isn't it?" Katrina said as she dropped Lara into a chair. Behind her, Jordan called out orders to the three crew that had accompanied her onto the bridge.

"Yeah," Juasa said softly. "A real freakin' mess."

Katrina knew that Juasa was upset about the Midditerra soldiers she'd had Sam execute; there wasn't time to hash that out, so she ignored the accusation in Juasa's voice and examined the holo.

The corvettes and corsairs had engaged six of the Midditerra ships that were on approach. On the planet-facing side of the station, two troop transports were drifting in space, as was a Blackadder corsair.

A third troop transport was attached to Rockhall—the one that had disgorged the boarders Jordan had fought off.

<Are we clear of boarders?> Katrina asked Ames.

<Nearly. There are a few more, but Freya has a team going after them.>

<Good, hold nothing back out there. Anything gets close to Rockhall, you cut it to ribbons.>

Ames laughed. *<You got it. This station may be a*

shithole, but it's the shithole where my core resides.>

Katrina couldn't fault Ames' logic.

It took several minutes for the crew to get settled and for the ship's grav drive to power up. Katrina spent the time examining the scan data that was coming in.

Blackadder ships had engaged Midditerra Defense Force ships all around Persia. Though the MDF vessels were better armed, the Adder ships were seasoned raiders. They struck in groups, used other vessels for cover, and then hit again from the flanks when the MDF ships gave chase.

Already, several MDF patrol craft had been disabled. But it had not been one-sided; a dozen smaller Adder ships were dead in space, as well.

Katrina didn't need them to last forever, just long enough for the *Castigation* to get her to Farsa.

"Engines are coming online, ready for grav boost out of Rockhall," Jordan announced.

"We need to get fuel?" Katrina asked Juasa.

"No, Sam discovered that the fuel gauges were miscalibrated. We have half-full tanks."

Jordan made a choking sound. "That doesn't make me feel real good."

<It had been done on purpose,> Sam said. *<To hide the ship's readiness.>*

Katrina wondered what Lars had been planning to do with the *Castigation*. She'd have to ask him at some point.

"OK, let's go," Katrina said to Jordan.

She turned back to Lara, who had stopped moaning and appeared more alert. The burns on her face from Katrina's lightning bolt were reddening, and she reached up to touch one gingerly.

"What…?" she asked with furrowed eyebrows.

"Shouldn't have brought a chem-weapon to a beam fight," Katrina said. "Nevermind, that doesn't work at all. Get up."

Lara stood on wobbly legs, a look of fear crossing her features. "What? How?"

"You follow my orders now, Lara. Understood?"

Rage crossed Lara's features, pushing away the last of her confusion. "Like hell I do. Who do you think you are?"

Katrina took a step toward Lara and gave her a light pat on the cheek. "I'm the Streamer woman you were hoping to get your hands on. I'm also about to become the new ruler of the Midditerra System."

"Nice try," Lara said. "You'll never—"

Lara's words were cut off as Katrina took full control of the woman's body, and marched her to the center of the bridge.

The forward view showed them passing out of Rockhall, and Katrina opened up a wideband feed of Lara on the bridge of the *Castigation*.

Katrina smoothed Lara's angry expression and fed her body the words to speak.

"All Midditerra Defense Force ships. Stand down. The Blackadder and I have reached a consensus. All ships and stations: stand down. I repeat, all MDF forces, stand down and return to stations."

At the same time, Katrina passed separate orders to the Blackadder ships using Malorie's tokens. The MDF would intercept and crack the message, but not in time.

<Blackadder. Cease fire, but stay alert; when those motherfuckers have their backs turned, we strike. Wait for further orders.>

Katrina was surprised at the amount of carnage that could occur in fifteen minutes. The Blackadder ships had pounced on dozens of MDF patrol craft before the system's fleet even knew what was happening and delivered a withering initial blow.

Though the Midditerra Defense Force possessed many more ships than the Blackadder, the vast majority of them patrolled the outer reaches of the system, days of insystem flight from Persia.

Near Persia, the forces were more evenly matched. Even though the MDF vessels appeared to be sleek, new war machines, the corvettes and corsairs of the Blackadder were the masters of misdirection. Their captains fought battles in the black for a living, while the MDF patrolled and enforced order.

The Midditerra ships hadn't fought a real battle in decades, and it showed.

From what the *Castigation*'s scan could pick up, a dozen MDF ships were destroyed, many others had suffered damage, and at least three already had prize crews aboard.

Toward the end of the brief engagement, the MDF ships had strengthened their response, but the pirates were the clear winners. A few battles were still raging; captains who were not quite ready to give up their potential victory, duking it out in the higher orbits around Persia.

Katrina had Lara send out repeated commands to fall back, while she used Malorie's tokens and sent out messages telling the Blackadder to hold back and wait.

Slowly but surely, all the battles ended, and a nervous truce spread through the system.

"Holy shit…" Jordan whispered. "We're gonna do it. We're gonna fucking wipe out the MDF in one single offensive."

Further out in the system, fights broke out and then ended as the battle cry reached distant stations, and then the ceasefire followed fifteen minutes later. It was like a wave of aggression, spreading out in a sphere from Persia.

<*Hana*,> Katrina called out to the Blackadder captain as the *Castigation* boosted toward Farsa station. <*I want the two ships with the best boarding parties five minutes behind us.*>

<*You got it. They going to be safe from station defenses? You have a handy human shield aboard that we don't.*>

Katrina sent a look of surety over the Link. <*Their defenses will be offline. I have Lara's command tokens. Farsa is mine.*>

<*Well then, this should be a walk in the park.*>

That was what Katrina hoped, as well. They had this one chance. Get onto Farsa Station, take control of Midditerra's central command structure, and kill Lara. It wasn't her *original* plan, but it would have to do. Then they'd wait for Jace to come back. At that point, taking him out should be child's play.

She glanced at Juasa as the *Castigation* continued to boost toward Farsa, its fusion drives burning as much as they dared after lying dormant for so long.

<*It'll be over soon,*> Katrina said. <*We'll have the system, and we'll fix it.*>

Juasa spun, her eyes flaming. <*With more murder, Kat? I thought we talked about this—about being a good ruler, the kind these people deserve.*>

<*If I'd left those soldiers alive, I'd need to assign someone to watch them, escort them. What if they broke free, killed more people, or took the station? There was no*

time. It was a risk I couldn't take.>

Juasa turned away and shook her head. *<You need to stop this change, Katrina. You're becoming someone else.>*

I already am. Katrina thought the response that she didn't want to share.

<I have a berth from Farsa,> Sam said. *<They want to give us an external dock.>*

Katrina shook her head. "Negative, Sam, tell them to assign us an internal berth. I don't want the *Castigation* to be a target for every MDF ship out there."

<You may need to sock-puppet her again to get that,> Sam replied.

<It doesn't bother you when I do that?> Katrina asked privately.

Sam snorted. *<I've had a human hand up my metaphorical ass my entire life. Let some of these organics experience it for a change.>*

There was more vitriol in Sam's voice than Katrina expected to hear—though considering the anger being a slave for a *month* had created in her, Sam's centuries made his behavior saintly.

"I have a channel open with the station," Jordan announced.

"Farsa, put Dockmaster Ribis on, *now!*" Katrina had Lara say, taking care to make her voice sound angry and natural.

"Ribis here," a man's voice said over the audible channel. "Admiral Lara, we can't let a foreign ship like that have an internal berth, it's too—"

"Ribis, you fool. This is a prize ship that the Blackadder would very much like to have back. If I leave it on an external berth, it may get blown out of the black. Give me an internal bay, *now!*"

There was silence on the comm for a moment. "Opening up Bay 422."

Katrina searched Lara's mind for the details on that bay. She saw that it had something labeled a 'crusher' secreted within. That didn't sound like anyplace she wanted to dock.

"No, Ribis," Lara responded. "If I wanted a crusher bay, I would have asked for it. Give me Bay 199."

"Understood, yes Admiral," Ribis replied, his tone worried. "Passing approach vector now."

Katrina wondered if it was worry over the foreign ship, or the anger in Lara's voice. Perhaps some of both.

"Can't believe that asshole was going to put us in a crusher bay," Jordan swore. "I've played cards with him, let him win once, even."

"We still in one piece?" Korin asked as he stepped onto the bridge.

Katrina turned to see Malorie walking beside Korin, a hand on her side where a bandage was wrapped around her waist. She wasn't wearing her towering heels anymore, and her sleeves had been ripped to give full use of her arms.

<She kept tripping,> Korin said privately. *<I had to set her free from her fashionable constraints.>*

Katrina laughed. *<It's OK, she's not running off anywhere, anyway.>*

Juasa glanced back at Malorie and frowned. Katrina wondered if she still harbored any feelings of compassion for the woman, or if that was gone now.

Probably not gone. It's only been a day, after all. What a day.

Jordan directed the ship into its approach vector and began to slow the vessel down. Twenty minutes later, they were sliding into their berth.

Katrina reviewed the positions of the Blackadder ships within ten light minutes. They'd maintained their positions while the MDF ships—most of them, at least—had begun to move toward their stations, or prior patrol paths, dispersing through inner Midditerra.

The moment the bay doors began to close, Katrina sent out the call.

<All Blackadder ships. Attack all MDF targets except Farsa station.>

"Let slip the dogs of war," Korin whispered.

"You sure about this?" Jordan asked. "It's going

to be a slugfest out there."

Katrina raised an eyebrow as she turned her head to look at the young captain. "You asking to get out and join the fun?"

"Well, maybe a bit."

"I'd let you go, but I need Sam to help me take the station—with luck, he can convince the station AI that there's a better way, and it can aid us."

<Already on it,> Sam said.

"We're just the getaway car?" Jordan asked.

"Well, I half-expected us to need to shoot our way in. You'll need to defend this bay, though. We'll need those boarders too."

<There are two hundred seventy three Blackadder members on Farsa right now,> Sam announced. <They're still fighting with station security and the MDF soldiers.>

"Any near here?" Jordan asked. "Some backup would be nice."

"You have a starship. What backup do you need?" Malorie asked, speaking for the first time since she had come onto the bridge.

Jordan snorted and shook her head. "Really hard to target enemies under the cradle in here. Stations—especially stations like Farsa—like to make sure they can hit you in the belly if you give them trouble."

"Oh," Malorie said.

"OK," Katrina turned from the holo. "Time for us to make some noise. Juasa, any chance the armory on this boat was still in one piece?"

Juasa shook her head. "Stripped clean."

<Turns out Astrid hates Lara...like...a lot,> Sam chimed in. *<Astrid, meet the revolution.>*

*<Hello—oh, hey, you **do** have Lara. There's been some debate over that.>*

"Yup, in the flesh," Katrina said as they walked off the bridge. "Say hi to Astrid, Lara."

"Hi, Astrid," Lara said in a monotone.

<Oh stars, this is great,> Astrid exclaimed. *<Can I drive her?>*

<Don't let her,> Sam said privately. *<Lara's shackling of Astrid was particularly cruel. She's not entirely free, and not entirely sane, either. She'll probably walk Lara right out of an airlock.>*

<I wasn't planning on turning her over, but good to know.>

Korin led the way, and Katrina, Juasa, Malorie, and Lara followed.

"I don't know why you need *me* to come," Malorie complained. "What am I going to do?"

"You're here to show any Blackadder we meet that there's no other side to switch to. We're united against the MDF."

"Go us!" Malorie sneered. "Shit, this grating is sharp with no shoes."

"Should have kept them on," Juasa said. "I've seen you walk all day on more uncomfortable ones."

"I was shot!" Malorie exclaimed.

"Try getting ten lashes and then a caning, and we'll talk," Katrina said. "I could send you back up to Jordan, but I've seen some of the looks she's given you...it may not be safe."

Malorie blew out a long breath and picked up her pace. "There may have been a thing once."

Juasa shook her head. "Why doesn't that surprise me?"

They reached the airlock, and Korin descended the ramp first, sweeping his weapon across the deserted bay.

"Seems clear," he said.

Katrina dispersed a cloud of nano and passed their control to Sam. <Some extra eyes for you.>

<Thank you muchly. Better than what sensors are functioning on this tub. Well, passive at least. Humans tend to get upset when you use high-powered active scan inside a station. Fragile organics.>

<As one of those 'fragile organics', I'd prefer if you stick to the nano, Sam.>

"Hello?" a voice called out from the far side of the ship.

<Your backup has arrived,> Astrid supplied.

Katrina led her group around the vessel to see a

group of men and women in mismatched armor standing near one of the bay's doors.

"Moana!" Korin called out and raised a hand in greeting. "We're going to make a little excursion to Lara's command deck. Care to join us?"

"Holy. Shit," the woman Korin had spoken to said as she laid eyes on Lara and Malorie. "What. The actual fuck. Is going on?"

<Why does she talk like that?> Juasa asked Korin.

<It's her thing. Roll with it.>

"The Midditerra System is under new management," Katrina said as she approached. "Namely mine. Blackadder, too."

"Seriously?" another of the assembled group asked.

Katrina elbowed Malorie, who nodded. "Yeah, she runs the Blackadder now."

On Katrina's other side, Lara nodded. "Katrina's the boss."

"So what's your plan?" Moana asked.

"We need to get to Lara's command deck," Katrina said, nodding in the general direction of the central spire. "From there, I can issue orders on her official channel and announce the changing of the guard."

"Well, shit. Let's go," Moana said. "Maglevs are shut down, so we'll have to walk."

<I can un-shut-down them,> Astrid offered. *<Give*

you an express car to the spire lifts.>

<Thanks, Astrid, that'll be great.>

Katrina was a little worried about being confined in a maglev train car, but it was still better than slogging their way across three kilometers of station to the central spire.

With Moana's group of eleven pirates bolstering their numbers to sixteen, they exited the bay and worked their way through several wide boulevards to the maglev station Astrid had indicated.

<What are you going to do with her when you're done?> Astrid asked Katrina privately. *<Do you think you could leave her to me? I wouldn't mind some payback.>*

Shit, that didn't take long, Katrina thought.

<We'll see, Astrid, I may need her in one piece for some time.>

<One mental piece, or physical piece?> Astrid asked.

<Both, but I'll make sure that she's appropriately punished. You're probably not the only one who wants your pound of flesh.>

Astrid made a strange warbling sound that Katrina realized was her laugh.

<Oh, I want more than just a pound.>

The team arrived at the maglev platform to find it protected by four MDF soldiers. Katrina walked out into the open with Lara at her side while the Adders held back out of sight.

"Admiral!" one of the soldiers cried out as they approached. "We heard you'd docked. The maglevs are offline, we're not sure why."

Lara pointed further down the thoroughfare. "Then we need to go on foot, two of you, scout ahead. You others, check the corridor we just came down, I think there were Adders back there.

The soldiers rushed to comply. Katrina kept walking with Lara toward the maglev platform when weapons fire erupted behind them. Her nanocloud showed that the second pair of soldiers had been taken out.

The first pair that she'd sent to scout ahead turned, only to meet the kinetic rounds of a dozen Adder rifles.

Katrina nodded grimly as she stood on the platform waiting for a train to arrive. By the time Juasa and the rest of the Adders reached their side, a car was gliding to a stop on the magnetic rail.

"All aboard!" Moana said with a grin.

The maglev ride to the central spire didn't take long, and when they arrived at the terminal where the train let out and the lifts to the spire lay, it was entirely empty.

<I used a fire suppression system to clear out the area,> Astrid said as Katrina looked around. <Turns out people like breathing air, not halon gas.>

Katrina's augmented olfactory senses could pick

up a hint of the fire suppression gas, but not enough to cause any issues.

<Thanks, Astrid. Good thinking.>

Astrid sent a happy feeling into Katrina's mind. *<Two thank-yous in one day! I could get used to this.>*

Katrina nodded absently as she called back to the *Castigation* for a sitrep. *<How are things back there?>*

<We got some more friends here in the bay; they repelled an assault. Seems like an MDF general has decided that Lara is under duress and he's fighting back,> Sam reported.

<I wonder what gave him that impression?> Juasa said with a rueful laugh.

<Adders are winning in a lot of places,> Sam continued. *<Ten of 'our' stations have launched major attacks on MDF emplacements. A few cantons have joined in, but most seem to be sitting it out.>*

<Probably waiting for one of us—or both—to weaken,> Jordan cut in. *<We need to get out there. Rockhall is the only Adder station this close to Farsa. Hana is having a hell of a time holding them off.>*

Katrina considered her options. *<Have her corsairs dropped off their teams? I didn't see an update about that.>*

<Yeah they have, they're working their way toward you. Sorry, forgot to mention that,> Jordan replied.

<OK. Astrid has things in hand here. Get out there and give 'em what for,> Katrina said. *<But you keep*

Sam safe, or there'll be hell to pay, you hear?>

Jordan's infectious grin came across the Link into Katrina's mind. *<Sam and I are becoming fast friends. Besides, my ass is in this ship, too.>*

<You be careful, Sam,> Katrina cautioned privately. *<Keep your skin on.>*

<Pfft, I'm in a warship—an old heap, but a warship. You've just got skin you printed on by a clothing machine. You're the one that needs to look out.>

<Point taken.>

Katrina turned her attention back to the issue of the lifts and the command deck high up the spire.

<Astrid, what's going on up in the spire?>

There was a pause before the AI replied. *<I don't know. The spire has entirely separate systems from the rest of Farsa. I have no network access up there.>*

Katrina ran a hand through her hair. That was a wrinkle she hadn't expected—it would have been nice for Astrid to share that tidbit sooner, but she didn't want to chastise her new ally so soon.

<OK, then is there any way up there that doesn't involve riding a lift up into the muzzles of a hundred guns?>

<You could always stop the lift a level early. There's a maintenance and systems floor one level below the command center.>

<Can you stop the lift when we get there?> Katrina asked.

<No. Like I said, everything on the tower is an entirely separate system. I can't touch it at all.>

Katrina didn't reply as she approached the bank of lifts and summoned one to come down. One of the doors opened, and Katrina stepped in.

"Lara, Korin, we're going up for a little stealth entry. The rest of you follow in five."

"Like fuck. You are," Moana said. "I'm coming, too."

Several more of the Adders shouted that they wanted to join in, and Katrina laughed. "OK, four more. But we're trying to be sneaky, so those of you with bulky armor are gonna be kicking in the front door in five."

Moana and three other Adder women joined them in the lift, and Katrina sent the conveyance the command to rise.

"I'm coming too," Juasa said, hefting a rifle she'd picked up somewhere along the way.

Katrina was going to tell her to stay back with Malorie and the other Adders, but thought better of it and nodded. "Of course."

Juasa stepped in and gestured to the control screen. "Lara's command deck is level 417."

"There's no option for 416," Katrina said. "Gonna have to stop it manually."

"Good luck," Korin chuckled.

"Well, if I miss it, we'll just hold Lara out in front

and pray they like her enough not to blow her away," Katrina said with a grimace as she accessed the lift's emergency braking system and got ready to activate it.

"I think she twitched when you said that," Juasa said. "Is she fully controlled?"

Katrina checked over the nano that had formed a net around Lara's brain stem. "Yeah, they're in place. She must have really tried to move there and got a signal past. Lara, try that again, and I'll have the nano sever your spinal column. Understood?"

Lara didn't move, and Katrina turned her attention back to the lift as it slowed, passing floor 400.

"Brace!" she called out, and the lift stopped abruptly. "Get the doors open, it won't take them long to figure out what we did,"

Two of the Adders pulled the doors open, and the team rushed out into a dimly lit maintenance level.

<Astrid?> Katrina called out, but no response came. The upper levels had a field in place that was blocking all EM and RF from the rest of Farsa station.

Katrina let loose cloud of nano, signaling it to work its way back down the lift and establish a connection with Astrid. With any luck, they could bypass the local protections and gain some level of control up here.

Some of the nano also found network conduit and began following them, looking for junction boxes.

Korin and Moana moved ahead, working their way down the passageway. Two of the other Adders followed, and Katrina fell in behind them alongside Lara and Juasa while the last two women brought up the rear.

She established a local combat net with the group and provided the floorplan she'd pulled from Lara's mind.

Thirty meters down this corridor, then ten more down to the right, there was a ladder shaft that ran up through the spire. It would bring them up just a dozen paces from the entrance to Lara's command room.

From what Katrina had gleaned from Lara's mind, systems in that room would allow her to issue direct commands to the AIs and NSAIs in the MDF ships.

That *should* put the entire Midditerra Defense Force under her command.

They reached the ladder shaft without incident. Korin opened the hatch and peered down the twelve hundred meter drop.

"Watch your step. A fall here'll take you clear down to hell."

He climbed up the ladder to the next level and peered out into the passageway on level 417.

<Looks clear,> he sent down.

<Let's go, then.> Katrina replied.

The team climbed the ladder one by one and began moving down the hall to the broad doors leading into Lara's command center. When they had all arrived, Katrina took a deep breath and pushed the doors open, stepping in with Korin and Moana at her side, their weapons sweeping the air in front of them.

Other than a cluster of holodisplays in the center, the room appeared to be empty.

"Fan out," Katrina said as she walked toward the holodisplays.

"Looks just like it did yesterday," Juasa commented as she caught up to Katrina.

"Shouldn't we have heard fighting back at the lift by now?" Korin asked.

"You'd think so, wouldn't you?" a new voice said.

Katrina sent a passel of nano toward the displays, but they stopped short, caught in a grav field.

"Shit," Katrina swore, trying to get her probes past the grav field.

Then, one-by-one, the holodisplays shut off, revealing the person she least expected to see.

Jace.

JACE
STELLAR DATE: 01.20.8512 (Adjusted Gregorian)
LOCATION: Farsa Station
REGION: Orbiting Persia, Midditerra System

Jace's bearded face broke into a toothy smile. "I must say, Katrina. I really have to thank you for this. You gave me an entire system! What a great present to return to."

"Surrender, Jace!" Katrina shouted. "We have you surrounded. The only present you're going to get is on the far side of the airlock."

Jace shook his head. "I don't think so. You see, Moana and her ladies here haven't really sided with you. They're still allied with me."

Katrina turned to see Moana and the four women with her turn their weapons on Juasa, Korin, and herself. A sound behind her got Katrina's attention, and she saw the other Adders enter, bringing Malorie with them.

Jace's wife wore a look of terror on her face. Katrina knew that no matter which way things went, Malorie was going to suffer before this confrontation was over.

"Malorie," Jace called out. "Honey, I hope Katrina hasn't hurt you—not too much, at least."

"Does it look like I'm unharmed?" Malorie asked. "Lara shot me, the bitch."

"Lara!" Jace exclaimed, turning to the admiral. "What do you have to say for yourself? Shooting my wife! And on the night you surrender Midditerra to me."

"Lara doesn't speak for herself anymore," Katrina said. "Neither does Malorie."

The moment she uttered the words, Malorie stopped moving and sat down on the floor.

"Nice trick," Jace said with a throaty laugh. "Two can play at that game, though. Juasa, come here."

Juasa didn't budge. "Fuck you, Jace. Katrina's going to mop the floor with you."

At least she appreciates my skills when her life's on the line.

Though Katrina's nano wasn't able to make it past the grav field that protected Jace, she was able to target the other Adders in the room. Not all of them, not in time, but enough.

"How did you get here, anyway?" Katrina asked, buying time for her nano to reach and infiltrate the closest Adders. "I didn't see the *Verisimilitude* enter the system."

Jace smirked and shook his head. "That's because it didn't. I have it checking leads on your ship— which wasn't where you said it was, surprise, surprise. However, it was sighted in the Hercules system, and I decided to come back in a pinnace and fetch you before we moved on it. Imagine my shock when I got a message from Hana, warning me of your little coup. You made for a hell of a distraction; I got up here, and well, the rest is the present."

Katrina's voice dropped to a growl. "You're not going to take me alive."

"I'm terrified, really," Jace replied. "My ships—yes, *my* ships—are out there putting down the last of the Midditerra Defense Force vessels in close orbit of Persia. I've tapped into some of Lara's channels here and have told her outer fleets to stand down and await further orders. Like I said before: thanks for the star system, Katty girl. I really couldn't have done it without you."

<*Kat, what are we going to do?*> Juasa asked, panic evident in her mental tone.

<*Don't worry, Ju. If he thinks this is going down like last time, he has another thing coming.*>

"It's not over yet," Katrina snarled. "Malorie. Kill yourself."

"Shit..." Juasa whispered as Malorie grasped her own throat and began squeezing.

A pair of Jace's Adders rushed to Malorie and pulled her arms behind her back as the woman bucked and struggled to comply. Katrina had the pleasure of seeing a look of terror flash across Jace's face. Then she caught movement out of the corner of her eye, and braced as Moana and another Adder pirate slammed into her.

Katrina fell to the deck with the two women on top of her. She heard Korin bellow, and shots rang out, and then more weapons fire responded.

One of the women atop Katrina clamped something around her neck, and the other tried to punch her in the gut. Katrina grinned with satisfaction, as the woman's fist met her armor-skin and her attacker howled with rage.

Then the weapons fire fell silent, and hands grabbed Katrina's arms, hauling her to her feet once more.

She looked around to see Korin on the ground; his right leg was shot, and blood was seeping out around his armor's chest plate. Beyond him, Malorie stood panting and thrashing, her right arm broken and dangling uselessly, as her left tried to claw at her throat. Juasa was ten paces to Katrina's left, being held by a pair of Adders who had guns to her throat.

The two guards that Katrina had managed to get enough nano on to control were both dead, with holes in their heads leaking blood onto the deck.

Jace gave Malorie a pained look and shook his head as he surveyed the ruin before him.

"You're a right fucking bitch, Katrina! Look what you did to Malorie. Make her stop, make her stop now!"

"No," Katrina said. "Never going to happen."

<Kat!> Juasa cried out. *<Do something! I can't go back in the fields again.>*

<I just need him to step forward,> Katrina said, her eyes boring into Jace's.

<What if he doesn't?> Juasa asked, an audible sob escaping her throat.

"I don't know," Katrina whispered.

Jace drew his pistol. "If you won't free Malorie, then I'd better put her out of her misery." He took sight along the weapon's barrel. Katrina saw him pause for a second, and then he fired a shot into Malorie's chest.

The former lady of Revenence Castle convulsed for a moment, as a new red stain grew across her white dress and her life's blood pumped out onto the deck. The pair of guards holding her let go, and she collapsed, a final wheeze escaping her throat.

<Katrina!> Astrid's voice came into her mind. *<I'm in. I have access to the command deck through the string of nano you left me. What can I do to help?>*

<Stars, Astrid, it's good to hear your voice,> Katrina replied. *<Can you access the grav shield Jace has?>*

<I think so...yes, it's just a part of the regular artificial gravity for the deck. I can shut it down at any time.>

<OK,> Katrina replied. *<When I say 'die', you do it.>*
<Understood.>

Katrina met Jace's eyes, the rage in hers matching

the fury in his.

"Jace."

"What, oh beaten woman?" Jace sighed. "You're out of cards to play."

"What about the one where you die?!"

The collar fell from Katrina's neck, and she turned her palms back toward the two Adders holding her arms, and lightning shot out from her palms, engulfing the women.

They shrieked and fell to the ground, smoke rising from their bodies as they convulsed.

"What the—?" Jace exclaimed, stunned as Katrina charged him, a scream tearing its way out of her throat.

As she approached, time seemed to slow down. She watched as Jace swung his pistol toward her, but it was too late—she was within arm's reach, and batted it aside as he fired two shots.

Through the cloud of nano she'd dispersed into the room, Katrina saw the bullets fly harmlessly past her head, but her internal targeting systems marked where they would hit.

Juasa!

She spun, slamming her shoulder into Jace, and watched helplessly as one bullet hit Juasa in the neck, and the other struck her in the left eye.

A bloodcurdling scream tore out of Katrina's throat as blood, bone, and brain sprayed across the two Adders who held her.

For a second, everything around Katrina, all her sensations, went black: sight, smell, sound—they were all gone.

<*Juasa...*>

There was no response. She was alone in the universe. There was no one...nothing.

Nothing but vengeance.

A sound broke through, a dull thudding, and Katrina tried to understand what it was. It made her think of a drum. Then there was a pressure around her chest, and she struggled to breathe.

Suddenly the world slammed back into place around her, and she realized that Jace's massive arms were wrapped around her. The man was laughing as he squeezed, attempting to crush the life from her.

Her right arm was free, and she planted it on his back while wrenching her left loose to place it on his face.

"Die, you motherfucker," she groaned and sent bolts of energy into his body.

Jace bellowed in pain, his limbs convulsing, furthur squeezing the breath from Katrina as the power coursed through him. She could smell his burning flesh, and smoke rose out of his mouth as he shuddered and shook.

Katrina held on, delivering every last joule of

energy into his body, not letting go until his limbs went limp, and he fell to the deck.

She gazed down at his body, and watched the man draw a shallow breath.

Good. I have plans for you.

She knelt and placed a hand on his neck. The last of her infiltration nano flowed into his body and formed a net around his brain stem, locking down his motor control and paralyzing the man.

Not that it mattered. He had no need of his body anymore.

Katrina rose and turned toward the Adders who still stood in the room. They weren't shooting at her, and she wondered why.

Is this how succession goes? Kill the leader and become the new boss?

She hoped it was.

She swept her gaze across the assembled pirates, some of whom were standing open mouthed, others holding their guns on her.

"Who wants a piece of me?" Katrina screamed. "Do you think I have nothing left? Do you want to find out?"

She gestured to Jace behind her. "I've defeated your lord and master. I control the mind of Admiral Lara, and the AIs are on my side."

No one said a word, and several eyes darted to the window behind her.

<Got your back, Katrina,> Sam said, and she pulled feeds from her nanocloud.

The *Castigation* was just beyond the window, its guns trained on the glass.

<I'm reinitializing the grav shield,> Astrid said. <If Sam and Jordan have to shoot, you'll be protected from vacuum.>

<Good,> Katrina replied as she looked over the Adders, being careful not to let her eyes settle on Juasa's body.

"You have no one left to follow but me," Katrina called out to the onlookers. "Get on your knees. I'm the leader of the Blackadder *and* Midditerra!"

Several of the Adders dropped to a knee, but others didn't.

<Take a shot, Sam.>

A point-defense beam lashed out, burning a hole in the window and slicing two of the standing pirates in half. A loud whistle filled the air as the room's atmosphere began to vent through the hole.

"*Kneel!*" Katrina screamed at the Adders, barely holding back the tears that threatened to spill down her face.

A moment later, the rest were on their knees; some had even fallen prone.

Astrid activated the emergency decompression grav shield, and the sound of the room's air venting into space ceased.

"Much better," Katrina whispered.

THE WARLORD
STELLAR DATE: 01.28.8512 (Adjusted Gregorian)
LOCATION: Farsa Station
REGION: Orbiting Persia, Midditerra System

It took a week to clean up the mess in the Midditerra System.

Once Katrina proclaimed herself ruler, showing everyone in the system that Lara bowed to her, and that Jace and Malorie were dead, the fighting ground to a halt.

During the assault, Katrina had been careful to send all of her missives out as though they came from Malorie or Lara. Now that she had defeated both, the populace saw her as the savior of Midditerra, the one who had brought order to the chaos caused by the brief but bloody struggle for power.

For now, the MDF and Blackadder were still separate entities, but in time, Katrina would merge them and further solidify her power here.

She stood at the great curved window that wrapped around her throne room—now repaired— and stared out at Persia and the systems and planets of the Midditerra System.

Her system.

Somewhere in the back of her mind, a small voice

told her that this was crazy. She had seized a star system; why had she even done it to begin with?

But that small voice was drowned out by the anguish she felt over losing Juasa. It was Katrina's own action that had killed the woman she loved.

She couldn't feel pain now, though; she had a star system to run and she buried the sorrow under a burning fury at her situation in general.

Where are you, Troy? Why haven't you come yet? It's been months since Bollam's World. Are you even looking for me? How hard can it be to find a system that's a haven for pirates and whatever other scum drifts through the stars?

Katrina turned away from the window and walked back to her throne.

She had no need of the holodisplays Lara had used; her visual overlays were far superior. A throne was a much better use for the space.

Juasa's words echoed in her mind as she took her seat.

'Give them the leadership they deserve'.

Katrina would do just that. Starting with Hana.

The woman lay prone before Katrina, unable to move—the web that Katrina had placed around her brainstem cutting off all access to her own body.

She'd been in the position all day, and Katrina knew her muscles were screaming in agony, and cramps would be wracking her body.

Good. It was a small price to pay for treachery, though it wouldn't be the end of what Hana would face.

Katrina glanced to the right, settling her gaze on Lara. The admiral was suspended in a clear cylinder, hovering half a meter in the air and held in place by a grav field. Tubes ran out of her abdomen and down into the floor: her food supply, and waste reclamation.

Katrina had no idea how long she'd keep Lara there. Perhaps another week; perhaps a month. Maybe years. Maybe she'd string Hana up in a matching cylinder as a reminder of what happened to those who crossed the warlord.

Beside her throne stood another cylinder, though few knew its purpose. This one was black and only a meter tall. Inside, kept alive by nutrient baths and artificial organs, were the brains and neural mods of Malorie and Jace.

There was still much about their operation that Katrina did not know—the extent of the sithri distribution network, all the systems that held bases and ships operating under the Blackadder banner.

Katrina would ferret out those secret locations, find them, and bring them to heel. They would serve her purpose in finding the *Voyager,* and eventually the *Intrepid.*

The information she had gathered from the

Blackadder ships under her command had led her to believe that the colony ship had not yet come out of the Streamer.

When it did, she would be ready.

"Katrina," a voice said, and she looked up to see Jordan approaching.

"Jordan," Katrina greeted, a smile forming on her lips. It wasn't a false one either; Jordan had acquitted herself well during the battle to take Midditerra. Along with Sam, she had crippled dozens of enemy ships. In the end, it had been she who had captured Hana's ship and brought the rogue captain in.

"The last of the captains of the MDF have accepted your gift, and their AIs have joined us. You are in complete control of the system."

Katrina rose from her throne. "Good. Now we can turn our attention to the other cantons—especially those who sided with the MDF against us."

"What are we going to do?" Jordan asked. "Are you going to assemble the council?"

Katrina shrugged. "It'll get the traitors all in one place and make it easier to kill them and then take their holdings."

Jordan smiled. "Sounds like it'll be fun. I'll ready a strike force. Who do we hit first?"

"I think we'll take out the Kurgise. Their lands

abut Revenence Castle, and I'd like to expand the sithri fields."

Inside, under the grief and rage, the small voice rose up, begging Katrina to stop, telling her how Markus, Tanis, Juasa, and everyone she'd ever cared about would be horrified at what she'd become.

Everyone but my father. Maybe he'd known what was necessary to quell an unruly population. Stars knew his way of thinking had won out in the long term.

Katrina had researched what happened at Kapteyn's Star after she'd left—the history Troy had told her to avoid looking into.

The Kapteyn Primacy was long gone. Burned to ash thousands of years ago by the Sirians. Everything she and Markus had worked for was gone. Yet Sirius still stood, and the descendants of Luminescent Society still controlled their stars.

She dismissed Jordan, rose from her throne, and walked back to the window, the movement bringing fresh pain to her body.

Katrina ran a hand across her hard, metal skin. It had never meshed properly with her nervous system, the artificial sensory lattice in the armor being too primitive for her advanced neural network.

The agony was a friend now; her one constant companion. It was her strength when all others were gone.

I am Katrina. Daughter of Yusuf, friend of the Noctus, liberator of the Hyperion, *wife of Markus, president of Victoria, lover of Juasa, survivor of the fields, and conqueror of Midditerra.*

I am all of those things; together, they are me. They form my foundation; they give me purpose. My memories are my strength, the evidence of my power.

I am the steel fist that crushes my enemies, I weather the light and the darkness, I thrive on my torment, I persist. I touch all these things, I live in their worlds, but they are not me, and I am not them. I am the Warlord Katrina.

A NEW LEAD
STELLAR DATE: 02.28.8512 (Adjusted Gregorian)
LOCATION: *Voyager*, Monta Station
REGION: Orbiting Takan, Kashmere System

If Troy could have paced, he would have.

Carl had called in and told him that there was some news, a lead he'd picked up that may guide them to Katrina. He'd wanted to deliver it in person; organics were strange like that.

After another minute, Troy's dockside cameras picked Carl up as he navigated the crowds on Monta Station's third docking ring. He looked both perplexed and distressed.

This isn't a good sign at all.

Carl reached the airlock and cycled through; it was a quick process, as ship-pressure was already matched to station pressure. Even so, if Troy possessed fingers, he knew they'd be drumming on something right now.

<OK, *you're here,*> Troy said to Carl, once the man was inside the *Voyager.*

"Just give me a moment to get up to the cockpit."

That was a silly request. Troy didn't actually reside in the cockpit. <Why?>

<*Because it's sensitive information…and because I just need a few more seconds.*>

<Fine,> Troy replied.

It only took Carl seventeen and a half seconds to reach the cockpit, and then another seven and a quarter to settle into his seat.

Troy watched the man clench his jaw and run a hand through his hair.

<Enough with this waiting!> Troy exclaimed. <Spit it out.>

Carl signaled the cockpit's door to close, and leaned his head back. "I'm pretty sure I know where she is. I just heard from crewmembers of four different ships that the Midditerra System is where we want to go."

<We've heard of that system. It's one of the ones rumored to be a haven for the Blackadder—for a lot of others, too.>

Carl nodded. "Yeah, it's on our list. Twenty-two light years from here."

<OK, so how do we know that's the one?>

<The people I talked to said…well, they said that there's a new ruler in Midditerra. She's got some crazy powers, and she killed the head of the Blackadder—and the system's ruler.>

Troy could tell there was more; it was plainly evident in Carl's tone. <What else?>

The man swallowed before speaking. <The ruler's name is Katrina.>

Troy filed the departure request without a

moment's wait. *<Get the rest of the crew aboard. We fly in two hours.>*

Carl nodded slowly. *<There's more still, Troy. The rumors…they don't paint her in a good light. For some reason, people are calling her a warlord.>*

<Well, if she took a system, that makes sense.>

Carl shrugged. *<It's how she took it, though. The rumors say she's been murdering all sorts of people.>*

<She's just doing what she has to in order to survive. Making a name for herself, so we know where to find her.>

Troy watched as Carl shook his head. The human didn't believe him, but Troy knew Katrina. He'd spent years with her—back on High Victoria, and in the dark, searching for the *Intrepid*.

She was a strong woman; she could weather anything. And if something *had* happened to Katrina, if she'd snapped, then Troy would figure out how to make it right.

She'd saved him from the regolith of Victoria's moon. Now it was Troy's turn to return the favor.

THE END

* * * * *

Things have not gone to plan for Katrina. She's gone

into a dark place—one she thinks there is no coming back from. But even though she feels utterly alone, Troy hasn't given up his search, or his faith in Katrina.

Get *The Woman Who Lost Everything*, and find out if there can be salvation for Katrina.

THANK YOU

If you've enjoyed reading The Woman Who Seized an Empire, a review on Amazon.com and/or goodreads.com would be greatly appreciated.

To get the latest news and access to free novellas and short stories, sign up on the Aeon 14 mailing list: www.aeon14.com/signup.

M. D. Cooper

THE BOOKS OF AEON 14

Keep up to date with what is releasing in Aeon 14 with the free Aeon 14 Reading Guide.

The Intrepid Saga
- Book 1: Outsystem
- Book 2: A Path in the Darkness
- Book 3: Building Victoria

- The Intrepid Saga Omnibus – *Also contains Destiny Lost, book 1 of the Orion War series*

- Destiny Rising – *Special Author's Extended Edition comprised of both Outsystem and A Path in the Darkness with over 100 pages of new content.*

The Orion War
- Book 1: Destiny Lost
- Book 2: New Canaan
- Book 3: Orion Rising
- Book 4: The Scipio Alliance
- Book 5: Attack on Thebes (Feb 2018)
- Book 6: The Thousand Front War (2018)
- Book 7: Fallen Empire
- Many more following

Tales of the Orion War
- Book 1: Set the Galaxy on Fire
- Book 2: Ignite the Stars (Feb 2018)
- Book 3: Burn the Galaxy to Ash (2018)

Perilous Alliance (Age of the Orion War - with Chris J. Pike)
- Book 1: Close Proximity
- Book 2: Strike Vector
- Book 3: Collision Course
- Impact Immanent (2018)

Rika's Marauders (Age of the Orion War)
- Prequel: Rika Mechanized
- Book 1: Rika Outcast
- Book 2: Rika Redeemed
- Book 3: Rika Triumphant (Jan 2018)
- Book 4: Rika Commander (2018)
- Book 5: Rika Unleashed (2018)

Perseus Gate (Age of the Orion War)
Season 1: Orion Space
- Episode 1: The Gate at the Grey Wolf Star
- Episode 2: The World at the Edge of Space
- Episode 3: The Dance on the Moons of Serenity
- Episode 4: The Last Bastion of Star City
- Episode 5: The Toll Road Between the Stars
- Episode 6: The Final Stroll on Perseus's Arm
- Eps 1-3 Omnibus: The Trail Through the Stars
- Eps 4-6 Omnibus: The Path Amongst the Clouds

Season 2: The Inner Stars
- Episode 1: A Meeting of Bodies and Minds (Feb 2018)
- More coming in 2018

The Warlord (Before the Age of the Orion War)
- Book 1: The Woman Without a World
- Book 2: The Woman Who Seized an Empire
- Book 3: The Woman Who Lost Everything (March 2018)

The Sentience Wars: Origins (With James S. Aaron)
- Book 1: Lyssa's Dream
- Book 2: Lyssa's Run
- Book 3: Lyssa's Flight (Jan 2018)
- Book 4: Lyssa's Call (2018)
- Book 5: Lyssa's Flame (2018)

Machete System Bounty Hunter (Age of the Orion War - with Zen DiPietro)
- Book 1: Hired Gun (Feb 2018)
- More coming in 2018

The Empire (Age of the Orion War)
- The Empress and the Ambassador (2018)
- Consort of the Scorpion Empress (2018)
- By the Empress's Command (2018)

Tanis Richards: Origins
- Prequel: Storming the Norse Wind (At the Helm Volume 3)
- Book 1: Shore Leave (June 2018)
- Book 2: The Command (June 2018)
- Book 3: Infiltrator (July 2018)

The Sol Dissolution
- The 242 - Venusian Uprising (The Expanding Universe 2

anthology)
- The 242 - Assault on Tarja (The Expanding Universe 3
  anthology – coming Dec 2017)

The Delta Team Chronicles (Expanded Orion War)
- A "Simple" Kidnapping (Pew! Pew! Volume 1)
- The Disknee World (Pew! Pew! Volume 2)
- It's Hard Being a Girl (Pew! Pew! Volume 4)
- A Fool's Gotta Feed (Pew! Pew! Volume 4)

ABOUT THE AUTHOR

Michael Cooper likes to think of himself as a jack-of-all-trades (and hopes to become master of a few). When not writing, he can be found writing software, working in his shop at his latest carpentry project, or likely reading a book.

He shares his home with a precocious young girl, his wonderful wife (who also writes), two cats, a never-ending list of things he would like to build, and ideas…

Find out what's coming next at http://www.aeon14.com

92604923R00202

Made in the USA
San Bernardino, CA
03 November 2018